Please return on or before the latest date above.
You can renew online at *www.kent.gov.uk/libs*
or by telephone 08458 247 200

CUSTOMER SERVICE EXCELLENCE

Libraries & Archives

00884\DTP\RN\07.07   LIB 7

POACHER'S MOON

When nursemaid Kate Cooper rescues poacher, William Thorpe, from a mantrap on her employer, Sir Titus Wiggins's, land, they are unaware of the consequences of their meeting. Wiggins, a cruel, heartless lecher, dismisses Kate. Finding work with childhood friend Tom Ridley, a local landowner, she struggles to keep a professional distance from him, aware he is to marry elsewhere. Healed by his lost love Judith, William joins Ridley on the night of the poacher's moon when matters come to a head and passion and disaster collide at the Wiggins mansion leaving all searching for answers and the elusive happiness they so desire.

POACHER'S MOON

POACHER'S MOON

by

Ann Cliff

Magna Large Print Books
Long Preston, North Yorkshire,
BD23 4ND, England.

British Library Cataloguing in Publication Data.

Cliff, Ann
   Poacher's moon.

   A catalogue record of this book is
   available from the British Library

   ISBN   978-0-7505-3812-1

First published in Great Britain in 2012 by Robert Hale Limited

Copyright © Ann Cliff 2012

Cover illustration © Michael Thomas by arrangement with
Robert Hale Ltd.

The right of Ann Cliff to be identified as the author of this work
has been asserted by her in accordance with the Copyright,
Designs and Patents Act, 1988

Published in Large Print 2013 by arrangement with
Robert Hale Limited

Magna Large Print is an imprint of Library Magna Books Ltd.

Printed and bound in Great Britain by
T.J. (International) Ltd., Cornwall, PL28 8RW

Thank you, anonymous friends.

ONE

Kirkby, Yorkshire, 1852

'Have you heard? The Weaver lass's taken up with young Thorpe. You'd think she'd have more sense.' Neighbours, talking to neighbours in the butcher's shop shook their heads or nodded, according to preference. 'I only hope it doesn't end in tears.'

That William and Judith were walking out together the whole village knew, thanks to those who felt it their duty to pass on scraps of gossip. It was news because of Judith's very proper parents, who ran a successful bakery and went to church on Sundays. Until this summer, Judith had been a model daughter with angelic fair looks, but now there was some doubt. Long summer evenings were a trap for village lasses, it was said.

Most of the lasses rather envied Judith because of William Thorpe's crisp brown hair, beautiful cheekbones and pure profile. He was slightly uppish though, had an impatient way with him and folks who remembered his father said he was just the same, but more respectable.

One mild evening in late summer William

9

met Judith at her garden gate with his dog Fern, so named because of her feathery tail. Fern, like William, was not quite respectable. Her bloodlines included greyhound and a touch of terrier, with a dash of collie, the sort that folks called a 'dinner dog'. She could run down a hare and catch rabbits with ease, which was strictly illegal, but exciting.

Judith, a small and slender girl, loved both William and Fern, whatever they did and whatever the villagers thought about them. Of course her parents did not approve of either of them, which made things awkward at home. Judith's mother was a woman who looked for trouble and usually found it. She was tolerated in Kirkby because she made an excellent loaf.

The couple walked demurely down the village street and passed the church beadle, who looked at them thoughtfully. No doubt he would report to her father, who was very involved with the church. 'Saw your lass out with that lad again...'

William turned into a green lane with high hedges running between fields of grass and corn stubble. He held her hand and they both gazed round at the perfect evening; rooks flying home to the wood and the dying sun touching the fields with gold. Judith sighed, relaxing at last. It had been a busy day and it was good to get out of the village, away from her mother's eagle eye.

'Let's sit on this gate,' William said, slipping an arm round her waist. 'It's grand to see you, Judith. I wish your mother would let you out more often.' He helped her up and they both perched on the broad top of the wooden field gate. He looked at her closely. 'Is she working you hard? I bet she is.'

The dog Fern sat at their feet, waiting for something to happen. Her ears pricked, she kept looking over the stubble to a line of trees at the far side of the field. Sleepy pheasants cackled in the wood, going to roost for the night as the sun slipped below the western ridge. 'Why are you wearing a coat on such a warm night?' Judith wondered.

William laughed. 'To make your mother think I'm respectable. Posh people wear coats.'

'She knows you too well.' Judith sighed. Her father was a devout man, a church warden, while her mother's family were farmers. Both parents were uneasy about young William, a lad with too much easy charm and no prospects as far as they could see. Judith was grudgingly allowed to see him one evening a week, for an hour or two. Thank goodness there were quoits matches on the green where they could sometimes exchange a word, even with the rest of the village looking on.

William leaned over and kissed her, and Judith forgot about prospects. How could old people understand? His clear, laughing blue eyes looked into her grey ones and Judith knew she'd never love anyone else.

'You're a bonny lass, Judith,' he murmured, stroking her long fair hair. 'I hate to leave you here even for a minute, but there's a job I have to do.' William slipped from the gate. 'Just stay here, I'll be back soon,' he said quietly.

'Will, I wish you wouldn't go after rabbits ... it'll get you into trouble.' Even as she looked at him, her heart seemed to turn over. If only he wasn't a poacher and they could have a normal courtship, things would be so much better. Judith was afraid of losing him; the thought of life without Will was un-bearable, but trouble would take him away from her.

Poaching was the easiest way for a lad to get into trouble in Kirkby, with game run-ning round all over the place and angry landowners trying to protect it. Most of them thought more of the game than they did of their servants and they handed out harsh punishments to poachers.

William's chin went up in a determined way. 'It's not like pinching someone's goose, or a stray sheep. You know I never steal off the farmers. Face facts, lass. Never mind the game laws, rabbits are wild animals. They're there for the taking. The manor can spare a rabbit now and then.' He laughed quietly and melted away along the hedgerow with his dog. To Will, it was enjoyment.

'We need to go home well before dark,' Judith warned, but he was gone. She wouldn't be allowed out again if she went in late. If only William could better himself ... but at the farm where he worked, he was the 'lad', and the poorest paid. He wouldn't be a farm foreman for years, if ever. He was quick and useful with his hands and he should find a better job. But even then, they wouldn't let her marry him. Mother said that seventeen was too young to know your own mind.

Time passed and the dusk deepened. Why wasn't he back? Judith was aware that his mother was a widow. Will's job was to put meat on the table, with no questions asked and a rabbit or a hare made a good meal, with a pie the next day, two days if the animal was a big one. Will and his mother were both thin; they were sometimes short of food and Judith gave him stale bread from the bakery when she could.

Suddenly the dog moved as two men erupted from a little wood and ran across the stubble; the general's gamekeepers, the sworn enemies of all the village lads. The general was hardly ever at the manor, he was in the army, but he was hard on poachers. The keepers had been employed to frighten all the local lads away.

He'd been seen, after all. Will would be caught this time for sure.

Judith jumped down from the gate and stood in the shadow of the hedge, her heart beating fast. Sitting up there, had she drawn attention to him? Could she warn him? She felt the silky brush of Fern's tail against her skirt, and then the dog vanished.

Oh Will, don't let them catch you ... she could just see William skulking along the bottom of the hedge, on his way back to her. The keepers had seen him too and they let out a shout as they charged towards him. Two big men, with the law on their side, one of them with a gun. They had him cornered with his back to the thick and thorny hedge.

The dog decided to intervene. Judith watched, fascinated, as Fern danced up to the keepers, barking happily, leaping and turning. What did she do that for? They might shoot her, they hated dogs that could run down a hare. But she moved so fast, she would be hard to hit.

'You mongrel!' one of the keepers growled and Fern ran between his legs, toppling him over. He fell heavily against the other man and there was a roar as his loaded gun went off. There was a lot of swearing and when Judith looked again, Will was nowhere to be seen. The dog loped off in another direction and the keepers, one of them limping, followed the dog. Judith breathed out slowly;

14

Fern would lead the men away from William. Had he trained her to do that?

Silence descended on the fields. After waiting for a while, she decided that Will was not going to come back to her. He would go home by a roundabout route. Judith walked home quickly, trying to hold back tears. Her mother was right, Will was not the man for her; she would have to forget him.

William did catch up with her just before she reached the village and he was laughing. 'Did you see that dog of mine? It was priceless! She upskelled them bullies and then she led 'em away! And you know, lass, I got a couple from the snares tonight. Ma will be pleased, we haven't had much meat lately.' He opened the big coat and she saw rabbit ears peeping from his pockets.

Angry, the girl faced him. 'You only take me for a walk to make it look right, to look like a courting couple with nothing else on our minds. Not because you like my company. You're really just a poacher. Anyway, you'd best go ... they'll catch up with you soon.' If she didn't love him so much, it wouldn't matter.

Will looked hurt. 'There is nobody I would rather be with, Judith. You're my girl. I thought you'd enjoy a bit of excitement! I love it myself, the riskier the better!'

Judith opened her gate and he put his hand over hers, but she removed it. 'Women can't afford to take risks, Will. That's for lads, and wild lads, at that. I was going to talk to you – about risks, and being responsible, but I think it's too late. You'll never change.' She went into the house weeping and went straight to bed.

The next day, Judith was at work in the bakery when the shop bell rang. She went through to serve the customer and blushed when she saw who he was: Mr Price, one of the gamekeepers they had seen last night.

The man bought his bread and paid for it, then lingered by the door. 'I was sorry to see you with that lad Thorpe,' he said quietly. There was no one else in the shop. 'Did you know that men can be transported to Australia for poaching? That would be a good start for a young couple! He'd likely never come back.'

'Er ... yes, Mr Price.' Judith felt miserable; he was right. She hoped her mother couldn't hear them.

Joe Price looked at her with some sympathy. 'General Ridley, he's not a hard man. But he's an army man, he believes in discipline and teaching thieves a lesson. If anybody steals his game, they can expect no mercy. You'd better tell that young ruffian to mend his ways. For your own sake, an' all.'

Judith's anger had evaporated by the next week, when William turned up at the gate without his dog. 'I'm sorry about last week, lass, I hate to upset you. You've enough trouble at home without me making it worse. I won't go rabbiting tonight, I'll just stay with you.'

He shouldn't go rabbiting any night, but Judith hadn't the heart to lecture him. She wished she could ask an artist to paint that face, just as it was, as he looked down at her.

'We'll make the most of it, Judith. Soon be bad weather and there'll be no walking out then.' He grinned. 'I'm planning to take you to Ma's house when it's raining.'

Judith smiled and put her hand in his. Will did understand, he did love her and perhaps in time, she could persuade him to give up poaching. One day, her mother might relent...

Years afterwards she could remember every detail of that evening. They walked up the hill out of the village to the west this time, towards the perfect sunset over Skeldings moor. The heather had faded and far away on the skyline, men were cutting peat for winter fuel. Kirkby was on the edge of the moor and there was a bit of the moorlander in William, Judith thought. Something free, independent, decent enough but not bound by too many rules. 'High Siders,' the moorland folk were called and there was bound to be High Side blood in this bonny lad.

William spread his coat for her on a bed of deep bracken and they lay, looking at the rosy evening sky. When he turned and took her in his arms, she could not resist. They were made for each other. This was happiness, this was how life ought to be. Gently, he made love to her.

'We must stay together, my love. All our lives.' William was serious tonight. They were quiet together for a while, with no need for words.

The evening star appeared; it was time to go. 'One day,' Judith teased him, 'you will bring me up here to cut peat like those folks over there. Will you still love me when I'm an old village wife?'

'I always will,' he said simply. 'Never forget it, Judith – we belong together. It might not be easy, but we'll find a way.'

Could you be so sure, at nineteen and seventeen, of the way your whole life should go? Judith thought you could. They wandered back to the village hand in hand, perfectly happy.

The fragile happiness of that night did not last long. The next week there was no William waiting at the gate. At the quoits ground where Judith went for news, old women were crowing. 'They've caught that young Thorpe with pheasants on him, have you heard? He'll be for Australia, mark my words!' The older people smiled and the young lads looked uneasy.

'No, they'll not do that, will they?' Young

Fred Easby was a friend of Will's and Judith turned to him for the truth. 'He's not a criminal!' A cold shudder ran through her. But after last week, something serious must have kept him away from her. It must be true.

Fred, a farmer's son, looked down at her with a hint of pity. 'Best forget him if I was you, Judith,' he muttered. 'Keepers have a set against him and the general's on the bench, when he's here.' He smiled. 'Maybe you'll walk out with me, in a week or two? Your ma might like that!' Everybody in Kirkby seemed to know her mother's views on Will.

Some girls could change from one lad to another, just like that. Judith shook her head and decided to be honest. 'If I can't have Will, I'll die an old maid. Sorry, Fred.' He was probably only trying to cheer her.

'A little lass like you'll never stay single!' Fred thought a minute. 'They say Australia's not so bad in some parts, better than being in gaol. He might come back in a few years, seven years it is I think...'

Judith bit back tears. 'But that lad of Brown's was transported for life!'

'Aye, but he shot a gamekeeper... My turn to throw, I have to go.' Fred moved up to the game of quoits and picked up the heavy steel ring. His next throw was a ringer; he threw the quoit clean over the hob and there was a burst of clapping. Judith stood alone, watching with unseeing eyes.

'Offence: entering enclosed land and unlawfully destroying game, to wit a pheasant.'

He'd been a fool to get caught, too careless. William and Fern had reckoned on two keepers, but there was a third, hidden in the wood and he was caught red-handed. It was a grand bird, too.

They locked him up straight away of course, really enjoyed throwing him in the tiny cell at Kirkby police station. There was no chance to see Ma or Judith ... he hoped they would understand. Two weeks later Will was up in court. He made himself as clean and neat as he could in the circumstances and decided to make it easy for them by pleading guilty. There was no point in doing otherwise.

'You are a disgrace to your family, young man,' growled the magistrate.

The sentence was three calendar months' hard labour for one pheasant, not a very good deal. William said nothing, trying to look quiet and respectable, although the keepers knew better. His mother would take care of Fern while he was inside. The officious beadle promised to go to see her.

Time went slowly in Ripon gaol and the work was hard and usually pointless, moving heavy stones from one place to another. It was grim, it was cold, so cold and the food was never enough; stale bread and thin gruel. It was the most cheerless Christmas he had ever known, but the thought of Judith's bonny face kept him sane. He would work hard to prove to her that he was a steady lad.

The thought of poaching pheasants was not so appealing to him now. Maybe the old folks were right and it was time for him to grow up, to be responsible – that was what they said. Judith was more important than chasing about after game.

The first thing William did when he got out of gaol was to walk back to Kirkby. The January day was bitterly cold and his coat was thin, but it was so good to walk in freedom under the sky. The exercise soon warmed him and he felt quite cheerful by the time he reached the village.

Home was just the same, the cottage kept bright and clean by his mother. She had more grey hairs than he remembered and her cough was worse. Ma wept to see him so pale and even went so far as to put her thin arms round him, which was very unusual. Of course, his dog nearly knocked him over with delight.

'You look so like your pa, when he took ill. Are you feeling well, William?' Will's father had died when he was ten. He remembered a pale, thin man with a cough; Martin Thorpe had once been a schoolteacher, but his health was poor and so he took an outdoor job, working on a farm. But the work was too heavy and eventually, the cough killed him. Will was his only child.

'I'm very well, Ma, don't worry about me. Never going to poach again,' he said firmly, and believed it.

William chopped some wood for his mother and then went to the baker's to look for Judith. He felt his face go stiff with shock when her mother said flatly, 'She's gone.' He had to wait until she'd served a customer.

'Gone where? Surely she'd leave a message for me?' He'd known there would be some explaining to do, some remorse to show and he would have to convince Judith that it wouldn't happen again. But they had their lives in front of them, and his boss had promised he could have his old job back at the farm. That was the main thing. He'd planned to find a cottage to rent.

'Gone away to better herself, a good job in service. There's nothing and nobody in Kirkby for our Judith.' The woman's face was hard. He'd get no help from Mrs Weaver.

Even then, William had the instinct to keep his pain to himself. 'How will you manage then, Mrs Weaver? She was – a right good help in the bakery.' He turned away to hide the tears in his eyes. Lads didn't cry, especially over a lass.

Village girls often went away to work in big houses – that in itself was not surprising.

Judith was well spoken, she'd make a good lady's maid, although she did like to be outdoors. But...

'Her sister Bessie's leaving school, she's helping us now. Judith won't be back, so you can forget about her. Find yourself another lass.' Her mother could not meet his eyes. 'The best advice I can give you, young man, is to mend your ways. Come to church on Sundays like a Christian. You're right lucky that you've still got a job to go to, but you'll have to mind your manners. Nobody wants a gaolbird about the village.'

Judith would write to him, he desperately hoped, explain what had happened. Once she was away from home, her mother couldn't stop her getting in touch by letter. Every day he looked for the postman, but no letter came. Slowly, he began to realize that a young lady's maid would probably not write to a lad who'd been in prison. She was trying to better herself, not sink down with him. Judith was gone.

Life dragged on; William worked at the farm, summer came and went. Every morning brought the same dull ache when he woke and remembered that Judith was gone for ever. He asked quietly in the village, talking to anyone who might be in touch with her. But nobody knew where she was and he could tell that her friends, the girls she'd known all her life, were just as puzzled as he was. 'You'd think she'd have said something, even if it was just goodbye,' one of them said sadly. Judith's sister Bessie was as tight-lipped and disapproving as their mother.

It was two years before William could think of courting another girl and even then, it was only because Lily had chosen him in her quiet way. Lily was a plain girl, a helpful person and a hard worker. She'd helped his mother get through the terrible time when he was in prison. She was often in their house and eventually, slowly he got used to her presence. His mother urged him to marry her and eventually, he did.

Lily was a Methodist and to please her, William signed the pledge, promising to take no strong drink. He didn't drink much beer in any case. His addiction was to poaching.

TWO

Kirkby, 1875

Sir Titus Wiggins rode out on his expensive chestnut mare to look for trouble. It was a fine afternoon, but there was bound to be trouble somewhere. He was away from his country estate for much of the time, looking after his woollen mills and he was always uneasy in the role of country gent. That was to please Lady Wiggins, who had been brought up in 'county' circles while he was sweating his guts out in a factory, and to prove that a working class lad could rise and rise and own a fine estate.

Somebody had to make the brass to pay them, but Bellwood Hall servants were idle. These country turnips knew that he was out of his depth in all this farming business and they tried to take advantage of him. Fletcher, the stupid groom, had a sly look to him as he saddled the horse – what did he know? No doubt Fletcher had noticed that his master was not at his best on horseback. The brutes didn't seem to like him for some reason.

And then there was the nursemaid, too pretty by half – Fletcher would be after her no doubt, and she looked as though she'd encourage it. She looked just ready for a tumble in the hay, if he was any judge, and he ought to be. Sir Titus smiled to himself. Lady Wiggins tried to keep her husband away from the women. He knew things like that.

The girl needed discipline, like all the others. That nursemaid talked proper, as if butter wouldn't melt in her mouth, but he knew different; she was from the gutter. A foundling, he'd heard. She probably looked down her nose at a master who came from the slums of the West Riding ... there she was, the girl herself. Walking along with her head in the air, down the drive where she shouldn't be. What was going on? He spurred his horse forward.

'Where do you think you're going, woman? I don't pay you to wander about the country-side!' The rough West Riding voice was bruising to the ears, more suited to shouting in factories than addressing a respectable children's nurse.

Kate could tell from the purple tinge in her employer's plump face that Sir Titus was not in the best of moods. On this lovely late August day, the green lawns and stately trees framing the big house were peaceful, but he was not. He hardly ever was, come to think of it.

'Well, sir, I'm looking for Polly, she took Master George for a walk.' Kate gazed round hopefully, but there was no sign of Polly on the gravel paths. 'I'm sure they can't–' She stepped back as he edged the horse close to her,

'It's your business to look after bairns, not maid's! What do I pay you good brass for? Any more of this and I'll turn you off!'

Sir Titus should have been on the stage, he was so good at working up to a scene. Kate watched with interest as he ran a hand through his sparse ginger hair, leaning heavily down from his horse to threaten her. How did Lady Wiggins cope with him?

Kate started to move away again but the man nudged her angrily with his horse's shoulder and her own anger began to rise, anger against a man who was not kind to anyone, even his own children. 'Don't do that! You nearly knocked me down!' Oh dear, you don't talk like that to an employer...

'You slut, you were going to see a man, I know! You're out looking for some man. You need a good thrashing to put you in your place!' Shaking, Sir Titus raised his whip and struck out. Kate jumped back, but a pain ran down her arm and blood began to flow. 'Get back to yer work!' The man whirled his horse sharply and took off down the drive, leaving her in a cloud of dust.

Kate wiped her arm with a handkerchief

and looked at the wound. Superficial, Father would have called it, but it certainly smarted and the fact that he'd called her a slut was unforgivable. Surely he didn't mean it, or he would not allow her to look after his children. She would not forget, but meanwhile, what about them? Should she go back to the house, or carry on down the drive, looking for Master George? It was nearly time for nursery tea and little Bella would be waking from her afternoon sleep.

There were bloodstains on her nurse's grey dress. Sighing, the girl looked back across the neatly raked gravel to where the house basked in mellow sunshine. Bellwood Hall was a lovely place, it was a beautiful time of year – why did the estate have to be owned by a rough factory man with no idea of how to speak to servants?

Kate had not gone far when Polly appeared from the bushes at the side of the drive, her cap falling off and her apron torn. 'I got lots of brambles,' she said happily, showing her basket full of purple berries. 'Cook can make us some jam.'

'Polly, where's George? I thought he was with you!' She spoke more sharply than she intended and saw Polly flinch as Kate put up a hand to straighten the girl's cap. The poor little maid was often in trouble from the housekeeper.

'Nay, he said he was going home,' Polly

said, miserable now. 'Said that now he's five, he knew which way to go, like. I never thought nowt of it.'

How could she? Kate bit back a comment. 'How long ago?' Wayward George had innocent blue eyes and no fear. And he loved water ... the ornamental lake was not far away.

'Dunno.' Polly looked blank.

Poor little George alone in the park – what if he fell in the water? Kate fought the panic and said crisply, 'Now go back to the house, Polly, and see if he's there. I will go on and look for him, and you come back, bring a few others if he's not at home. And ask Mrs Mason to look after Bella for me.' She tried to smile, but it was an effort.

For only six months Kate had looked after him, but she loved the little heir to the Wiggins fortune. Instead of his father's rough mop of ginger hair, he had silky copper curls and a far nicer nature than Papa. But George was an independent little being if only she hadn't let him go with Polly! This was how children had accidents, fatal accidents. If you were responsible for them, you should never let them out of your sight. Kate broke into a run.

There was no little figure by the lake; the water was ruffled by a slight breeze. Kate usually loved this tranquil spot, but today the dark water was menacing.

A family of ducks sailed past, almost full grown and the waterlilies rocked in their wake. What was that floating on the water? Kate's heart gave a lurch as she saw, just out of reach, something out there ... it looked like George's blue jacket.

It was too late. Sobbing, Kate kicked off her shoes, hitched up her skirt and waded into the cold water. She snatched up the waterlogged jacket, but there was no sign of the child. 'Where was he? Lying on the bottom, white and cold...

'Hey, there!' A shout travelled across the water. A man on a horse was on the far side – perhaps he would help? Gasping, Kate struggled out of the muddy reeds and ran towards him.

'Please, there's been an accident...' She looked up at the rider. A young man, broad shouldered, sitting easily in the saddle. Thomas Ridley was grinning at her, the playmate of her childhood. And in front of him, high on the horse and clapping his hands, was the missing boy.

'George, where have you been? I thought you were drowned!' The nurse's voice was high with tension.

Thomas swung down and lifted George after him. 'I'm sorry you were worried, Kate. Master Georgie has been with me, inspecting my sheep and I was taking him home.' He smiled down at the bedraggled Kate.

'Haven't seen you since the doctor died ... it seems a long time.'

Thomas belonged to her former life and it did seem a long time ago that she was the doctor's daughter and knew everyone in the village. 'I thought – George's coat was floating on the water, so I–' She stopped as George came up to her.

'I had a lovely ride, Nursie,' he said, and the touch of his warm little hand made Kate relax a little. George was not lost after all.

'Thank you for bringing him back. Have you thanked Mr Ridley, George? We'd better go back to the house.' Kate was still holding George's wet jacket. She wanted to get away from this big man with his smiling eyes, who was probably laughing at her. She knew she looked wet and woeful.

'I'll come with you. George has walked quite a long way.' To the child's delight, he was put back on the horse. 'He'd lost his coat before I caught up with him.' The man looked up. 'George, hang on to the front of the saddle, there's a good chap. Now, Miss Cooper, what are you doing here, so far from the house?'

Kate pulled herself together. 'I could ask the same of you, Mr Ridley, since this land is the Wiggins estate. I seem to remember that you, er, adventured a little as a boy.' That was putting it politely.

'Who, me? You must be mistaken. Doctor

31

Cooper was always digging shotgun pellets out of Kirkby boys, but not me.' Tom was laughing openly now. 'But since I've been away I don't know half the people in the village ... and I find things very different since Sir Titus took over here.' They were coming out onto the drive and Kate looked hastily around in case Sir Titus was coming back again. If he saw her talking to Tom, she would be dismissed.

'You went off after finishing your degree? There was no time to ask, at the funeral.' Kate had wondered where Tom was.

'I did, I worked on an estate in Scotland, learning how they managed the woodlands and the farms ... that sort of thing. Then old Brown, our manager, retired and my father decided I was old enough to take charge here. So if the manor goes bankrupt, it will be my fault.' Tom didn't look very worried.

'Well, thank you, we must be going. Please lift George down, Mr Ridley.' The nurse tried to smooth her fair hair.

Thomas stopped the horse and looked at Kate. 'This is not the place for you,' he said, very quietly. George was busy talking to the horse. 'I saw him strike you, Kate. I was up on the ridge over there and I saw him raise his whip – couldn't tell who you were, but now I can see the cut on your arm. He can't be allowed to do that.' There was a danger-ous glint in the dark eyes.

Wiggins must have seen the rider on the ridge and supposed she was going to meet him; it was Thomas who'd got her into trouble. 'Who can stop him? Sir Titus employs us all, and jobs are hard to get. He's in Bradford for much of the time...' Kate wiped her arm, which was bleeding again. 'You know all about us, and Sam works for you now. Our father died and I have to earn a living.'

'So do I, lass, so do I. I've just taken over the farm, so there's plenty to do. The place has been neglected for years, since Pa decided to spend most of his time in Jamaica. Poor Brown was never allowed enough money to do repairs.'

'You like the work?' He looked like a happy man.

'Love it. I've always loved the manor, and Kirkby. And I suppose you like nurse-maiding. George thinks you're wonderful, he told me about it.' Thomas grinned and then was suddenly serious. 'But don't take any nonsense from them, Kate. I hate to think of you working for that brute.'

'No, Thomas, I won't,' Kate said, with more confidence than she felt, and was rewarded with a heart-warming smile. 'I'll keep a hat pin ready. That's what ladies are supposed to do, isn't it?'

'I think I had better keep an eye on you,' Thomas said, as he gently lifted the reluctant

George from the horse's back. 'I always used to, didn't I?' He looked at her in the old way and Kate reminded herself that Tom Ridley was a flirt. When they were sixteen he'd pretended to be madly in love with her, but it was all a game. It was years ago now; behind the laughter there had been real friendship between them: Kate, her brother Sam and the young squire of Kirkby Manor, Thomas Ridley, who had no mother and spent most of the school holidays at the doctor's house.

Polly was coming down the drive with another maid and she ran up to them, crying with relief. 'I dusn't tell Mrs Mason we'd lost him...'

'Thank you, Uncle Tom,' said George politely as he was led away. Kate was relieved to hear from the maids that Lady Wiggins was still in her room; there would be no enquiry as to how her son had spent the afternoon.

'Serve nursery tea, please, Polly, I must change my dress,' and Kate ran lightly up to her room.

When she joined the children, three-year-old Bella was throwing pellets of bread and butter and George was making gurgling noises with his milk. A firm hand was needed, so Kate diverted their attention. She showed Bella a whole strawberry in the jam and then said to George, 'Who said you could call Mr Ridley Uncle Tom?'

'He did,' George said importantly. 'One

34

day when Mama took me visiting in the trap and left me for *hours*. Uncle Tom came and talked to me.'

Trust Lady Wiggins to leave her child with a groom who was not sympathetic to small children. Kate sighed. 'That was kind of him.'

George drank his milk thoughtfully. 'He said not to worry about Mama, she had important things to do. He said that you can't choose your relations, but you can have extra uncles. So now he's Uncle Tom. I've seen him a few times, he lives just over the hill.' He looked up. 'Can we go and visit him, Nursie? There's peacocks and things. Bella would like it. And he's got a lovely dog.'

There had been a black labrador dog, Kate remembered, sitting at attention in the background while she talked to Tom.

Kate washed the children and put them to bed and then had supper in the kitchen with the other servants. She was mending George's torn coat in the nursery when Polly tapped on the door. 'Your brother to see, you, Miss.'

The nursemaid ran down to the now deserted kitchen, worried that someone would see him. Servants were not allowed visitors and she was treated as a menial. She usually saw Sam on her days off, when she walked to his cottage.

Sam was dressed in his gamekeeper's tweeds and his normally cheerful brown face was serious. 'I'm working tonight, Kate, there's poachers about after pheasants. Season opens soon and they can sell them from now on.'

Kate frowned. 'It sounds dangerous – anybody with you?'

Sam grinned. 'My trusty dog Chloe, of course.' Chloe was another black labrador, the proper dog for a keeper. She was utterly loyal and would probably attack anyone if he asked her to. 'Thought I'd call here on my way through to Piper's Wood... Boss said you've had trouble from old Titus.'

Kate looked round nervously. 'Ssshh! Sir was annoyed when he saw me out looking for George ... he caught my arm with the whip. It's nothing.' She wouldn't say that he'd called her a slut.

Sam sat in a chair by the kitchen fire, head in his hands. 'What would Father have thought about it all? You here, treated as a servant and working for a man like that!'

Kate laughed. 'He'd be proud of the way we both found work! Of course, he thought that you would go to university to study science and I would may be train as a teacher...'

Doctor Cooper had never realized that by the time he died, there would be no money and no house left. Father had been good to his patients; he only charged them what he thought they could afford. There were not many rich people in Kirkby, so his income was small. While he'd been ill, villagers had found other doctors, so by the end there had been no practice to sell. The doctor's house and surgery was sold to cover debts.

Sam brooded over their situation, but Kate had never worried. 'We're better off than many folks, those that can't find work.' After a series of bad harvests there was poverty in Kirkby but they were among the lucky ones, with plenty to eat and a roof over their heads.

Sam looked over at his sister, the dark face creased with worry. They were a contrasting pair, Kate fair and slim while Sam was sturdy, with curly black hair and a tanned, outdoor face. 'You don't have to stay here, lass. You could live with me in the keeper's cottage, until we find something else for you.' His tone lightened as he said, 'You might get married, stranger things have happened!'

'I'm not going to marry someone just for security! You don't meet many eligible young men in a children's nursery – and then, you know, they wouldn't want to take up with a servant. We're servants now, Sam, both of us.' Perhaps one day, Kate thought, she might be promoted to governess, slightly higher on the social scale. 'And also – there's our past, re-member.' It was their serious drawback and there was silence for a while. 'But let's look on the bright side! Once you're head keeper, that will give you a lot of prestige ... all the village girls will be sighing for you!'

Sam stood up, laughing and shaking his curly head. 'I'm the only keeper at the manor, so there's no prestige and no promotion. That reminds me, I must be off, got my career to think of!' He reached for his stick. 'The boss, Thomas that is, was talking about marriage the other day. He's going to marry a rich young lady in the spring, a girl from York. Some people have all the luck.'

Kate walked with her brother to the door, where the faithful Chloe was waiting, lying across the doorstep. 'Do take care, Sam. I worry about you meeting poachers in the woods... oh, I know some are just local lads out for a lark, but is it true that there are criminal gangs coming out to here make money from poaching? It sounds dangerous.' She looked at the stick he carried – was it for attack or defence?

'That's what we've got to find out. I report to Tom every day – he doesn't mind losing one or two birds. But if things get busy he's going to give me a hand. He says it's a drawback that our best game preserves are on our boundary with old Titus's land. Wiggins isn't exactly popular round here; he's managed to upset most folks. Kirkby lads might go in there just to stir him up, and that would disturb our pheasants and partridges as well.'

'It sounds as though Tom Ridley won't have much time for shooting, so why is he worried about his birds?' Cook had said that once the season opened, Sir Titus would be inviting weekend parties for the shooting and that would mean a lot of work for the servants. It was an important social event for the Wigginses, establishing them as landed gentry, at least in their own eyes. But by all accounts, Tom's ancestral home wasn't ready to receive guests, having been neglected for years.

'It's income for the estate, lass. Tom has let the shooting rights to a syndicate and then he'll sell some game to hotels in London, it goes down by train. So we can't afford to let poachers get away with it.'

There was no moon and it would be very dark under the trees. 'Don't poachers – er, poach by moonlight, Sam?'

Her brother shook his head. 'Not when they think we're watching, they don't. If the coast is clear and they're shooting, of course they need light. But we've put the message about in the Queen's Head that Tom has several keepers out at night, so they'll try to sneak pheasant in the dark.' With a grin he went off down the drive followed by Chloe, a dark shadow at his heels.

THREE

Polly came in the next morning to light the nursery fire. 'It's a bit parky this morning, miss, so Mrs Mason said bairns need a fire.' She struggled in with a bucket of coal as Kate dressed the children in their Sunday clothes ready for church, but with a pinafore in case of spills at breakfast.

'Can you bring me some more tooth powder, Polly, we've none left–?' Kate broke off as she saw that the normally cheerful girl was near to tears. 'Whatever's the matter?' She plonked George at the table with a boiled egg and put Bella beside him.

'Oh, miss, Sir Titus is in a rage and her ladyship an' all. There's trouble downstairs this morning ... we all have to go to the dining-room straight after breakfast. It's one of them days.' Polly was still breathless from her climb up three flights of stairs. The servants used the back stairs, a steep, twisting metal staircase, to carry up everything needed in the nursery. It was not a convenient house for the people who did the work.

The children stopped eating and turned scared faces to the maid, then looked at each other. They were both afraid of Sir Titus, as was everybody at Bellwood Hall, except perhaps Lady Wiggins and Kate, who was beginning to despise him.

'All? Does that mean me – and George and Bella? Just stay with these two for a moment, Polly.' Kate ran down to the kitchen and found Cook serving the staff breakfast. The buzz of conversation was quieter than usual.

Everyone at the big table looked serious except John Fletcher, who was showing his white teeth in a laugh. Fletcher was handyman, part-time groom and sometimes gamekeeper as well because Sir Titus believed in keeping people busy. He was not a local man and the other servants were wary of him as yet.

The housekeeper should know what was happening, but she wasn't there.

'Mrs Mason's in her room, you can take her tray in if you don't mind.' Cook smiled at Kate as she handed over a breakfast tray. Kate liked to help out in little ways when she could and her help was repaid many times over when she needed another hand with the children. It was a harmonious household below stairs as a rule.

The housekeeper was standing at her window, looking out into the park. 'Good morning, Kate, I suppose you've heard the news?' Kate shook her head and Mrs Mason walked over to the table, severe in the black dress she wore for church. She must be about fifty and she looks tired, Kate thought. 'Sir Titus is going to speak to the staff in the dining-room ... I think there's been a misunderstanding about something.'

What, again? Kate sighed. 'Can't you tell me more?' She went to the door, knowing that Polly would be in trouble if she stayed too long.

'We'll have to wait and see,' the woman said wearily. 'All I know is, Sir Titus is furious.'

The atmosphere in the dining-room was tense as Kate went in with the children after breakfast. They tried to hide behind her and Bella had her thumb in her mouth, which wouldn't create a very good impression. Sir Titus stood on shallow steps at one end of the room with his lady sitting beside him. Both wore grim expressions and maintained a frigid silence. Since everybody wore their Sunday clothes, it reminded Kate of a funeral. There was trouble brewing for somebody.

Suddenly the gravelly voice boomed out and the maids jumped. 'It seems that none of you can be trusted,' Sir Titus began, puffing out his chest. 'Items have been stolen and I intend to get them back. Moral standards in this house, on this estate, are lax and this will not be allowed to continue.' He sounded as though this was a prepared speech, very much in Lady Wiggins's pompous style. In his more normal, woollen-mills voice he went on, 'Think on, then, all of you. I'm going to mek you suffer! Nobody gets the better of me, so be warned. Others have tried and it were the worse for them.' He looked round, to see the effect of his words. 'Stealing is a sin!'

The servants looked at each other uneasily, evidently wondering who was due to suffer – and how.

Fletcher looked unhappy; the maids and the housekeeper were just as shocked as Kate, judging by their expressions. Sir Titus and his lady spent much of their time in town and the staff at the hall was not large. If somebody was dismissed, Kate thought, there would be more work for the rest – including herself.

'Dishonesty I will not stand! Some of you will know that pheasants are being stolen from this estate.' The indoor staff breathed out slowly; this was not their problem. Everyone looked at Fletcher, the part-time keeper, who stood with his eyes on the ground. Maybe he was in for trouble?

'This points to criminal activity. Those birds are my property, do you hear?' The harsh voice rose. 'You have a duty to tell me who it is. Everybody in this village must know who steals my game. I'll have them in prison, I warn you.'

But when was a pheasant a wild bird, and when was it someone's property? That was a poacher thought, Kate realized; the law said that game was the property of the land-owner. She thought of what her brother had said. After a few years of bad harvests, Kirkby folks were poor and had got used to taking birds for the pot, especially Wigginss birds. There was no tradition of loyalty to him.

Once pheasants were released from the breeding coops they could fly where they liked. Most stayed on the estate, but not all. But if Fletcher was still feeding them, they were more like farmyard poultry than free spirits, and as easy to catch. How could a part-time gamekeeper watch over them all the time?

Sir Titus had not finished. 'But that is not all. Last month there were fifty cattle in the park, and yesterday I could only count forty-five. You people must think I can't count. Where are they?' he shouted suddenly, and George hid his face.

A slight sigh of relief went through the room and Kate relaxed a little. This was a scene for the sake of one. Everybody – except Sir Titus, it seemed – knew that Jim Robson, the farm manager had sold five fat cattle during the week, because it was the right time of year and they were ready. Mr Robson wasn't there to explain, of course. He lived in the village and was entrusted with looking after the farm, which included buying and selling livestock. But Sir Titus was letting his people know that his beady eyes watched their every move.

Surely it was over now? Kate began to relax, but it was too soon.

'Worst of all!' The servants braced themselves all over again. 'Worst of all, valuable silver has been stolen from this very room,' Sir Titus boomed, pointing dramatically to the sideboard behind him. There was still a gleam of silver urns and candle holders – what could be missing? 'My napkin rings, serving spoons, small objects easily taken and sold! Some person here must be a thief. I shall send a message to the Ripon jewellers, to look out for my silver. We've no butler, that means the housekeeper's responsible. Mrs Mason, what have you to say?'

The housekeeper shook her head miserably. It was like the Wigginses to have a public scene like this without telling Mrs Mason of the problem. She caught Kate's eye with a despairing look.

Now there was horror on every face, as the servants calculated their chances of getting another job if they were turned off without a character. Sir Titus was likely to throw them out on mere suspicion – he'd done it before. There were very few big houses in the parish and none with places for more servants, everyone knew. That meant a move away from home and a struggle to find another place.

Kate herself started to think about her options. She would have to start looking at advertisements ... and she would probably have to leave Kirkby.

Polly was crying quietly into her apron, but the rest of the staff merely looked grim, as though they were wondering who would be daft enough to steal the stuff. It wasn't antique, it was silver-plated, showy and cheap, not even Elkington's. Even Kate knew that. If you polished the Hall silver too hard, the plating wore off.

'Before we leave this room I demand to know where my silver is! One of you must know!' Sir Titus shouted and Lady Wiggins's cold gaze raked the faces in front of her, looking for signs of guilt.

Kate felt both children shrink closer to her; this was frightening for them. She put a hand on George's shoulder and found that he was sobbing. Turning his face into her side, he muttered something.

Kate bent down to hear him and Bella started to cry in sympathy. 'What is it, Georgie? Tell me,' she whispered. As his father launched into a lecture on morals, George raised a tearstained face.

'I took it. It was – a game.'

'But why, George?' How could he ... she'd been with him nearly all the time. Kate went cold as she realized that on the Friday, her

46

ladyship had taken up several hours of the nursemaid's time, to act as lady's maid. They had sorted out Lady Wiggins's wardrobe, looked over her winter clothes and planned what she would wear for a charity ball. You didn't refuse anything that Lady Wiggins ordered.

That afternoon George had asked to play in the gardens, and promised to be good. Polly was to keep an eye on him ... she must have taken her eye off him for at least half an hour.

The room was quiet and into the silence George gulped and said loudly, 'I did it.' He shook the copper curls over his eyes.

What should she do? Kate wanted to protect the little boy from his terrible father, but ... and then it was taken out of her hands. George had been heard and all eyes were on them.

'Come here, boy,' his father shouted and Kate walked slowly forward with the two children, Bella clinging fiercely to her hand. 'Do you know what happens to thieves? They go straight to hell to burn in everlasting fire! How will you like that?'

Lady Wiggins held out a languid hand. 'Let us hear what he has to say for himself. Some thief may have persuaded George to steal the silver for him. Who was it, child?' She was not a warm mother, Kate had always known, and this morning she was like ice. But she was fairer than her husband and less vindictive.

Kate stood between the children, holding their hands. No doubt the blame would fall on her.

George took a deep breath and raised his head. 'It was nobody else, just me and Bella. We were playing pirates. We needed buried treasure and I ... I couldn't get gold, so I took some silver instead. I didn't really steal, Papa, just borrowed it. I'll put it back ... it's in the orchard, under an old apple tree.'

Bella nodded; she stood sturdily beside her brother. 'I was a pirate as well.'

There was a shocked silence and then a ripple of relief ran round the room. The silver plate was not lost and they would all keep their jobs for the present ... except, perhaps, Miss Cooper. Cooper was in for trouble now. Fletcher shot her a look that might have been sympathy, but he was grinning.

'Right!' Sir Titus took out a gold watch from his waistcoat pocket. 'It's time you all went to church. You will hear more of this, especially you, Cooper.' He glared at Kate. 'Gross negligence and neglect of duty! And the bairn shall be whipped.' He paused and George shivered.

'On the matter of poaching, be warned that drastic action has been taken.' Sir Titus licked his thick lips. 'This'll stop further trespassing in my woods. I intend to stamp out dishonesty in this place for good. You're a disgrace to the neighbourhood, d'ye know? A disgrace. I never found my Bradford workers to be dishonest, never. I mistrust the lot of yer. For two pins I'd turn you all off and start again.'

Mrs Mason raised her eyebrows in disbelief and Kate caught her eye. He was more likely to get rid of one servant or at the most two, than dismiss them all at once. That would be far too inconvenient for the family, although it could be done. There were plenty of people without jobs, just waiting to step into their shoes.

In hard times, it was good to work in a place like the Hall, with three meals a day and a good bed at night. A lot of rich people bullied their servants, but you had to put up with it. Most of them stayed because they had no alternative.

The ancient church was dim and quiet, with the organ (donated by Sir Titus) playing softly. Kate took a deep breath and settled into the pew with a child at either side. Church was a relief after all the drama at the Hall, in spite of the usual jolly sermon. They heard the vicar's favourite theme today, the terrors of hell fire and the virtues of knowing your place in the world, being satisfied with your humble station in life. The vicar would obviously please Sir Titus with this one. Hell fire was a favourite notion of his, reserved for all who displeased him and he liked to keep people in their humble stations, even though he had climbed up the social ladder himself.

Kate was sceptical; she had come down in the world because of circumstances and she wished luck to anyone who could improve their situation. As a small girl living at the doctor's house, she had never imagined that one day she and Sam would be servants. Not that Sam felt it very much; he worked for Thomas Ridley and they were friends. Tom had mixed with all classes at the doctor's house and Kate could see the difference. To some of the gentry, servants were invisible at best.

Poor George was still trembling and Kate put a protective arm round him, but she couldn't shield him from his father and what was to come.

After church, Polly came to fetch the little boy, crying herself as she looked at him. She was very fond of both the children. 'Sir Titus is in the library,' she whispered. The library was a gloomy room, rarely used by the present owner of the Hall.

Kate stood in the corridor outside the library, listening to the whoosh of the cane descending time and again. The man was inhuman – he should have talked to the child, not hit him. What could she do to distract George's mind when it was over? There was very little she could do with children on a Sunday; most of their usual games were forbidden and when Sir Titus was at home, they could never make the slightest noise. Now she could hear him crying as though his heart would break.

At last the door opened and George hobbled out, his face white, followed by Sir Titus, flushed and triumphant. He must enjoy inflicting pain.

'You! Cooper! Any more of your laziness and you will be dismissed.' He smiled, and it was not a nice smile. 'Just to remind you, I will deal with you next.' He grabbed her by the arm, pulled her into the room and shut the door so quickly that she had no time to resist.

Kate stood with a straight back as she faced her employer. Words wouldn't hurt her but would he stop at shouting? Surely a nursemaid was safe? With a shock she realized that she was not safe. Sir Titus came towards her, came closer.

The man was not tall, but he was immensely powerful and must have developed his muscles when young, working in the mills. And now she was at his mercy and he wanted to inflict more pain. His face was flushed and to her horror, Sir Titus grabbed his cane and snatched at Kate's shawl, under which she was wearing a rather thin dress. 'You are neglecting your duty to the children,

Cooper,' he said in a quiet voice that was more sinister than his ravings. 'For this, you too shall be thrashed.' He struck her with the cane several times across her back, although she dodged and turned and kicked out at him.

Kate pulled away from him and ran to the door, but it was locked. Wiggins followed, pushed her up against the door and twisted her arm up her back, then pulled back her dress until she was exposed. She scrabbled frantically but could make no impression on him. The man was mad, she was sure of it now, as he pushed himself against her, forcing her back against the door.

'You are enjoying this as much as me. I know you are, you slut,' the man gloated. 'You're a foundling, I found that out. Bad blood, it always shows in the end ... your mother were a slut and so are you. This is how you always behave.' He was scrabbling at her clothes.

Kate started to protest but he shouted her down. 'When I saw you going to meet Ridley I knew what you were up to. You looked so pure and innocent, but now I know, I can see the look on your face ... you chase after men. Leaving your post and meeting in the woods ... well, you may show me your talents now.' His face was close to hers as he whispered, 'It's my turn now ... show me what you did with Ridley. Show me!' His fingers were digging into her flesh and Kate could hardly breathe.

At that moment there was a loud knocking on the door. 'Sir Titus! Please, Sir Titus, you're wanted urgently!' It was Mrs Mason, coming to her rescue.

'You are a stupid, incompetent woman!' Sir Titus began to roar at the top of his voice as he unlocked the door. 'Remember what I told you – one more episode like this and you are dismissed!'

Kate did not stand to be shouted at, but hurriedly pulled her shawl over her shoulders and ran out of the library and up to her room to calm herself. She stood for a moment or two, looking out from the attic window over the park, serene in the midday sun. The episode had given her a sick feeling. No one had ever before accused Kate Cooper of being a loose woman; it hurt more than the bruises. She had never been attacked like that before.

It was time to go up to the nursery to look after George. His buttocks and legs were bleeding and already beginning to bruise. It had been a vicious attack on a helpless five year old and Kate felt her own tears flow as she looked at the little boy.

George lay face down on his bed, sobbing into his pillow. Kate calmed him, gave him a drink of milk and put salve on his wounds, talking in a soothing voice. She brought up some food from the kitchen and Polly brought in Bella to share it with them.

'Tomorrow, we'll go to Bluebell Wood and collect some plants for our botany book,' she told the children. 'We might even find some blackberries.'

'After you, was he?' Polly said quietly, once the children were settled for an afternoon sleep. 'I've had to dodge him many times and I told Mrs Mason where you were. That's why she came up and knocked on the door.' She looked at Kate and then said, 'It's not easy to get away from him, you know. He beat me, once ... but then Mrs Mason came. I'm – afraid of him, miss.'

'Let Mrs Mason know if he assaults you again, Polly,' Kate said firmly. Something should be done about him, but – what? Perhaps Lady Wiggins should be told, but she might not believe the word of a servant.

'Well, tomorrow the Wigginses go back to Bradford,' Kate reminded the girl. She didn't want to talk about what had happened in the library. She was shaken and bruised and she wanted to leave the Hall and never set foot in it again ... except that would mean she abandoned George and Bella.

How could a man who had so much power be such a monster? Sir Titus Wiggins had been knighted for his donations to charity and was seen as a benefactor; among other things he had given money to the orphanage in nearby Ripon. But those who worked for him got no charity. It was all for show.

While the children were sleeping, Kate thought about her situation. Walks in the grounds were obviously to be avoided when the owner was at home and she would watch carefully to make sure that he never trapped her in a corner again. When George went to school Miss Cooper would have to find another job and next time, she would be more careful, if she ever had a choice of employer.

How had Wiggins found out about her past? A few people in the village knew. When she was a little girl, the Coopers had told her gently that she and Sam had both been adopted. 'We couldn't have children of our own, so we chose you,' Dr Cooper had told them both as soon as they were old enough to understand. 'But it makes no difference, you know. We are your parents now and we're a happy family.'

They had been happy until Dr Cooper died, and his wife soon after him, leaving Sam and Kate to face an uncertain future. Not for the first time, Kate wondered who her real parents were and why they had given her up. She'd come to the Coopers from the orphanage, but how had she got there? They could have died in a cholera outbreak...

Kate sighed and got out some needlework. If ever she wanted to marry, her past would be important, but marriage seemed unlikely. She would have to make the best life she could out of being a governess.

FOUR

A bright Monday morning was all the brighter as Kate watched the Wigginses roll down the drive on their way to the railway station, driven by Fletcher in the brougham. They would be in Bradford for at least a week; Cook said she didn't expect them back for a while. Fletcher might know when he next had to collect them from the station, although Sir Titus liked to keep them in suspense as to when he would return, and often surprised them. 'Tries to catch us out,' Fletcher often said.

Kate sighed and relaxed. Days of peace stretched ahead, a tranquil time in which to enjoy the autumn sunshine and dabble in a little learning. The Wiggins children were supposed to be cared for, rather than educated. That would come later, with a boarding-school for George and perhaps a governess for Bella. But Kate believed that you were never too young to learn interesting things about the world and she encouraged their curiosity.

George was rather quiet and still sore, but Bella had recovered from yesterday's fright and worked out how to deal with it. 'I'm not going to be a pirate no more,' she announced as Kate brushed her golden hair. 'Pirates get into trouble.' She was a year younger than her brother, but somehow, already Bella liked to think things out for herself.

Perhaps that was a valuable lesson in life, but it was all behind them now. 'We need a new game,' Kate said to them both. She herself was trying to forget about Wiggins and her Sunday ordeal. He was just an unpleasant fact of life and she would avoid him as much as she could. She too wanted to keep out of trouble.

George looked out of the window where across the park they could see the woods, old woodland that was part of the land his father owned. 'Robin Hood! And you can be Maid Marian,' he said graciously to Bella.

'No! We had a story about that and he was a ... a robber and then he got into trouble.' Bella was wise beyond her years, Kate decided. They needed a game that seemed adventurous, but was safe.

'Let's be explorers. We could venture into unknown places, far from civilization and discover, er, rare plants that nobody has seen before ... or at least, that we haven't got in our collection.' Kate stopped short of the idea of discovering lost tribes in the parish of Kirkby.

The children considered this as they ate breakfast and decided that it had some promise. 'As long as we don't have to miss our meals,' Bella decided. So to make it more of an adventure, Kate asked the kitchen for a bottle of water and some bread and cheese, to which Cook added chocolate and an apple each. Cook liked the children and spoiled them when she could. She had grown up children of her own, so she understood that exploring is hungry work.

The expedition set off down the drive, each member with a pack and a stick to walk with. They carried food and water, a bag in case of blackberries and a small can for plant or insect specimens. They wore sun hats instead of the helmets that explorers usually wore.

George seemed to brighten as they went along. 'We'll have to go right into the woods, very far in,' he told the others. 'Maybe I should lead the way 'cos I'm a boy.'

Kate was not keen to get lost in the woods and she didn't know that part of the estate very well. You could walk round in circles in places like this and take hours to come out again, especially when the leaves were still on the trees.

The boundary with Kirkby Manor, Ridley's estate, formed one side of Bluebell Wood and if they walked parallel with that hedge, she would always know how to get home again.

'You can lead the way,' Kate conceded. 'But let me decide the direction. We must draw a map of our journey later, explorers always do, so I need to keep the map in my head.'

The sudden alarm call of a pheasant reminded her of the game. They were not supposed to frighten the pheasants, especially not to send them over the fence onto the neighbours' land. 'And we must walk quietly, so we don't disturb the birds. We'll see more birds and maybe a squirrel, if we keep as quiet as we can.'

At the edge of the wood they came to a newly painted notice:

TRESPASSERS BEWARE!
ENTER AT YOUR PERIL!

George tried to spell out the words and then asked Nursie to read it for them.

'We're not trespassers, we live here,' she told the startled children. 'This must be intended to keep poachers away.' It must be a bluff, she decided. What sort of peril could lurk under the trees?

The explorers walked in single file ever deeper into the wood, with the Ridley hedge, or sometimes stone wall, just visible to Kate on her right. Eventually, the leader halted under an enormous tree with spreading branches and leaves that were yellowing with the first touch of autumn. 'Look!'

A red squirrel peered down at them, then flicked its tail, scampered along a branch and disappeared. 'I've never seen this tree before. These are acorns, so it's an oak tree,' George pointed out. The acorns were green, but one or two had fallen and Bella picked them up.

'Fairy hats,' she said happily. 'We can draw them later.'

'This tree must be very old ... how old is it, Nursie?'

This was ancient woodland, Kate knew. 'My brother told me that where you get bluebells, it's a very old wood,' she said. 'This tree will be hundreds of years old, I think. Let's take a leaf or two and an acorn for our collection. The squirrel probably has a hole up there, where he sleeps for the winter.'

They walked on, talking about the wood of the oak tree and what it could be used for. None of them had been here before and they were beginning to feel like real explorers. Bella found a plant bright with scarlet berries 'Pretty!' she said. 'Can we take them home?'

'That's Jack in the Pulpit and the berries can poison you, so we'll leave it alone,' Nurse said firmly. 'Perhaps we'll find blackberries later.'

When it was time for lunch, they sat on a fallen log in a small clearing where sunshine filtered through between the trees. 'Let's keep really quiet and see how many birds we can hear,' Kate suggested. But the birds had fallen silent, the breeze had dropped and the air was utterly still.

Kate became aware of a mysterious atmosphere in the darkness under the trees at the edge of the clearing, where the dense canopy shut out the light. Ancient woods such as this one had a pagan feel to them. She thought of fairy-tales, some of them quite dark; people lost in forests, or meeting wolves or witches. It was easy to see where these stories had come from. No one knew, even in civilized Yorkshire, just what was buried in the green depths of a forest.

George seemed to pick up her train of thought. 'It's like the story of Babes in the Wood, Nursie,' he whispered. 'But we won't get lost, will we?' He smiled when he heard from far away the sound of a hammer hitting wood; someone repairing a fence, perhaps. They were only on the edge of the dark wood and there were people not far away.

Lunch tasted good, out in the open air. This adventure, in its quiet way would help to restore both children after the terrors of yesterday. Kate herself felt the healing influence of the ancient woodland; it was a different world to the Hall. She handed out the chocolate to complete their happiness.

Suddenly George sat up straight. 'Listen! No, not the hammer, someone shouting!'

'Probably a ploughman with horses...'

Kate began, and then she heard the sound, 'Aaaaagh...!' A hoarse and chilling cry. Then silence again.

The children's eyes were round as they looked at Nurse. 'Where did it come from?'

A shiver went through Kate in spite of herself, it sounded so like the call of an ogre who ate little children, in one of the stories she'd heard. She was being too fanciful. Pulling herself together, Kate raised her voice to a shout. 'Where are you?' Nothing, except for the alarm call of a pheasant in the distance. Had they imagined the sound? A feeling of danger persisted; whatever had made that sound, there was trouble ahead, in the dark under the trees.

Kate packed up the remains of their lunch while the children sat quiet and then they heard the hoarse call again. This time there was no mistake; it could be a cry for help and they would have to find out.

As they hurried along, Kate wondered about the wisdom of taking the children with her, but she couldn't leave them. 'We're coming, keep shouting!' she called and her voice echoed through the trees. This time it was answered.

'Here! Here...' A man's voice, hoarse and weak. It sounded like someone in pain.

The sounds led them to a long woodland ride with patches of blackberries and rabbit holes dotting a sandy bank. They called again – and the answer came from a clump of bracken. Kate looked carefully round and saw a hand waving in the air, just visible above the green and yellow fronds. The ogre had been found.

A man was lying on his back and at first Kate couldn't see why, but as he struggled to sit up she saw that his leg was clamped by two steel bars, holding him down. He was in a trap.

'Oh, my goodness! How long have you been here?'

'All night ... lying here waiting to die.' The man flinched and groaned as he tried to see who they were. 'You're the bloody Wigginses! You're responsible for this – I'm going to have the law on you!' He didn't look like a poacher ... though dirty, but who were poachers anyway? And he was ferocious, dangerous even in his pain. 'My leg's caught; I'm fast, in case you hadn't bloody well noticed. This is a man trap, for killing men...' His voice faded. He must be quite weak.

Kate took the children back a little and then went up to the man alone. What would her doctor father have done? Kept calm, for a start. She took a deep breath. 'How are we going to get you out of there?'

The man trap had smooth jaws, not teeth, but even so his leg might be broken. Kate suddenly boiled with rage. These things had been illegal for years but that hadn't stopped

Wiggins and he wouldn't care if a man died, so long as his game was protected. Or – what if his own children had walked into it? She tried to force the jaws apart with her walking stick, but it snapped.

'I'll go for help. As quickly as I can, we'll get you out of there.' She would go back to the boundary fence and try to find the workman who was hammering. The man continued to swear about Wiggins, so she needed to get the children away. He hardly seemed rational, but then he had been suffering for hours.

Kate left a trail of broken bracken fronds to lead them back to the spot again. They walked fast and little Bella's legs could hardly keep up.

To their relief, Kate's brother Sam was working on the boundary fence, watched by Thomas Ridley who apparently had just arrived; he was sitting in a trap. The young horse impatiently swished his tail at the flies and stamped his feet. Just what was needed; Kate felt weak with relief. It was dreadful to think of that man's suffering and it would take two men to free him.

The men were amazed to see Kate and the children rush up to them, flushed and breathless. 'We found a man and he's hurt!' George babbled, while Bella shrieked.

When Tom heard the story, he immediately selected some tools and he and Sam jumped over the fence to the Wiggins side.

'We'll have to get him out quickly, men can die in those traps,' he said quietly. He picked up George and put him on his shoulders, and Sam did the same for Bella. 'It's a cruel, inhumane instrument of torture – invented for poachers. Do you know who the fellow is?'

Kate turned to her brother as they strode along. 'Do you remember Lily Thorpe, Sam? She was one of Father's patients she died just before he did. I think the man is her husband...'

'William Thorpe,' Sam said at once. 'Works at Village Farm. He's not a poacher surely?'

'He called us bloody Wiggineses,' Bella reported, mimicking the man's accent.

'Please go and collect bracken, children,' Kate ordered when they were set down.

The man was still swearing when they got back, but as Sam and Thomas set to work he fainted. Kate could hardly imagine what he was going through, what his wounds might be. Added to the pain, he'd been out in the cold woodland all night.

It was hard work, but slowly Sam and Tom together prised the jaws apart with a crowbar. 'Lucky it's not one of the old type,' Sam said between his teeth. It took them some time to pull him free and lay him on a bed of bracken that the children had picked.

Kate moved away the torn trousers and

looked at the leg. It was badly bruised and lacerated and the foot was white because the blood supply had been cut off. 'We need to get him to a doctor,' Kate said. She ran her hands along the bones, but none seemed to be broken. He was not bleeding very much; she gently wiped off what blood there was with a handkerchief and noticed green stains where vegetation had been forced into the leg.

William Thorpe was conscious again by this time. 'No doctors,' he growled. 'Can't afford it. Just take me home, will you?' He peered up at Kate. 'Well, it's Dr Cooper's daughter ... oh Lord, this leg! Your dad would have looked after me right, but this new bloke's too dear.' He was wet, soaked with dew.

Sam shook his head. 'You won't be able to walk for a while; you need looking after ... and there's nobody at home, is there?'

'Not since Lily died. Take me home, will you, Mr Ridley? I just realized who you are.' He smiled bitterly. 'Thank God it wasn't Wiggins found me, he'd have finished me off.'

Tom looked down at William, his face full of concern. 'Sam and I can carry you to the trap ... and then I think we should take you to someone who can care for you. If that wound turns bad, you're in trouble. And you've had a mighty shock.'

'Miss Weaver, the herb woman,' Sam suggested. 'We could take you there, William, she'll know what to do.' Kate thought that was a very good idea, but the patient didn't.

'Nay, not there! Anywhere but there!' Thorpe tried to stand up and fell heavily. This time he lay still.

Grimly, Sam and Tom lifted the inert body between them, locking hands behind his back. 'I'm afraid there's no choice, let's do it as quickly as possible.' He looked at Kate and the children. 'Would you like a ride?'

'Thank you, but we'll walk, it's only a mile or two back to the Hall.' Kate wanted to get George and Bella away from the scene, to talk to them about something else. It had not been a good experience for them.

The children looked up at this and then Miss Arabella Wiggins made up her mind. 'Won't walk,' she announced, sitting firmly on the ground. Feets hurt.' George was looking wistfully up at Thomas. They were all rather tired, it would be nice to have a ride ... Kate gave in. 'Thank you, Thomas, we'll come with you.'

Miss Weaver lived on the moorland side of the village, not far from Bellwood Hall. They had to look after the injured man first before they could go home.

As they bowled smoothly along Tom looked sideways at Kate. 'I think this is the best option for him, but it's a lot to ask of poor Miss Weaver,' he said quietly.

Kate nodded. 'Judith Weaver will cope, I'm sure. My father said she was good at medicine – he used to send people to her for salves and tonics. That's probably why Sam thought of her.'

Goats were being brought into the shed for milking as they reached the cottage, goats of various colours and sizes, prancing and jostling. Their owner walked behind them, a woman of about forty with a straight back. She wiped her hands on a black apron and came forward to greet them at the gate.

'Mr Ridley, good day to you. And to you, Sam. How can I be of help to you?' Miss Weaver's voice was low and pleasant. The goat lady, as she was known, was straight and slim and had steady grey eyes. Her fair hair was just beginning to show a few grey streaks. Kate thought she looked kind but firm, just the sort of woman to deal with William Thorpe.

By this time, Thorpe was struggling and had started to swear again. Tom stayed with him, while Sam explained the situation. 'He's been caught in a trap all night, he needs care and we thought of you,' he said simply. 'Will you be able to look after him for a few days?'

The woman came through the gate and walked up to the vehicle. 'Now, William Thorpe, there's no call for swearing. You're in trouble and this is the best place for you.

Bring him inside,' she said firmly to the men and a strangely subdued Thorpe was carried in and laid on a sofa at the back of a big kitchen.

'Of all the places,' he muttered to Kate, while Miss Weaver went to fetch water, 'this is the last place on earth I would want to be.'

Kate wondered what on earth he had against the goat lady. Why couldn't he keep quiet and be grateful?

After the trap had gone on its way, taking the children back to the Hall, there was silence in the cottage. Judith Weaver gave the patient a long drink of water and then put the kettle on the fire. Into a basin of warm boiled water she poured a little lavender oil, while William lay on the sofa with his eyes closed.

The man's leg was now blue and very swollen, with dark blood collecting under the skin in places. Judith bathed it gently and then said, 'I must milk the goats now. Are you hungry?' There was no reply, so she left a piece of bread on a plate beside him and went out quietly.

While she milked five goats and went through her peaceful evening routine, Judith was wondering what she could do to help the turbulent spirit in the house. It had been a shock to see William. They had not met for over twenty years, but she had never been able to forget him completely.

No wonder he didn't want to be nursed by her. When she came back to the village he was married to Lily and they had avoided each other ever since. There was too much bitterness for either of them to forget the past. He had let her down by going to gaol – and she had gone away. She had never married and now she was set in her ways. Having him here was going to be difficult.

By the time the goats were turned out again and the milk was sieved and put to cool, the sun had set and Judith felt calm again.

He needed help; that was enough. The pain would get worse before it was better.

'I never wanted to come here,' was the first thing her patient said when she went back inside. Deliberately Judith went about making up the fire and preparing supper. She gave him a cup of willow bark tea to deaden the pain and William shuddered at the bitter taste, but he drank it.

'Of course not. I understand that.' Judith helped him into a sitting position and put a shawl around his shoulders. She gave him a poached egg on toasted bread and he ate most of it.

They sat in the warm firelight. William Thorpe was still a handsome man, Judith decided, although at the moment he needed a shave and his face was pale with shock. 'I'm content to have you here, William. When you have healed and gone home, we need not meet again. But for now, please accept what cannot be changed, as I have done many times. Mr Ridley and Sam did right to bring you to me.'

The man sighed and passed a tired hand over his eyes. 'Well, I suppose its not your fault ... and they had no idea that this was the last place on earth... I'll go home as soon as I can walk.' He looked at her for the first time since his arrival. There were hollows under the high cheekbones; William looked haunted, but that might be because he wasn't eating enough. Times were hard in Kirkby.

After the supper was cleared away, Judith took up her knitting and the patient fell asleep. The willow bark would take away some of his pain and sleep was a powerful healer. When he woke, she helped him outside to relieve himself. Then she took him to a bed in a small downstairs room and climbed the twisting stairs to her bedroom in the attic. Tomorrow she would make comfrey compresses and bind them to his leg. Tomorrow was another day.

For a few days after his ordeal William seemed to improve, but then he worsened. He didn't want food and was feverish. 'This leg's gone bad,' he said. 'I can feel it. It's all over with me now.' Judith cleaned the wound again, this time using honey as a dressing.

It was nearly midnight. A chill wind howled round the cottage as William tossed and turned, muttering and crying out by turns, half unconscious. He was cold and clammy to the touch. Judith made up the fire and wrapped another blanket around him. He was quiet for a while after this, then asked for a drink. 'I'm deathly cold, lass.' Judith spent the rest of the night with William in her arms, gazing into the fire and thinking of times past. Once he looked at her. 'Judith, girl, this is how it should always have been. Now it's too late.' Eventually, he slept with his head on her shoulder. She thought that he might not wake again. When wounds went bad, they poisoned the whole body. That she knew.

FIVE

The more he talked about the mantrap in the woods, the more angry did Tom Ridley become. 'If your sister hadn't come along, the old boy would certainly have died,' he told Sam. 'What a terrible death! Wiggins should be prosecuted – I must tell the police about it. What's the name of the inspector at Ripon?'

'Won't that land William in trouble?' Sam suggested. Sometimes Tom had to be held back from rushing into things. 'He shouldn't have been in the wood. I think we need to talk to him in a day or two, before we tell the police.'

Tom, driving the trap, looked straight ahead with a set face. 'We can just tell someone in authority that the terrible thing is there, that it's been sprung, but it could be reset. No need to mention Thorpe. At the very least it should be destroyed. I wonder who made it? It could be an old one, of course, from the days when they were legal and poachers were transported to Australia, if they survived the trap. It was barbaric – but they've been banned since about 1827. My pa told me about it.'

'It's been hauled there and set recently, I saw the wheel marks of a cart. I'm not sure about the legal side,' Sam said tentatively. 'But I understand that certain types of trap are still allowed, if fair warning is given and Kate says there's a notice at the gate into the wood. I think Wiggins will stop short of anything illegal, he's very keen to act the part of a leader in the county. I can't stand the man!'

They clattered into the stable yard and when Tom had unyoked the mare, Sam wheeled the trap into position in the shed.

'I wonder if there are any more?' Tom said suddenly and they looked at each other. 'We'd better warn Kate not to go into the wood again.'

Sam looked up at the sky which was fading into the dark blue of evening. 'I think she'll be very wary of the Wiggins woods in future. Poor Kate, I wish she didn't work at the Hall. Oh well, time to feed pheasants, it'll soon be dark.' In a building next to the stable the food was waiting on benches. 'It's a mix of grain they get now.'

'No wonder it costs so much,' groaned Tom.

'You can help, if you don't mind, sir.' They both laughed; in their schooldays the two had formed a bond and their relationship was not formal, but Sam reminded his employer quite often that he was in charge.

'You'll see how the birds have grown since they were in the coops.' He was proud of the birds, the first he'd ever reared.

'I'd love to spend more time with the game.' Tom picked up two buckets. 'There's so much forestry work at the moment, selling timber and organizing to plant trees ... how do things look for the season? The guns will be here soon.'

'Since they were moved to cover, I don't think we've lost many birds,' Sam told the boss, as they walked across to the edge of the little wood, each carrying buckets of grain. 'They've been out here three weeks now and the broody hens have gone home, so this is the most dangerous time.' The young pheasants were out in the wood, learning to fend for themselves.

Tom looked at the birds. 'They have grown, haven't they? I'm hoping to earn some money from the shoots this year, Lord knows we need it. There's plenty of interest, we've got several bookings so you're going to be busy! We'll have to think about hiring beaters soon. Let's hope the poachers don't get in first... I wonder if Thorpe was after pheasants?'

They scattered the grain and the young birds clustered around them like chickens in a farmyard, hundreds of pheasants now in beautiful adult feathers. Many of them would disappear into the wild population, but some would be shot by the guns and sent to restaurants. It was an industry in this part of Yorkshire and a potential source of income for the estate. These birds would help to pay Sam's wages.

'Rabbits, more likely,' Sam told him. But he knew the temptation, had felt it himself. At this time of year it was so easy. The birds were roosting on low branches. They'd been reared under broody hens and were used to being fed. You could throw out some grain and then pick them up and wring their necks without a sound. 'Maybe you should call on Mr Thorpe, one day when you've an hour to spare.'

A week later, Kate was driven to the village by John Fletcher on her usual round of charity from the Hall. Lady Wiggins liked to distribute soup and other food to the deserving poor, but, as she was often away, the job increasingly fell to the nursemaid.

She had been given a list of families, but as time went on her ladyship tended to trust Kate's judgement. 'You were the doctor's daughter, you will know the cottagers,' she said. 'But don't take the children on visits, they may catch some dreadful disease.'

Kate smiled at this; she'd heard a different story. When Lady Wiggins was told that Cook was ill one day, she wouldn't allow it. 'The lower orders are never ill,' she'd announced. It obviously meant *when they are supposed to be on duty*.

Her ladyship was from an 'old' family, the servants said, from generations born to order people about – and who also felt at times a need to dish out soup to cottagers. Some said it was true charity and were thankful, others thought it was all for show and to be patronizing. It was hard to please Kirkby folk.

Lady Wiggins's own family had spent all their 'old' money, which was why she'd married Sir Titus, people decided. He was new to riches and climbing the social ladder with some difficulty. The knighthood, earned by generous donations to the right causes, helped, and his wife made him more acceptable in some circles.

Sir Titus was trying to make a good impression on the villagers with gifts of money to the church, as well as food for the cottagers. But Kate knew that the folk at Kirkby were very independent and any help had to be given tactfully. After bad harvests for the last few years, many people were feeling the pinch and so the food was welcomed, especially by women with big families to feed. The general feeling was that Wiggins was making plenty of money in his Bradford woollen mills and could afford to give food away.

Fletcher liked to call at the Queen's Head for an illicit glass of beer while Kate made her visits and he took no interest in where she went. It was a moment of rare freedom for Kate, one of the few times she was able to get away from the demanding children at the Hall. She loved them, but it was good to have a break sometimes.

After visiting two cottages and chatting with the mothers and children, she strode quickly along to Miss Weaver's house. The goat lady sold cheeses and herbs and had never needed charity, but now she had another person to feed for a while.

'I wondered how you were getting on,' Kate murmured, when she met Judith Weaver in her garden. The day was cool and breezy, whipping Kate's shawl above her head. 'Mr Thorpe seemed to be difficult, but he would have suffered a lot. How is he?' She put down her basket, lighter now.

'He'll mend, but it will be slow.' Judith straightened up and smiled, which made her look much younger. 'It was kind of you to come, Kate. Yes, I was worried for a night or two, but he's over the worst. William's not a happy man. But come in and see him.'

The patient was reading the local paper by the window. He was dressed in clean clothes, but the scowl was still there. 'Suppose you've told the whole bloody parish about what happened to me? Women can't help but gossip,' he muttered. 'Well, listen to this: I don't want folks to know that I'm here, or why I'm here. You just remember that.' His blue eyes were cold and hostile.

'I was going to ask the vicar to say a special prayer for your recovery in church on Sunday,' Kate said cheerfully. 'That would spread the news round the parish!'

Thorpe growled, but then looked up and saw that she was teasing him. A slight smile crossed his face and for a moment, Kate caught a glimpse of a kinder man, the husband of Lily. He'd sometimes come to the surgery for his wife's medicine; he was always polite and he paid for it immediately, which was unusual. The Coopers had all liked him.

Judith busied herself with making tea and, just as the kettle boiled, there was a rattle of hoofs outside the gate. Tom Ridley knocked at the open door and then walked in, fresh faced from the drive. His eyes seemed to light up when he saw Kate, in the old flirtatious way. 'You visit the wounded as well as nursing the children, Miss Cooper! How to do you find the patient, or should I ask the man himself?' He walked over to the sofa with hand outstretched, but it was ignored. His broad shoulders seemed to fill the low room.

'No better for your asking.' William turned his head away. 'If folks would leave me alone, the woman here could get on with her work. Have you nowt else to do but hang about getting in the way?'

'Ah, I see you love to have visitors.' Tom grinned. 'The pain's still bad, is it? I can sympathize, broke my leg once. Fell off a horse. I was just as cross as you are now, William. But you're in good hands, the best. Miss Judith will have you right in no time.'

Judith looked resigned as she handed round tea and gingerbread. Kate drank her tea quickly; Fletcher would be ready to go home by now. In the scullery, she gave Judith the ham and soup in her basket. 'I hope this improves his temper,' she whispered. 'He's not an easy patient, is he? You'd think he would be grateful. He's much better off here than alone at home.'

Judith smiled. 'Thank you for thinking of it, Kate. He'll probably settle down. The pain is still quite bad as you can imagine. That leg was cut to the bone and it was starting to go bad, I was afraid of gangrene. He's still weak, but he's an impatient soul, William. He hates sitting about, he likes to be up and doing. I know how he feels.'

Kate was impressed. 'You are so patient with him – I hope he appreciates it.'

They moved back into the kitchen where Tom was still talking to Thorpe, uphill work for them both. 'Let's be straight, William, I'm not telling anybody you were involved. But just between you and me, what were you doing in Bluebell Wood?' He took another slice of gingerbread and winked at Kate.

Kate wanted to see what the man said, so she perched on the edge of a chair.

William looked out of the window and sighed, then turned to Tom. 'You wouldn't understand ... I was after a couple of rabbits. Just to keep my hand in. You've got to keep doing something and I've no work just now. Jim Dale turned me off, can't afford a foreman this season.' Judith Weaver gave him a surprised look; perhaps she hadn't heard a civil word from him until now.

Tom laughed, but it was sympathetic. 'Couldn't you dig the garden to keep your hand in, something less dangerous? Mantraps apart, you could've met with a keeper's truncheon, or been peppered with shot! Poaching ... well, it's a chancy business.

Especially with landlords like that one,' he finished grimly. 'Wiggins!'

'It gets into the blood ... I can't explain it. I love being out at night, hunting with the foxes. But I never struck a trap like yon before, never in my life.' William was more animated now.

Kate thought it was a pity he'd been so rude to Tom if he wanted another job. But Tom had been brought up in Kirkby, he knew the local ways. To an outsider, ordinary conversation in these northern villages often sounded like an exchange of insults. Her father had said that the Kirkby folk polished their insults like the vicar polished his sermons. He'd also said that while parsons see people at their best, doctors and nurses see them as they really are.

'Well, leave my pheasants alone, William. Can't afford to lose 'em,' Tom said pleasantly.

William shrugged. 'I'm no threat to anybody's game right now, am I? Any road, I've never sunk so low as to take birds out of season and it hasn't started yet. As I said, I was after rabbits.'

Tom nodded. 'I believe you.'

The poacher put his newspaper down and leaned forward. 'Tell you what, Mr Ridley, it's the Taylor gang you need to look out for. I've heard they're back together again. He's recently done time in prison, but they say he's out and they'll take pheasants any way and any time they can. There's a good market for the birds, of course, and no questions asked.'

'Lord, I hope they don't come down our way. I've heard some bad things about those gentlemen.' Tom looked serious as he made for the door.

William's high cheekbones jutted out of a thin face and Kate wondered whether he'd had enough to eat lately, since he'd lost his job. Maybe he'd been after a rabbit for a stew. You couldn't blame a hungry man for that. She stood up. 'Goodbye and thank you for the tea, Miss Weaver.' She smiled at William. 'I won't say a word to the vicar, you'll just have to get better without the help of the church.'

'Your father's daughter, you are. Always one for a joke, Dr Cooper. And do you know, he used to say that most folks recovered in time, with or without a doctor. That was honest, that was.'

Tom opened the door for her and followed Kate out of the room. 'I'm going to the post office, may I walk with you?' When they got into the street he went on, 'Kate, that man is low in spirits. See how he brightened after a while when we talked to him. Probably been on his own too long. I wish I could find him a job, heaven knows there's enough work, but the cash won't stretch to it. And now he's laid up for a while ... what do people live on in such cases?'

'Good will, credit and the help of neighbours, I suppose. Father never charged a fee when people fell on hard times...' Kate's voice died away. That was why she had no inheritance, but she had no regrets. 'But he'll surely never get a job if he goes on being rude to people. We're used to folks saying what they think in Kirkby, but he's impossible.'

Tom looked down at Kate as she walked beside him. 'Wiggins is the impossible one and I'm – well, Sam and I are both worried about you. Why don't you take another job?' His eyes were anxious. 'I would hate anything to go wrong for you, Kate,' he added very quietly. 'You mean a lot to me, you know.'

With an effort, Kate dragged her eyes away from his. He was still a flirt, after all.

'Please don't worry about me, lad,' she said lightly. 'I love the place, and the children. Wiggins is not at home during the week, so we get by very well.' Kate looked along the street. 'There's Fletcher waiting for me ... goodbye, Tom.'

'Just a moment, he can wait,' Tom said firmly. 'I thought you should know ... last week I had business in Bradford and just out of curiosity I went to see one of the Wiggins mills. The conditions there are terrible, Kate! Small, ragged children crawling under machines ... the dust and oil in the air and the noise! I couldn't bear it for more than a few minutes and the workers are in it for most of their lives.'

'I suppose they've never known anything else.' Kate was saddened by the thought. 'Life is very hard for some people – I suppose it always has been.'

'Harder still if you work for someone like Wiggins,' Tom pointed out. 'He's exploiting the poor people, especially the children. I know you could say that we landowners have always done that, but some of us look after our people very well.'

'But is there not a law to stop people putting young children to work?' Kate was appalled.

'I suppose their parents need the money they earn. But yes, since last year no child under ten is supposed to be there. I asked several urchins how old they were and they all said "Ten, mister", except one tiny mite who said "Dunno". Wiggins is using cheap labour, of course.'

Kate quickened her pace a little. They had reached the post office and Tom stopped walking. 'I can't forget that he struck you! That's why I think he has no principles at all – and that you should get away from Bellwood Hall. It's no place for a young woman!' Tom stood in the street, earnestly making his point. He seemed to feel very strongly about it.

It was a good job he didn't know that Wiggins had assaulted her. 'Getting away is easier said than done, Tom. But I suppose it's not just the Wiggins mills, all factories and mines must be bad for the workers. However kind the bosses are, it's dirty work. The varnish works in Ripon smell horrible, you'll have noticed that yourself.'

'I might have agreed with you, if I hadn't spent some time in York. There, things are different.'

'With your fiancée, I believe,' Kate said brightly. 'Sam tells me you're getting married, Mr Ridley.'

'Well, yes, Selina and I will be married next spring. But as I was saying, the chocolate

86

factory in York is different. It's run by the Rowntree family and they look after their people. Provide classes to teach young people to read and encourage them to learn skills and better themselves. They pay decent wages and for some, they provide housing. A different world, Kate, to the Wiggins factory I saw. And knowing Wiggins, I can imagine that the children would be bullied and possibly beaten. So, my real point is, leave the Hall, Kate. You can find a job somewhere else, I'm sure.' Tom didn't seem to mind who heard what he said.

The less said about Wiggins, especially in public, the better, Kate decided. 'So chocolate is made by happy workers, that's nice to know. I must go, Thomas.'

Tom's smile as they parted lingered with Kate until she reached the trap and Fletcher, who was anxious to be gone.

'Posh friends you've got,' Fletcher commented, as they rolled down the street. 'Tell you what, if you say nowt about where I've been, I'll keep quiet about the company you keep. How's that for a bargain?'

SIX

Sir Titus and his lady came back to the Hall on the next Saturday and below stairs, the usual apprehension spread like a grey cloud through the lower floors. What would go wrong this time? Fletcher, who drove them from the station, reported that they seemed to be in a good mood. 'Long may it last,' muttered Cook, looking over her shoulder.

After dinner Kate was summoned to Lady Wiggins's sitting-room. Nurse stood by the door, hands folded, waiting for instructions. Had her ladyship got wind of the scene in the library? Last year, a maid had been dismissed after Sir Titus took too much interest in her.

'Your services will not be required in future, Cooper,' Lady Wiggins announced in a bored tone of voice, after a few minutes of unnerving silence. She was dressed in a dark red gown with many frills and flounces. Kate concentrated on the frills while her mind tried to take in her ladyship's message. Not required...

'I am taking the children to visit my family in Chester, to a house where there is a capable children's nurse. During October we may return for the pheasant shooting season, but we have employed a governess for the future who will travel with us when we go to town. The children have been neglected and I cannot allow this to continue. They will stay with us in Bradford during the week.'

'Oh, ma'am!' Kate couldn't hold back, not now. 'The children are far better off in the country!' Poor little George and Bella how could they be happy, with Papa watching them the whole time?

Lady Wiggins looked right through Kate. 'You will leave tomorrow as soon as we have gone. Your wages will be ready. That is all, Cooper.' She turned away and then looked back. 'I wish you well, of course.'

Kate was stunned. The woman was notorious for saving money, especially on servants' wages and she obviously did not care whether Kate had anywhere to go. A nurse was one of the 'lower orders'. 'Very good, ma'am,' she said quietly and went out, resisting the temptation to bang the door. It had happened; she was dismissed, with no notice.

Mrs Mason the housekeeper raised her eyebrows when told the news. 'You'll go to your brother, dear? If not, you can stay here – I don't see why they should turn you out!' All hands in the kitchen were hoping that with his wife away, Sir Titus would stay in Bradford and leave them in peace. 'I saw a middle-aged woman come here the other day. She'd be the new governess.'

'Heaven help her.' Kate was still coming to terms with the situation; she felt unreal. A middle-aged woman was perhaps less likely to be molested by Wiggins, or at least should be clever enough to look after herself. The lesson learned, Kate had decided she would never be cornered like that again. 'I hope she'll be good to George and Bella ... I'll miss them,' she said with a catch in her voice.

The housekeeper nodded. 'You will, but I'm sure you'll find another position, dear. I will give you a character if Lady Wiggins doesn't. I wouldn't bother asking Sir Titus.'

'I don't think either of them would say a good word for me. Lady Wiggins said the children had been neglected, Mrs Mason.' In spite of herself Kate had been deeply hurt by the criticism.

'What nonsense! You're an excellent nurse. Don't let that sort of remark affect you, Kate.' Mrs Mason was indignant.

The children were excited to learn from their mother that they were to go on a train to visit their cousins. Kate didn't tell them she was leaving; the holiday would make it easier for them to cope with the change.

That morning Bella and George were at their angelic best and it was hard to fight back the tears. Leaving the Hall is good for me, Kate told herself. Thomas would be

90

pleased, and so would Sam.

The day was spent in packing clothes for the holiday and Kate wondered why she hadn't been told before. More time to organize would have been useful.

It was a fine evening and once the children were in bed – early because of the journey next day – Kate left Polly in charge of the nursery and set out to walk to Sam's cottage.

'Of course you'll come here, I've always wanted you to leave the Hall,' Sam said at once. 'We'll start looking out for another job, one without an old goat in charge. I heard the other day that he assaults women – have you had any trouble with him? A village lass who works in the laundry at the Hall has been telling some tales.'

'I can believe it.'

They sat in Sam's garden in the twilight, in a bower of roses planted by the previous keeper's wife. The cottage was on the edge of the Ridley woods, with good views of the surrounding countryside and Sam wanted to keep an eye out for any unusual movements as the sun went down. 'I hope you don't mind sitting outside,' he said apologetically, but Kate loved the old garden.

'A keeper's work is never done! It's nice to get some fresh air.' She paused, thinking what to say. 'Now, Sam, I don't want to be a burden to you. I've saved a little money, so I want to pay for my keep,' Kate told him.

'And perhaps I can–' She broke off at the sound of fast hoofbeats on the lane.

Tom Ridley threw the reins over the garden gate and strode in. 'Sam, we've got a crisis on our hands!' He saw the visitor. 'Katherine, how good to see you!' His smile was friendly and Kate felt the now familiar flutter as she looked at him. Living at Sam's for the next month would probably mean seeing more of Tom. That was not a good thing, but it couldn't be helped. Kate decided not to worry about it; after all, she'd known him all her life. It was just that they'd both grown up.

'Had a letter today – my father is coming. Been in Jamaica for years and now, suddenly, he wants to visit. It's important, he wants to discuss business. And, as you know, we're not fit for visitors – have to get some rooms ready as best we can.' Tom was agitated.

Sam sat back with arms folded, always the calm one. 'Surely the general can't expect too much? He's an army man. He must have slept on campbeds before now! Give him military board and lodging.'

Tom laughed. 'Pa left the army years ago, he's been in the lap of luxury ever since. The problem is, Kate, we only have one servant in the house. Sadie does her best to cook and clean, but she'll panic when she hears the news. He'll be here next week, no servants with him thank goodness; he's coming on the train.'

There was silence for a while in the garden, but Tom said no more. Dusk was falling gently over the fields and the sleepy sounds of birds going to roost came to them from the wood.

Tom walked up and down the path, then flopped into a vacant chair. 'What on earth shall we do?'

Sam said deliberately, 'Kirkby Manor isn't really a big house. We can help – can't we, Kate? Kate's free and she's a good cook, Tom, and if it's only for a few days, I can take time off from the farm to help to put the house to rights. I can mend broken windows, you know!' He grinned.

Tom turned quickly. 'Kate? You've run away?'

Kate explained what had happened. 'I'm free for the rest of my life. I'd be happy to help in a crisis,' she said quietly.

Tom covered Kate's hand with his. 'More relieved than I can say, girl, for your sake – you've got away from the Hall. So you can join us for a while. Wonderful!'

'So – what exactly is to happen?' Kate tried to make her voice low and soothing, as she did with the children when they were upset. 'Let's look at the problem.'

Tom heaved a sigh and seemed to relax a little. 'The old boy – he's fifty – will be here for two or three days and then go to Harrogate to take the waters – seems his liver is giving him trouble. But...' Tom sighed again – 'he insists on meeting my – er, fiancée, so we'll invite her too. At least overnight. She'll be coming from York,' he added, 'if she agrees, that is. She's never been here – doesn't like the country – so she might feel obliged to stay for a day or two.'

Why did her heart sink suddenly at this news? Kate gave herself a mental shake. 'Well,' she said firmly, 'if a lady is to visit, a military welcome will certainly not be good enough. And she'll probably have a maid or a companion with her. What do you think is lacking at the manor?'

Tom rolled his eyes. 'Everything! I don't know where to start. Come over tomorrow, and you'll see. We have about a week to clear it up, that's all.'

Sam walked back with Kate to Bellwood Hall and promised to pick her up the next day in Tom's trap to collect her belongings. It was with mixed feelings that she packed her trunk. This was the end of an era and it was hard to imagine what the future might hold.

It would be hard to treat Thomas as an employer: they knew each other too well. What would he expect? Sam seemed to be more like a friend than a servant. No doubt they would have to act their parts properly when the visitors arrived.

One bright thought on Kate's last night at

the Hall, was that she might never see Wiggins again. The children cried a little at breakfast when they realized that Nursie was to be left behind, but were consoled by the thought of riding all that way on a train. It was probably Nursie who felt the parting most as they said goodbye.

Most of the rooms in the manor were unused. Dust covers shrouded the old furniture, cobwebs swung from the chandelier in the dining-room. How could they possibly make it habitable in a few days? And if they didn't what would be the result? Tom seemed to think that it was vital to impress General Ridley, his usually absent Papa. Kate could only just remember meeting the general, years ago when he was on one of his short visits. Tom's mother had died when he was born and after that, the general had spent very little time at the manor.

Tom guided the Coopers through the rooms, starting with a pleasant room with long windows looking out over the overgrown lawns that was used as his office, judging by the number of papers strewn about. He used a small bedroom on the second floor.

There were four other bedrooms, apart from the now empty servants' quarters in the attics and a big, formal drawing-room led off from the dining-room. The kitchen was big but old-fashioned and needed a good coat of whitewash. The cooking range looked serviceable.

Kate pulled back a few of the covers and decided that with a good clean and plenty of fires, the rooms would be acceptable. The fiancée could be given the bedroom with the most sun, and the general the largest.

'Have we plenty of bed linen? If not, we could borrow from the Wigginses, Mrs Mason would be pleased to help,' Kate said briskly. She was just beginning to appreciate her freedom. The future was uncertain, but she had no time to worry at the moment.

Sam organized a labourer to scythe the grass on the sides of the drive, to give the impression of neatness. It was still far short of the raked gravel and clipped lawns of Bellwood Hall, but it was the best they could do.

Large fires in all the rooms began to warm the air in the old stone house and Kate raided the garden and arranged flowers where she could. 'I am relieved that the kitchen garden is so good,' she said to Sam. Tom had told the gardener that he could sell surplus produce to eke out his wages, and the old walled garden was full of vegetables in season.

Kate began to enjoy herself; this was hard work, but you could see results. The smell of beeswax polish began to float through the house.

They had nearly finished the preparations,

on a bright and breezy day, when a brougham trundled up the drive and decanted a spritely man with a fiery complexion, followed by a mountain of luggage. 'Here I am, dear boy!' the general shouted, clapping Tom so hard on the back that he nearly choked. 'I'm sure you don't mind – I came a few days earlier, y'see. Want to have a good look at the estate. What's the matter, man?' He looked up at his son, who was wearing a scarf round his neck and an ancient jacket. 'Why are you dressed like a workman, may I ask?'

Tactfully, Kate intervened. 'Can I offer you refreshment, sir?' she asked, a model housekeeper in her black dress and white apron. 'Tea or coffee, perhaps? Dinner can be served early if required, Mr Ridley,' she said to Tom and was rewarded with a wink.

'Where d'ye get such a pretty housekeeper? They was always old hags when I lived here!' The general leered, but somehow he was not so repulsive as Wiggins. Perhaps he was just old-fashioned. 'Tea? Never drink the stuff. Tom can get me some whisky.'

While the general drank whisky in front of a roaring drawing-room fire, Sam carried his luggage upstairs. 'Feel the cold, y'know. Temperature's in the eighties in Jamaica...' He looked around the room. 'No changes, as far as I can see. How many years is it since I was here? You haven't engaged a footman, have you? That young fellow would look good in knee breeches!'

That was too much for Tom and he laughed immoderately. 'Sam's a general – er – servant, he works outside as well as in the house. I'd better admit, Father, that we – I can't afford many staff. The harvests have been bad for three years, livestock numbers are down and the timber's only recently been ready for felling.'

'You should come to Jamaica, Thomas. Our sugar crops are always good and the labour – well, there's no slaves now of course, *not officially*, but black labour's cheap. It is easy to make money, my boy! And it's warm all the year round! Mind you, I do miss the pheasant shoots and the fox hunting ... reared a few pheasants this year, have you? I must borrow a gun.'

Rushing back to the kitchen, where the newly whitewashed walls were still damp, Kate hastily checked the roasting chickens in the oven. Sadie was remarkably calm as she peeled the vegetables. 'I'm right glad you're here, miss,' she said to Kate. 'Mr Ridley, he's not a big eater so I don't make dinners like this as a rule. Do you think there's enough soup?'

'Quite enough. We can have cheese for supper later if there's nothing else left.' There were peaches for dessert – was there time to go to Village Farm for some cream? 'Tomorrow I'll work out some menus,' Kate promised. 'Is there any bacon for breakfast?'

Sadie pointed to the kitchen ceiling where a side of bacon was suspended from a hook. 'Cured it meself,' she said simply. Sadie was a farmer's daughter from the village, big and capable. Kate was glad that Sadie was there.

The dinner went quite well, Tom coming to the table with a hastily scrubbed look. Kate waited at table and Sam helped out in the kitchen. The general drank a good deal of claret and refused dessert, calling instead for Stilton.

'Sorry, sir, we've no Stilton,' Kate said with her best smile. 'Would you take fresh Wensleydale instead?' The general said he would be delighted. So far, so good.

As she brought in the cheese and biscuits, Kate heard the general say, '...looking for a wife, don't mind telling you. To keep me company in my old age, y'know. I'll go back to Kingston with a beautiful woman – might meet one at Harrogate, eh? Is there any brandy, boy?'

Tom came into the kitchen at the end of the meal to thank the staff. 'I couldn't have managed without you. That went very well but Sam, you need a rest. Don't go out after poachers tonight.'

'We'll see, sir,' Sam said evasively.

Afterwards, as they went back to the keeper's cottage, Kate asked, 'How often do you patrol at night? It seems hard, after a full day's work.'

'Tom's been doing his share, but obviously he's tied up tonight – and for as long as the general stays. It's quite dark, with wind ... just the night for pheasant poachers, they can't be seen or heard. I think I'll check on the young birds tonight.'

'Well, I'm coming with you,' Kate said firmly, but Sam shook his dark head.

'It's not the place for a girl, you know that.'

Kate did not go to bed. When she heard Sam go out she put on a cape her brother used in wet weather, and tied up her hair in a dark scarf. After some thought she picked up a stick from near the door and slipped out into the darkness.

Kate could see well in the dark and once her eyes had adjusted to the starlight, she went along the lane to the wood where the young pheasants had been released. She stood still and listened, but there was no sound other than the wind.

Grasping her stick, Kate crept under the trees. If Sam was in trouble she could at least make a diversion; if not, she would sneak home to bed. She felt a bump behind her knee and bending down, she saw a dim shape in the darkness. A rough tongue licked her hand. 'Chloe!' she whispered. Sam's lab-rador wagged her tail gently and after a few minutes she disappeared. The night felt lonely without her.

Time passed, but there was no sign of Sam – or of anyone else. What would she do if she met a poacher? Kate's plan had been to find Sam.

A twig cracked behind her and for a moment Kate thought the dog was back, but suddenly she was seized by rough hands and held tightly. 'Drop that stick!' a man's voice growled. She struggled, but could not get free.

The man turned her round to face him. 'Let me see who you are!' He seized her chin and held her face up to the dim starlight. 'Kate!' Tom Ridley was staring down at her, still holding her tightly. He started to laugh. 'It's you who's stealing our pheasants! Oh, Katherine! What are you up to?' He bent swiftly and kissed her, a long kiss that turned her knees to water.

As soon as he relaxed his grip, Kate moved away from Tom, trying to be calm. 'Looking for Sam ... he doesn't know I'm here, but I thought – if he needed help – I can see quite well on a dark night...'

'Do you realize how dangerous it can be? Dear girl, you're a rare one, a woman after my own heart. How many other lasses would do this? But I shouldn't have – I'm sorry, Kate. I apologize. It won't happen again.'

'I expect you say that to all the girls,' Kate

said lightly. Best not to make too much of one kiss. 'You're a flirt, Mr Ridley. You always were, even when you were a lad at school. You should be ashamed of yourself, you know. A young lady expected any day and you practically married to her! You'll have to try to be respectable, difficult though that may be.'

'Yes, miss,' Tom said meekly, but he caught both her hands in his. 'It's just that – well, no matter.' He turned away.

It really would not do, Kate thought. Apart from the difference in their station in life, the man was engaged to be married. She'd always had a soft spot for Thomas Ridley, and now she was in danger of ... it would not do.

At that moment they both saw a dim light among the trees. 'Stay here, I'm going to take a look.' Tom put a hand on Kate's shoulder. 'Don't move,' he whispered.' I don't want any harm to come to you, my love.'

Kate swallowed. There must be half-a-dozen girls swooning for Tom Ridley in this parish alone and she wasn't going to be one of them. Her father had called him Young Lochinvar after a Walter Scott hero, which had made them all laugh, Tom included.

Tom crept quietly towards the wavering light and after a minute, Kate went after him. She wasn't going to be left out. If only she had brought a lantern! Just for a moment she thought of William Thorpe and imagined how he must have gone through the wood as they were doing, until he met the terrible steel jaws of the trap...

Kate caught a whiff of a strange smell, something sulphuric. Standing perfectly still, she fixed her eyes on the light. Against the glow she could see the outline of shadowy figures, all gazing upwards into a tree.

As she watched, birds began to flutter down from the branches and into the waiting hands of the men. A quiet movement in the shadows and each bird was dropped into a sack. Tom's precious pheasants were being stolen, right under his nose.

Kate could see Tom standing under another tree, watching the men. Surely he wouldn't try to attack them, even if Sam turned up? And where was Sam? The fumes from the fire were making the men cough and spit. Sam had told her that an old poacher's trick was to burn brimstone under the trees so that the fumes would choke the birds. 'A nice quiet method, no guns – but then, they have to show a light,' Sam had said.

Suddenly the wood seemed to erupt. 'Will! John! Alan! Here to me!' It was Tom's voice, as rough as he could make it. The harsh alarm call of many pheasants echoed in the trees. There was a crashing noise in the undergrowth and the sound of thudding feet. The dim shapes made off through the trees, each in a different direction, taking the bags with them.

After they had gone there was a smouldering can, still burning sulphur and one dark shape left, lying in the grass. Kate's heart sank. She knew before Tom got to him that it was Sam.

SEVEN

That night there was a report of a suspicious cart passing through the village at an ungodly hour. No doubt it was Tom's pheasants, trundling to an unknown destination. It would be too public to put them on the train at Ripon, but somehow they would make their way to hotels in the city.

Tom was not thinking about his lost birds. He was worrying about Sam, lying very still and pale in what had been the housekeeper's room at the manor. Kate had stayed with her brother while Tom went to fetch a cart and between them, they had managed to get him to bed. Kate had felt his head gently and found a sticky patch of blood. A blow to the head had felled him and he was still unconscious.

Through the rest of the night Tom and Kate sat beside Sam, but his breathing did not change and he hardly moved. 'You did tell him not to go out,' Kate reminded the boss, who obviously felt guilty. There was silence for a while and then she said, 'I remember you called out to other people, there were noises in the bushes and then the men ran away. They must have thought there was a group of keepers in the wood. But there was nobody else, was there?'

Tom smiled. 'That was the idea, it must have saved a few birds. Sam and I planned to do it if we were outnumbered. First time I've had to use it. At least those extra lads came in handy. You knew who they were, of course, old friends from the past.'

Kate tried to remember the names. 'They were Robin Hood's merry men?'

'Clever girl. Little John, Alan-a-Dale and Will Scarlett. It was Sam's idea. We used to play Robin Hood games in that very wood when we were young ... it was just a joke. Never thought that Sam would be injured, though. It's not a joke any more.' Tom looked across the bed. 'Get a bit of rest, Kate. You have to work tomorrow.'

At first light Tom sent a man to fetch the doctor, who decided that all they could do was wait, and keep Sam warm. 'He's young and strong; he should get over it,' he said. 'His breathing is normal. I'll come back tomorrow.'

Kate prepared breakfast and brewed the general's favourite coffee, wishing fervently that Sam had chosen a different career. 'It's far too dangerous,' she told Sadie, who agreed.

The general took a different view, Kate heard, as she went into the dining-room. 'All part of life, that sort of thing. Young men have to take risks. Hope the young fellow recovers.' He helped himself to another slice of toast.

Tom was washed and changed but looked exhausted. 'Just thought of another problem,' he said. 'My fiancée Selina is coming today. She'll arrive at Ripon after lunch. Somebody will have to fetch her. I was going to do it, of course, but I want to see the police and I don't like to leave Sam. I feel responsible.'

The young lady's room was ready, Kate had seen to that, but she'd forgotten about the visitor after the events of the night.

Tom looked at his father. 'Would you be willing to go to the station, sir? Jake Benson will drive you, he's young but very steady. He's the, er, groom and general handyman. Selina hasn't been here before, so I can't send him alone.'

'Certainly,' the general beamed.' I quite fancy trying the paces of that young gelding of yours. Your man can come with me to help with the bags, but I'll hold the reins. Miss Fulford will be quite safe with me.' Kate thought she saw Tom shudder.

Every few minutes during that long morning, Kate slipped into the room where Sam lay. She could see no change. Tom went to see the police in Kirkby. 'I suppose they're not too keen to hear about poachers,' he told Kate as he was leaving. 'But assault is a grave offence, they must do something this time.'

At about noon, Kate was watching Sam when he stirred and groaned. He tried to sit up, but fell back. 'My head...' He saw Kate. 'Any chance of a cup of tea, lass?'

Kate's heart was beating fast, but she tried to be calm. 'Of course, I'll get you one. Do you remember what happened?' To her relief, a faint smile flitted over the white face.

'Taylor's gang, that's what happened. I caught a glimpse of the big man himself by the light of their fire. They were smoking pheasants out and then ... they must have hit me. I'd planned to go for Tom. How did I get here?'

Kate almost danced into the kitchen, she was so relieved. Sam was going to recover, his brain was working. She hadn't felt so happy for a long time.

Miss Selina Fulford was bored. She sat on a boring, dirty train with her boring companion, her old governess, Miss Ward, travelling towards a boring visit. Thomas, her fiance, had not seemed to be boring at first. He was easy to talk to, almost flirtatious and he was a gentleman. But after the first enthusiasm, he talked to her a great deal about his estate. She was beginning to suspect that he would be a tedious husband. Everyone knew that rural life was dull, which was why she'd avoided visiting the manor until now.

Thomas was tall and quite handsome, so

Selina's women friends had told her she was so lucky. 'You can't have everything,' one of her married friends told her. 'You'll be the lady of the manor, you know! He'll probably hunt a lot in winter, you'll be able to come back to York on visits.'

At thirty, Selina had to admit she was running out of options. Thomas was five years younger than she was, but that didn't matter. She watched the flat fields of the Vale of York slide past, while Miss Ward slept. Things could have been very different if Charles, her first suitor, hadn't died ... that was a sad time, but it was over now.

'What a wonderful match for you, Selina,' her father had said happily, soon after they had met Thomas at his aunt's house. 'This family needs a country estate and he seems to be a very decent young fellow.'

Life in York was most enjoyable; there were balls, trips to the theatre and boating picnics in summer. Selina and her friends read all the latest books. She loved to travel and had seen most of Europe. But she didn't want to be an old maid.

And now she was expected to give it all up, give up her friends and go to live at this place called Kirkby, which sounded as though it was at the back of beyond, on the edge of the moors.

Wuthering Heights, that's what it would be like. Reading that novel had made her realize just how uncivilized life in the country could be. It was horrid to imagine oneself living in a house miles from anywhere, surrounded by monotonous green fields – or even bare moors! The only people in the dreary landscape would be uncouth labourers.

Perhaps they would have a town house in time, and she and Thomas could spend some time in York ... money would not be a problem. Selina was an only child and her father was a very successful merchant. But would Thomas adapt to York? He had once confessed, 'Not too keen on city life, I'm afraid.'

The train was slowing down for Ripon Station and gave a melancholy whistle at a level crossing. Miss Ward woke with a start and peered through the grimy window. 'I can't see Mr Ridley, I hope he hasn't forgotten,' she muttered, as they drew in to the platform. Of course, Miss Ward thought Thomas was wonderful. He gently flirted with her, whereas most of Selina's friends ignored the ageing companion who was only there for convention's sake.

Selina patted her curls into place under her hat, the ladies alighted and Miss Ward found a porter for the luggage. Selina never travelled without clothes for every occasion, although this time ball gowns had not been included. Her mother had suggested that balls at Kirkby would be unlikely. There was a slight chance of good society at Harrogate, she had said, but not until later in the year. 'But do take some pretty clothes, Selina. The local ladies will be waiting with interest to see the York fashions.'

A gentleman with a military moustache approached them and raised his deerstalker hat. 'Miss Fulford, I presume?' He bowed with old-fashioned courtesy. 'May I present his profound apologies from my son Thomas? He is devastated that business prevents him from coming to meet you, but I am here in his stead. I am his father, y'see, James Ridley.'

Selina held out a languid hand. 'Very glad to meet you, General Ridley.' The father would be even more boring; he sounded very formal. 'This is my companion, Miss Ward.'

The general organized the porter efficiently, stowed the ladies in the trap and in no time at all they were bowling smoothly out of the station and up a hill on the Kirkby road. A groom was driving, so there had to be conversation, at first rather stilted. Then the general asked, 'How does the theatre at York look now? I hear that they've been refurbishing this year. I used to love plays at the Theatre Royal when I was stationed near York.'

Relieved, Selina was able to tell him all the latest news of the theatre. They talked on about life in York. Only once did she feel apprehensive when the general waved a hand to the western skyline. 'You can see the moors from here; the heather is blooming now – magnificent view.' A chill breeze whirled up leaves at the side of the road and Selina shivered. Moors were the last thing she wanted to see.

By the time they reached the big gates of the manor, Selina realized there had been no mention of turnips or sheep, nothing at all about the estate. At least the father was someone she could talk to.

They had climbed out of the river valley, but the countryside was gently rolling fields and woods, not 'wuthering' at first sight. There was a ridge of high land on the skyline, but before they got there, the vehicle swung in through wrought-iron gates. 'Here we are,' the general beamed. In spite of herself Selina was impressed by her first sight of the manor: it was stately.

When they reached the house, Thomas was on the steps to greet them. Taking Selina's hand, he smiled into her eyes. 'It is so good to see you here at last. I do hope you and Miss Ward will both enjoy your stay at the manor.' He turned to his father. 'You didn't drive after all?'

The general smirked. 'A lovely lady like this one deserves one's full attention, so I let Benson take the reins. You didn't tell me, Thomas, that you're engaged to marry a

112

beauty! I am so glad you have come to visit, my dear, before I go back to Jamaica.'

Selina blushed and Tom evidently thought it best to change the subject. 'Welcome to my home. We haven't entertained for some time, but I hope you will be comfortable. Jake will carry your bags upstairs when he has seen to the horse.'

What, no indoor staff?

A young woman was hovering in the background. 'This is Miss Cooper, Selina. She will provide anything you may need. When you have settled in, we will take tea in the drawing-room' – he caught his father's expression – 'and whisky for the general. Thank you, Miss Cooper.'

Selina looked round the entrance hall. The place looked faded, with a sort of shabby grandeur. The house was very old; the housekeeper was very young for such a position.

That evening, the guests were given a good dinner and Selina was asked to play the piano, which was only slightly out of tune. The general asked for Chopin and she played a sad nocturne, but Thomas had slipped out and didn't hear it.

She had to admit to herself that the house was pleasant, although she felt nervous when Thomas came back and talked about problems with poachers. It sounded as though the grounds were bristling with criminals at night. They were probably armed to the teeth

... Kirkby must be a wild sort of place.

'Pepper 'em with shot, that's the go,' the general advised. 'I'll have a pot at them myself if you'll lend me a gun. It's a long time since I was in a skirmish.'

'I gather that your army days are over?' Selina wondered why such a vigorous man would have retired.

'Better prospects as a civilian, Miss Fulford. My estates in Jamaica claim much of my time and that's where I like to spend my days.'

'Jamaica! How romantic! Tell me, is the climate pleasant?' Selina leaned forward and then she noticed that Thomas was creeping out of the room again. He seemed to have a lot on his mind.

The next day Thomas drove Selina and Miss Ward around the estate in a dog cart. Thomas pointed out his home farm and two or three tenanted holdings, the timber plantations and the woodland. They admired the sight of a ploughman with two horses, turning over corn stubble in a big field. 'We're short of labour, but I have made some improvements this year,' he told the ladies. 'We need to increase production on the home farm. But I'm not quite certain what breed of sheep we should keep...'

Selina smiled politely. For one day she could show some sort of interest, she told herself. 'You seem to be very involved with the estate. Why can you not employ more people, a manager perhaps?'

'I am the manager,' Thomas said briefly. 'I studied land management, you know, and it's good to try out the theory in practice.' The lady suppressed a yawn. 'Is that not a lovely view?' They could see a sweep of high moors beyond the woods.

Selina nodded, but already a sort of oppressive feeling was growing, of being shut in, away from the world. York seemed very far away, although from the highest point of the estate, Thomas said you could see York Minster on a clear day.

As they returned to the house, Selina decided that she would persuade Thomas to take them further afield the next day. 'I have heard that Fountains Abbey is a very picturesque ruin,' she said at dinner. There at least she might see some people and some civilization and get her fiancé away from his cares for a few hours.

Thomas looked up from his soup. 'Should you like to go there? We could get up a party – it's not very far from here across country, and I think you would like the gardens at Studley Royal.' He seemed relieved that she was showing an interest in something.

'I should like to go too,' put in the general. 'I used to know the owner in the old days.'

The next day was cool and clear, but Selina's plan did not run smoothly. Thomas was called away just as they were about to leave, by an individual who had come to buy timber. Selina thought he should have been sent off and told to come back another day, but Thomas didn't take her advice.

'So sorry, I really am,' he said and the deep voice sounded sincere. 'But I've been waiting for this chap for weeks and we really need to do business.'

The general unexpectedly supported him. 'Business comes first, we all know that,' he said brightly. 'I will conduct the ladies on a memorable tour of the ruins. Fear not, we will be home again before dinner.' And he swept them away.

The party, driven by Jake Benson in an open vehicle, trotted through the little village of Studley and came to the park gates. The general pointed out the avenue of limes, leading the eye to a new church built on a hill. 'I really think we should walk through the park to the abbey,' he said, looking at Miss Ward. 'Do you feel able to accompany us, madam?'

Miss Ward said she would stay with the vehicle and Selina and the general walked down into the little valley of the River Skell, which pleased Selina very much. 'After all those fields and hedges, it is so civilized!' The river widened out into a lake with swans and other waterfowl, bright against a backdrop of dark trees. There was a cascade,

116

statues and what looked like a Greek temple up the hill. It was landscaping on a grand scale, within its midst the imposing ruin of Fountains Abbey.

On the gravel walks there were people, ladies leaning on the arms of gentlemen, children with nursemaids. Selina felt she was back in the real world again. 'Some people have hermits and grottoes, but this – it's wonderful! General Ridley, do you not love a cultivated landscape such as this? Thank you for bringing me here.'

The general smiled down at her. 'It is such a pleasure to be here with a beautiful lady on a sunny day. Miss Fulford – may I, as your future father-in-law, call you Selina? My dear, I'm so glad that you like it. I've always preferred art to nature, I must admit. Kirkby is far too rural for me. That's why I've left it to Thomas.'

They exchanged meaningful glances. 'Yes, Thomas is very attached to his farm,' the lady said.

'Perhaps we may persuade him to visit Jamaica on your wedding journey? I suppose you will have done some planning for the future while you've been here.'

In fact, there had been no planning so far. Thomas had been too preoccupied with his timber. Selina sighed. 'That is a wonderful idea.'

The general left for Harrogate, to take the waters. He told Tom that he wanted to help him with the problems on the estate. 'You need more servants – wish you could see how many we employ in Jamaica!' Kate was pouring him a glass of whisky before dinner on the night before he left as he went on, 'I'm going to put a few thousand in the bank for you, Tom. It's the least I can do. If you're to get married in a few months, you'll need to make the house lighter and brighter. The grounds need attention and you need more stock on the land. You know what to do.'

'Certainly, sir. Thank you very much. It's just the lack of capital that's holding me back.' Kate saw the beam on Tom's face.

The manor was rather quiet after the general had gone. Selina took walks, read a book and took a drive to Ripon with Tom, but it was market day, so the atmosphere was rather too agricultural for her taste. Kate felt rather sorry for her. Tom was polite, but didn't seem to be particularly entranced by his fiancée, nor she by him. It was all rather sad.

'Surely Tom wouldn't just marry – for money?' Kate said privately to Sam.

'I think he's got into the engagement somehow, and is too much of a gentleman to back out.' Sam grinned. 'But the money will be useful, I'm sure.'

When the ladies went home, the atmosphere lightened. Kate and Sam had dinner with Tom in the kitchen that night and he told them what his father had said. 'So we'll hire another gamekeeper straight away. That will make your life easier, Sam. And Kate, will you stay on as housekeeper? Unless you have other plans, of course.'

'But you can't hire a servant without a character,' Kate said demurely, to give herself time to think. She quite enjoyed working at the manor, but she didn't want to be there when Selina took over as mistress. The lady had a slightly discontented look that probably meant she would be hard to please. And there was another reason: she didn't like to think of Tom as a married man.

Tom laughed. 'I've known your character since you were five, girl. Now ... Sam, do you know of anyone who'd make a good gamekeeper? We need a capable man who can turn his hand to other jobs, of course, but someone who knows about game.'

Sam rubbed the back of his head and Kate wondered whether it still ached. 'I do know a man ... he has all the qualifications we need but you might think him too well qualified.' He grinned. 'Just a suggestion.'

'He's a poacher, I suppose. Set a thief to catch a thief.' Tom sighed, then he sat up straight. 'You mean William Thorpe? It's not a bad idea. He's local, he's available – if his leg heals, that is. And I believe that he's an honest man.' He looked pleased with the idea.

Kate cleared away the plates. 'His leg will heal, I'm sure Judith Weaver will see to that. But I'm not sure about his temper. He's a miserable old soul from what I've seen – could you bear to work with him every day?'

'Just imagine, Kate, if you were in his position. No job, no wife – a bad injury and winter coming on. It's not surprising that he's unhappy. Well, Tom, perhaps you should have a quiet talk to him.' Sam stood up. 'I'll take a walk round the pheasants. Good night.'

EIGHT

Governments in London came and went, but life was much the same in Kirkby, dependent on the seasons, although there were those who thought that the weather was worse when Disraeli was Prime Minister.

Summer was now turning to autumn, the mellow stone buildings hoarding the last of the warmth while in the kitchens, pans of jam were boiling on the fires. The old and the sick began to dread the winter ahead; there were many families in the village that would find winter a difficult time. Anyone could dig peat on the moor for fuel, but unless you had a cart, or could borrow one, there was no way to bring it home.

Judith Weaver sometimes felt herself to be growing old, but she was still young enough to enjoy the change of the seasons and the extra work of preparing for the winter. She dried herbs, fragrant green bunches of sage, rosemary and thyme hanging from ceilings and walls. She made plum wine and elderberry cordial and blackberry jam, busy all the day with little time to talk. It was good to be busy when you lived on your own and she had been busy for fifteen years, since she came to the little holding.

Autumn was always an active time for Judith, but this year she was thankful that there was a good excuse not to spend very much time with her patient. An awkward silence had fallen between them and, strangely, it was since William had made an effort to be polite. Somehow, it was easier when he was grumpy.

The miserable, swearing, scruffy individual who had come to the cottage was nothing like the William Thorpe she used to know. His normal pleasant self was now coming back and it brought back the memories that had to be shut away.

Time was going by, the poacher was recovering and would soon be able to go home. Judith would once more be alone with her goats, thank goodness.

'Thank you for chopping the kindling,' Judith said to William, one day after he had hobbled out to the woodshed and spent half a day there. The man actually smiled, but said nothing as he put down a basket of neatly chopped sticks to dry in the hearth. That smile held the ghost of young Will, the lad of long ago.

William went out to the shed again a few days later and came back with something behind his back. He went up to Judith. 'Happy birthday, lass,' he said quietly as he presented her with a wooden tray, cleverly carved round the edges.

Judith was surprised by her sudden tears. How could he have remembered, after all those years? Today was her fortieth birthday, the day when you realize that without noticing it, you have grown old. Her sister Bessie had written from Leeds to wish her well.

She could find no words for a minute or two, but she took the tray carefully, as though it was fragile. 'You made this? It's clever, William. And it'll be useful, too.' They looked at each other.

William seemed to be struggling for words, his pale face earnest. 'I wanted to thank you. But for your sticky salve, I would be over in yon churchyard by now. You were always good like that, Judith. Do you mind the time—'

Judith stopped him. 'No! I don't want to remember the past, its over, it's done. Leave it be.' She turned away. 'I'll get supper ready.'

'Nay, sit down a minute and listen to me.' William pushed her into a chair firmly. They sat by the fire together, Judith trying to find her usual calm. 'When I came here, I hated you. After all this time, it still hurt, what you did to me.' He paused and Judith listened to the crackle of the fire. Did she deserve this? It had been for his good, hadn't it? Soothing wafts of the scent of drying herbs washed over her.

'In the end I got married to poor Lily and

she was a good lass, but – to be honest, it was to please her. And I think it did make her happy.' There was a tremor in his voice. 'Why did you go away without a word? Why, Judith? We were right, we were young – I'd planned we would wed, you knew that. I knew then that you were the only lass for me.'

Judith looked steadily into the fire. Should she tell him the truth, a truth that she had kept to herself for over twenty years?

'I did think that you were of the same mind. It hurt when I found I was wrong. You thought more of going after a good job than ... staying with me. Of course, your mother saw her chance while I was in prison, she'll have had a lot to say, my word. But you knew me better than she did – you could at least've told me!' William spoke very quietly. 'I'm not good at this. It's hard to say how you feel.' He eased his damaged leg on to a stool.

Take a deep breath, take it steady, Judith reminded herself. 'Don't upset yourself, Will. It was a long time ago.'

'Prison doesn't make a man a criminal, you know. It's there to keep us in our place, along with the parson. To warn the likes of me to keep off the rich folk's property, to keep off their land. I've thought about it a lot. There was only one or two hardened thieves in Ripon when I was there. The rest had been unlucky, or were slow in the wits.' William gazed into her face. 'Do you know, the only thing that kept me going in prison was the thought of my girl. I was planning our future...'

'My heart was broken too, it was a terrible time. But you can't go back – I live in the present day. I love my garden, the herbs – and the goats. I've a good life, settled, I don't want a lot of – feelings!' Judith looked up and saw his face, Williams beautiful face, that had haunted her dreams. That pain was over, she wanted to forget it.

'I thought you must have no feelings ... please, Judith? Tell me what happened to change you so much, so quickly. To make you so hard that you never tried to leave me a message... You could have seen my ma – anything, just a note or a word. But there was nothing.' William was agitated; it would not help his recovery.

'Hush, lad. Hush, bairn.' She laid a hand on his arm with the old words of comfort.

'Tell me, then I can go home knowing your side of things.' He sighed deeply and seemed to relax a little. 'It's important to me, lass. Since I've been here I've seen that you are the same woman, even if we're both forty and getting old. And I'm sorry I was so like a pig when I first came.'

William's face changed when he smiled.

'You were, too.' Judith sat up straight. 'Right, I'll tell you, lad. I'd no choice. We, you and I had made a big mistake. I left Kirkby because I was expecting a baby and it was a disgrace to the family.'

There was a quick intake of breath and William whispered, 'I'd no idea.'

'You know what it's like for young lasses who fall? That's what they say. Your good name is gone, the woman is always blamed. So we told no one. My mother was bitter ... said she thought I'd been brought up to be respectable. It's important to the Weavers, with my father a churchwarden and all. I disappointed them, Will.'

There was a shocked silence.

'So they wanted rid of me; the only way to preserve the business, that's what they said. They told me that folks wouldn't buy the Weavers' bread if they knew that the daughter was a fallen woman.' Judith smiled bitterly. Now he would know that she too had suffered. 'That was why nobody knew, none of my friends or yours. I was bundled off as soon as they found out. I had to do as they said – what else could I do?'

'My poor love. Strange, I never thought of that.' After a deep sigh he said, 'But why not tell me? It was my fault – my baby! You said to wait until we were married...' William moved restlessly. 'If I'd known, we could've been wed straight away. We were young, but other folks have managed before now. Your ma told me you'd gone off to better yourself. Taken a job in service. She managed to make me feel that I wasn't good enough for her daughter.'

'You were a wild lad, remember. Always poaching ... didn't impress my mother. You were in prison when I found out about the baby, not the way to start married life. Folks were sure you'd be sent to Australia in the end, that's what the keepers said. And then, we were too young – you were too young to be a father,' Judith said quietly. 'Only nineteen. Your mother relied on you, she couldn't earn her own living.'

'So you made the rules for both of us.'

Judith's eyes were full of tears. 'I really did. I thought it was best for you, as well as for me. It wasn't done to hurt you, Will. I knew what you'd want to do, if you found out about the baby, but it would have been too hard. And when I came back, you were married to Lily. She was a grand lass. It was all for the best.'

William shook his head. 'She was, but it was you I wanted. Do you understand that, Judith? We could've managed. So who did know? Where did you go?'

Judith sighed. 'Dr Cooper knew of course, he was the only one. I went to him in my trouble, like everybody else did. He looked after me, found me a place to go. He knew it was best to go away. I went to a farm over Pateley way, where they were kind to me, and I worked for them for a few years. To pay them back. And the wife taught me a lot. Cheese-making, and how to make salves and cordials and tonics... She gave me a living, Will.'

The grandfather clock ticked slowly, ticking their lives away. Judith decided she had said enough.

'So what happened next?' Will didn't ask about the child.

'Nothing, that's all there is to tell. I never think about it.' It was a lie.

The shadows of evening crept through the room, settling in the corners like ghosts from the past.

After a long silence William asked, 'Why did you come back to Kirkby, lass? You weren't looking for me, that's for sure.'

'Where else would I get a cottage and a bit of land to rent?' Her voice sounded hard and Judith said more quietly, 'I was known here, the family's respectable. Anywhere else, they wouldn't let a lone woman rent land. So I waited until there was a chance at Kirkby.' She put more wood on the fire.

William sat still. 'Now at last I have some answers. For years, it went round and round in my head...'

'My sister let me know when old Mrs Nunn died and this cottage was vacant, it was just the thing for me. I wrote to General Ridley – he was here then – and he let me have it. There's a couple of houses this side of the

128

village that belong to the manor. This was the only way I could make my own living, without being in service. I'd been planning it while I was away.'

'So you never got wed to somebody else? A bonny lass like you?' Will shook his head. 'You could have married a farmer. I remember young Fred was keen on you in the old days.' He chuckled. 'A fat farmer's wife, you could have been. Taking your butter to market on Thursdays, driven by a worker like me.'

'It's strange to think of the different ways folks' life could have turned out. I'll be honest, Will. It was you or nobody for me. I never looked at another lad. I never hurt a man by turning him down: I didn't let them anywhere near me. I knew you'd be upset that I was gone, but I thought you'd soon get over it and when I saw you were with Lily, I was sure. A lad like you was bound to be married after five years or so.'

Her answer was a huge sigh.

Judith made supper, brightened the fire and tried to get back her inner peace. The memories that had been locked away for years were now crowding in, the bitter regret flooding back, the thoughts of what else she might have done. At the age of seventeen, she had made the decisions for both of them – but William had not known. Only now did she fully understand how he had felt. He'd had a carefree way with him that hid his real feelings.

After a sleepless night, as the first light filtered through the curtains, Judith decided that William must still need to talk. He would soon be gone and the chance would be lost. Painful as it was, they must revisit the past again.

That morning, William was pale and quiet. He took several turns round the garden to exercise his leg and Judith, watching him, noticed that he hardly limped at all.

The day was warm, with bees working in the last of the lavender flowers and William helped Judith to pick plums from a gnarled old tree. After a while, they sat on a bench under the tree, enjoying the hazy sunshine.

Gently Judith said, 'I was wrong. I've kept down all the memories; but you're right, we should talk about the old days before you go home. Then maybe we can put it all behind us. Finished for good.'

'That's not my idea,' William said mildly. 'I might as well tell you, though it's not likely to happen very soon. If I can get a proper job, not so easy at my age. I still want to marry you, Judith. We could spend our old age picking plums.' He gulped and went on, 'I love you, you see. I want to protect you.'

Judith was speechless. She had never expected this. An old man of forty-two behaving like a young lad! She blushed. When had

Judith Weaver ever wanted protection? She was an independent woman who earned her own living. And she was respectable whereas William Thorpe was still just outside the law. It would never do, she told herself.

'I'd give up poaching, o' course. I'd...' He stopped as a horse and rider came up to the gate. 'Here's young Ridley again. I think he must fancy you, number of times he comes here.'

Judith smoothed her apron and stood up. 'He comes to see you, Will. Good morning, Mr Ridley. As you can see, the patient is doing well.' She moved away.

'That's good news,' Tom said heartily. 'As a matter of fact, I came to ask you what your plans are, William. No need to leave us, Judith, if William doesn't mind.'

Judith sat down abruptly on the bench at William's next words. 'Well, the truth is I plan to get work and then to get wed. To Judith.'

It was Tom's turn to be surprised. 'Really! And what do you think to this, Miss Weaver?' He smiled at them both. 'It sounds like an excellent idea to me ... as long as you can keep him in order, of course.'

'Since work is hard to come by in Kirkby, I'll have plenty of time to make up my mind,' Judith said tartly, to cover her confusion. 'Will you take a cup of tea, Mr Ridley?' She went off down the path to the house.

When she came back, Tom sat beside William and grinned at him. 'I have just the thing for you, to help Judith to make up her mind. How would you like to work for the manor estate?' He laughed as William sat back and stared at him.

Judith dispensed tea and ginger biscuits from the new tray, trying to look neutral. Young Ridley was going to give a poacher a place! A thing his father would never have done. This new generation seemed to have different ideas.

'You were a foreman at Village Farm, I believe? I need a man with experience ... for whatever job needs doing at the time. Such as lambing as we've no proper shepherd. And we certainly need help against the Taylor gang; they injured Sam as you've probably heard. So we have a position for a game-keeper and general worker, and we think you're the man for the job. For a reasonable wage, of course. We can negotiate about that.' Tom drank his tea and waited.

William Thorpe thought a moment and then said quietly, 'Thank you, sir.' It was so far from the way he had spoken to Tom before that the young man looked shocked. 'When do I start? The leg's right enough now, I can get about.' He paused and then added, 'I should tell you, Mr Ridley, that I have a criminal record. I was sent to prison for poaching ... twenty or so years ago.'

'Thank you for telling me,' Tom said cheerfully. 'Suppose I should be shocked, but it's a long time gone. I don't remember it. I was only five years old at the time, but I know my father was hard on poachers. The truth is, we need your, er, expertise with regard to poachers. You may be able to find out their plans, although I don't want you taking any risks on my behalf. One injured worker is quite enough, so take care.'

Judith looked serious. 'Mr Ridley's right, you don't want any more injuries at your age.' She knew it was a sharp remark and Will glared at her, then he laughed.

'I'm sure you won't be wanting to patch me up again, *old lass*, so I'll try to keep out of trouble.' It was the young teasing William, as he used to be, but it was also linking them together, as though she were responsible for him. As though they were together, in some way. It was a tempting thought, but Judith put it behind her.

If Will was amazed at the turn things had taken, he kept it to himself. 'I'd best go home, get my place cleaned up,' he said to Judith after Tom had gone.

'I'm pleased for you, Will, it's a grand job. But don't go making plans for me, I am right as I am.' Judith spoke firmly. His ideas had to be knocked on the head, she was far too old to entertain wild ideas of marriage. A spinster, that's what she was and used to having her own way. She didn't want to promise to obey anyone, not at her time of life.

'Ah, you're a hard woman.' Will didn't sound as though he was taking her seriously.

That afternoon, Will made his bed and folded up his clothes into a bag. Judith gave him another bag: a new loaf, cheese and an apple pie to take home.

'I don't know how to thank you,' he said, leaning on the door and watching her pack his food bag.

'To tell you the truth, it made me feel better to do something for you, after what happened, Will. I think we can say we've evened up the score.'

That was intended to let him know it was over, the past was gone and forgiven and could be forgotten. But William laughed and, as he left, he kissed her cheek. 'I'll bring you a rabbit or two when I can. Lawful ones, of course. I think young squire will let me loose on his rabbits.'

Judith watched him walking steadily down the lane, doing his best not to limp. He had got back some of the lightness she had loved in him when they were young. Her parents had been so solenm ... the poor things worked hard, and for what? Father was dead and Mother lived in Masham, a life of criticism and complaint. She had never quite forgiven Judith for being a 'loose woman', as she called it.

NINE

William Thorpe walked down the village street as twilight fell between the grey stone cottages, exchanging greetings with neighbours at their doors.

'Where've you been, lad? Thought you'd left township for good.'

'Aye, well, I've been laid up for a while. It's grand to be about again.' They would all have noticed that there had been no light in the window of his cottage for many nights. He was sure that nobody would know just what had happened, so he kept his answers vague. 'Bad leg,' he told them. That was true enough and the limp was just noticeable.

The new job was being kept quiet for the present. People were wary of a gamekeeper, as Will knew all too well; he'd been one of those folks. If it came out that he was working for Mr Ridley at the manor, he was to say he was the farm foreman. There were very few labourers to oversee, but the title pleased him. He hoped to impress Judith with it eventually.

William felt more hopeful than he had for years, in spite of Judith's coolness. She would come round, given a little more time. Now that he knew her story, all that he'd felt for her had come back and he was like a lad again, already thinking of ways to see her. She had the same fascination for him somehow, as she did at seventeen. He still thought that they could have managed if they'd wed, but he could see her side of things more clearly now. Maybe it wasn't too late; they might just get a second chance.

He turned in to the Queen's Head, the cosy, smoke-filled inn that was the centre of the village to all the men who liked a drink. Will hadn't been there for years, but nothing had changed; tobacco smoke swirled so thick you could have cut it with a knife and there was a cheerful buzz of talk. The place had a smell of smoke, beer and dogs. Some of the High Side shepherds took their dogs out for a drink.

Perhaps something had changed, though, Will thought, as he looked round. The place was not so crowded as it used to be. There was less money about in Kirkby these days and farm prices were poor, so less beer money, although men with families could hardly ever afford to drink, even in the good times.

Over in a quiet corner by the fire, a game of dominoes was in progress. William's eyes flickered over the group and away. He would join them in a while.

'By gum, it's not often we see Will Thorpe!

What brings you in here, lad?' A large man accosted him by the door. One of the two blacksmiths in Kirkby, Jesse Turner was a man who knew everybody's business. The forge was a centre of information and, sometimes, of intrigue. William knew that whatever he said to Jesse would buzz round the village in a flash and in this community, everybody would wonder why he was suddenly turning to drink.

Will had his answer ready; he had thought it out. 'Well, Lily's been gone two year now. She was a Methody o' course, and kept me on the straight and narrow, never a beer while I was married. But I reckon a lone man has a right to please himself.'

'And come in for a bit of company,' the blacksmith grinned. 'Why not?' He himself came there to get away from a nagging wife, folks said.

'Aye.' William took off his cap and edged nearer to the bar, looking round. A sheepdog nudged the back of his leg, reminding him of old Fern, long since laid to rest. He bent down and stroked the silky head.

It was almost too warm in the bar. The ceiling was low and oil lamps glowed through the smoky haze, through which you could only just see across the room. On the walls an array of horse brasses gleamed here and there. It was time they whitewashed the ceiling; it was dark brown with smoke. He

137

bought a tankard of beer from the landlord, who looked surprised, but said only, 'Evening, Will.'

As he sipped the beer Will saw that the domino players were looking over at him and talking quietly to each other. He waited to see what would happen. Eventually one of them looked up, caught Will's eye and came across to him.

'Never seen you here afore, lad!' Seth Simpson had worked with Will at Village Farm a few years before and they had set a few snares together. 'Seen any bunnies lately?' he whispered, and winked. 'Come your ways and sit by fire.'

Will went over with him and at the table, a big man leaned over and shook his hand. 'I'm Brad Taylor, you mightn't remember me. You know Seth, and these here lads are Ben and Shorty, used to work for me.'

'Evening, lads. My word, you've grown! I last saw you on your mammy's knees.' The lads giggled as though they thought he should realize that was history.

'Only old folks live in the past,' one of them said cheekily.

Will was right in the middle of the Taylor gang, rather sooner than he'd expected. He'd planned to gather news of them, but hadn't thought to be drinking at the same table. He suddenly felt his age; it was true that these lads were schoolboys the last time he'd seen them and he hardly recognized them now. Will was strong, but finer boned than they were and he'd lost his muscles since he stopped working. He wouldn't stand a chance in a fight with any of this lot.

He smiled and sat down, burying his face in the tankard to have time to think. How could the poachers meet here, with half the village looking on? But, of course, it looked less suspicious than getting together in a shed. The dominoes were shuffled about while the men talked quietly.

In the same quiet way Seth said without looking up, 'I suppose you lads know that Will here did time? It were bad luck he got caught.'

Will grinned. 'Thanks for telling the world, Seth. Aye, I worked for Her Majesty. Three months' hard labour for one lousy pheasant.'

The group shook their heads. 'Shame!' They were all on his side, of course. Shorty stood up, well over six feet and with broad shoulders. You wouldn't want to meet him in a wood on a dark night. 'I'll buy you a drink, Will,' he said jovially. 'We'll drink to the landlords, them that would rather see a man starve than let him take even a rabbit. Blast 'em!'

There were several farmers in the room, a couple of shepherds – about twenty men in all, laughing and talking. But in their corner, the domino players were secure and their words were not heard above the general buzz of talk.

Shorty came back with a large jug of beer. Taylor's face changed as he made the toast; he said something bitterly obscene and they all drank. Will was sitting next to Taylor and after a moment he said sympathetically, 'You've had a bad time from landlords, then?'

'Just the usual, they're all the same.' Taylor took a gulp of beer. 'Wiggins threw me off the farm – it was a good spot, my father and grandfather farmed it before me but we was only tenants, with no rights. I hope he rots in hell, that Wiggins. The slimy little–'

'That sounds like Sir Titus. He's not human.' Will thought of his own reasons for hating Wiggins. Only a criminal would set a trap like that.

The man clenched his fists. 'He – he bothered my daughter. She was milking the cows one day, late afternoon and I was raking hay. He came into the yard, pinned her up against the wall and had his way with her. It was months before she got over it. Poor lass was walking out with a lad at that time, but after it happened she wouldn't go near a man.' He sighed. 'It was no good telling the police, it was his word against hers. He told her so at the time.'

Will could see now why Taylor's men were so ferocious, so intent on grabbing as much game as they could. 'So what did you do?'

'So I waited until he rode out and horse-whipped him ... it were nearly murder, but I stopped in time. And we lost the farm.' There was a silence and the dominoes ceased to move.

'And we lost our jobs,' Shorty said briefly.

'You do all right, though, Brad,' the man called Ben told him. 'Carrier's job gets you round villages, you see over a lot of hedges and make a bit on the side.' He grimaced. 'All I got was a job carting muck. The night soil man, that's me.'

Will had sometimes seen the carrier's cart at the side of the road, the horse quietly grazing. No doubt Taylor sometimes slipped through the hedge and went after game. And then, poachers sometimes used the carrier to get the game home, which could be harder than catching it.

Taylor turned to William as though considering him. 'Your trouble was years ago; you'll not be worried about Wiggins, one way or the other.'

It was time to tell his tale, and he knew that the story would go no further than the gang. William took a deep breath. 'I was caught in a bloody mantrap on Wiggins's land,' he said heavily. 'Lucky to be alive.'

There was a shocked silence. Then Shorty said, 'But I thought there was no more of them things left. A mantrap's – it's from me

141

grandfather's day, or before. You mean it happened to you this year?' He obviously thought Will was still living in the past.

Will rolled up his trouser leg and showed the livid scar, which was still spectacular. 'Lay there all day and all night, until a young lass happened to hear me shouting.' He winced at the memory. 'By, it did hurt. Few weeks ago, that was.'

That did it. 'You are one of us, lad,' said Taylor, clapping Will on the back. 'Hey, boys, this makes a difference. If he's using traps we could end up maimed or dead. He didn't ought to set traps. It's against the law, but that's never stopped Wiggins. It's against the law to assault a woman and he makes a habit of it, from what folks say.'

'It's not going to stop us going after his birds, eh?' That was Shorty. 'We've got orders to fill.' He looked at Will. 'Not a word, o' course. You know the drill.'

'You don't think I'm going to run to Wiggins, do you?' Will was sarcastic. 'I thought you'd know better nor that.'

Taylor leaned back in his chair and looked round the table. After a minute or two he said, 'Nah. That's just what Wiggins wants: he wants to stop us. He didn't see you, did he, Will? But he'll know trap's been sprung, I suppose, if his keeper bothers to look... And that's another thing. Any keeper with a scrap of human kindness would check a bloody thing like that every day, just in case there's some poor bugger stuck in it, bleeding to death slowly. You could've died there, Will.'

'I nearly did,' Will agreed. 'I don't suppose Wiggins or Fletcher would ha' shed a tear.'

'He thinks to frighten us off. There might be another one ... wonder which smith made 'em? I would love to know.' Taylor paused, thinking. Shorty poured him some more beer and he looked at it sourly. 'Ale's flat tonight. What's up with the cellarman?'

'We could go somewhere else,' Shorty suggested. 'But it'll be best to clear Wiggins's place first. He really deserves it and apart from Fletcher, there's no keeper.'

'So we keep going, boss?' Ben looked anxious. 'One place or another? I've debts to pay, I was counting on cash next week.'

Taylor ran a hand through his tangled dark hair. 'Aye, we'll keep to the plan and go to Wiggins.' There was a sigh of relief round the table and the dominoes moved again.

'There's full moon next week and as long as we keep clear of bracken, anywhere a trap might be hid, we should be safe,' the leader said thoughtfully. 'Think of those big fat birds just waiting for us ... we'll take guns next week.' Taylor had already accepted the mantraps and worked round them. 'That idiot Fletcher, supposed to be a keeper – he's nothing like it. A fancy boy, that's all. I'll organize him, tell him to stay in bed. And look, here he is, just coming in the door. Well, well.' He stood up and sauntered over to the Wiggins groom and keeper, who looked nervous.

Will watched as Taylor bought Fletcher a glass of beer. He said something and they both laughed. Under cover of the bar, he passed something to the groom and Fletcher looked pleased as he put it in his pocket. They talked together earnestly for a few minutes.

The other men concentrated on dominoes for a while. 'How about some raisins?' Ben asked, his eyes on the game. 'Wiggins's birds aren't fed, but they might come for raisins. Scatter some on the edge of the wood, early next week?'

'Soak raisins in a drop of rum and birds'll die happy,' suggested Will.

'Do you reckon that works?' Shorty was doubtful. 'Never done it, meself.'

Will smiled mysteriously. He hadn't tried it either, it was one of those tales that went about. But he'd seen pigs drunk on fallen, fermenting apples in an orchard and they went to sleep. Drunken pheasants might fall out of the trees.

As the men talked on, William felt a divided loyalty. Life was hard for working men, even harder when they lost their place. Wiggins was a monster who deserved to lose all his pheasants. And yet he felt bound to Tom Ridley, who trusted him, even though Tom's father had put him in prison. Sam Cooper had been bashed when Taylor invaded the Ridley estate. Taylor had said that landlords were 'all the same'. One day it would be the manor's turn again to be poached.

Taylor came back almost jovial, when Fletcher left. 'Most helpful, the lad was. Says there was only one mantrap and it got damaged, like.' He imitated Fletcher's rather high-pitched voice. 'They'll send you a bill for repairs, Will, if they find out who done it.' He laughed. 'We'll keep a look out for traps in case he's lying, but I think he's maybe right. Anyway, he'll stay in bed o' nights all next week, with covers well over his head if I'm any judge. I wasn't daft enough to tell him which night, or why. Just general good advice, I gave him.' He grinned. 'It sounds as if he doesn't go out of a night much, any road. They keep him busy all day and a man needs his sleep.'

'When old Titus comes back at weekends, he's likely a bit more active then,' Seth suggested. 'It's like a hive of bees at Hall, when he comes home.'

For the present, William had been accepted by the gang. At the end of the evening, he had no real information about their movements, but he promised to meet them again the next week. Maybe he would be able to talk them out of poaching on Ridley's land.

Back at his cottage, which was scrubbed and cleared of dust, William ate some of Judith's bread and cheese. Already he was missing her quiet presence, wondering what she was doing. He would have to ask Tom for a rabbit for her, very soon.

Judith felt restless after Will had gone, although she was tired with the strain of looking after her troublesome patient. If he had died that night of fever ... would she have been to blame? Whatever other people thought, she would have blamed herself. He did not die; he was healed and probably healthier than he had been before the accident. And now he wanted to marry her! There was still a trace of the old Judith inside her, that wanted to go with Will wherever he led.

To take her mind off the problem of William, Judith decided to deliver a batch of cheeses to the village shop. She brushed her fair hair, tied it back neatly and put on a clean apron. Her big wicker basket was packed with cool ferns and the cheeses placed carefully in the basket.

A fresh wind blew down from the moorland and clouds scudded over the sun. Just as she was leaving, the goat Molly saw her and bleated, lunged forward and snapped her chain. Judith caught the animal before she ran off and shut her in the milking shed. She would have to call at the blacksmith's to get the chain repaired, but money from the sale of the cheeses would more than cover the cost. Her goats were allowed to run free for most of the time, except Molly who had found a way to get out through the fence and was chained up until it could be strengthened.

The cheeses sold, Judith went to see the smith, Jesse Turner. He was good at making goat tethers. Once her eyes had got used to the gloom in the forge, Judith could see that Jesse was alone, banging away at a piece of metal on the anvil. When he saw her, he smiled. 'What can we do for you today, Miss Weaver?'

Judith showed him the broken chain and the blacksmith offered to repair it on the spot. The goat lady sat on a stool to watch him. After a few minutes, Jesse looked across at her while he waited for the metal to heat up. 'I hear as you've been nursing yon William Thorpe,' he began. 'That right?'

Judith said lightly, 'Yes, my herbs have healed him up, I'm thankful to say. If he tells folks about it, maybe I'll sell more salve!' Might as well turn it into a joke, but how did Jesse know?

'What did you use?' The man asked with interest. 'I get called out to horses, and what put Will right might help out a farrier.'

147

'My secret and it stays with me,' Judith told him, glad to be off the subject of William. 'But for horses, I hear that comfrey's the thing. Heals cuts and it also helps broken wind if you put it in their food. They do say it mends broken bones, though I've not seen it. I've plenty of comfrey year round, if you need it, dried leaf and root.'

'Thanks, I'll try it. Folks seem to think you know what's what, Miss Weaver.' He nodded. 'Saw Will in the pub last night,' Jesse went on casually, while working on the chain. 'Don't know that I'm keen on the company he keeps. But you'll know him better than I do.'

What did he mean by that? 'I don't know him at all, except as a patient. But I don't think he drinks very much, as a rule.'

Jesse laughed. 'He downed a few last night, though. He was with Brad Taylor and them, poachers every one, playing dominoes. Too slippery to get caught, though! Old Will used to be a poacher ages ago, and it looks as if he might be thinking of taking it up again. He was working at Village Farm – did he get turned off?'

'I believe so,' Judith said coldly. 'A lot of farm men lost their places after last year's bad harvest and the farmers haven't recovered yet. How much do I owe you for the chain?'

Jesse called after her as she walked out into the bright daylight, 'Think on, if you see

Will, you might warn him to keep away from Taylor. He's a dangerous man.'

Walking home, Judith was breathing quickly. She was very annoyed with Will. Just as his luck was turning and he'd been given a good place on the manor estate, he was throwing away any chance of being respectable by taking up with poachers. She sighed. It was too much to expect him to change. Once more, Judith would have to forget about Will, let him go his own way. He had not learned anything from the past. It was hard to have to do it twice.

TEN

'You won't look for another place just yet, Kate?' Tom said persuasively one misty November morning, as his housekeeper cleared the breakfast table. 'Can't manage without you, you know!' He was looking up at her from his chair with the smile she knew so well. Why did he have to be so friendly? It would be much easier if he kept his distance as a proper employer should. She said nothing.

'I'm being selfish I suppose, but I've never been so comfortable in this house before. It seems lighter and brighter. You've made it into a home, somehow...' Tom broke off when he saw her severe expression.

'I'm getting the manor ready for a wedding. We have only a few months and I'm about to give you a list of what we need – material for new curtains, tablecloths, sheets and glassware, for a start. This is going to be quite expensive, but Miss Fulford will not be impressed if she has to refurbish her new home.' Kate picked up the tray.

Tom ignored the frosty tone. 'Speaking of Miss Fulford, I have a letter here from her, she wants me to go to Harrogate next week.

A special ball or something. Not my idea of pleasure, I'm afraid. It's connected with some charity. Her parents are organizing a party and they want me to join them.'

'That will be a nice change of scene,' Kate said, as lightly as she could. 'You've been very busy lately, with the shooting parties. Let Sadie know what clothes you'll be wearing, so she can press them and sew the buttons on.' Tom was sometimes carelessly dressed and at Harrogate, it would not do.

Tom stood up and drew a deep breath. 'Have to make the best of it, I suppose. I can see Father at the same time ... he goes back to Jamaica soon. When he goes to Harrogate he stays at the Crown; he said it has its own sulphur well. Wouldn't drink the stuff myself, but he thinks it does him good.'

Going back to the kitchen, Kate wondered whether she was wise to stay at the manor for very much longer. Perhaps she should start to look now for a change of scene for herself. She loved the old house and enjoyed housework, but there was no future in it. Eating her heart out for Tom Ridley was a waste of emotion. She'd managed to resist him – just – when they were growing up and she could do it now.

Kate even wished that Tom would show more enthusiasm for his marriage. She knew him well enough to realize that he wasn't interested in Selina's wealth, but why did he seem to be bound to her?

Later in the morning Kate gave her shopping list to Tom, who had just come in from riding round the farm. His coat was damp from the drizzle outside and his hair was plastered over his brow, but he looked happy. 'William Thorpe's ploughing the twenty acre at the moment, doing a good job. Thanks to Will, Sam and I have been able to relax a little about Taylor and the poachers. He finds out every week what they intend to do, and so far they've left us alone, thank goodness ...' He took off his muddy riding boots. 'Is it time for a cup of tea?'

Kate waved the list under his nose. 'This is important, sir. Perhaps Miss Fulford would like to choose the materials? If you have time, you might shop in Harrogate, while you both are there.' Kate made tea for Tom and for Sadie, who was at work in the scullery. The manor was a world away from the formal Wiggins household.

'Thank you, Kate. I'm sure Selina will enjoy looking at the Harrogate shops, but it's a much smaller place than York, you know.' He sat down at the kitchen table. 'Come and sit down with me.'

Sitting at the table with him, Kate wondered again how two people like Tom and Selina had got together, and how they could imagine a happy life together. She would enjoy a ball at Harrogate, he wouldn't. He disliked the town, she seemed to hate the country. Opposites must need some sort of magnetic attraction to bind them and she'd seen nothing of the kind with Tom and his girl. She ventured a question. 'Excuse my asking, Tom, but how did you and Miss Fulford meet, and – get to be engaged?'

'These things happen, I suppose. My aunt, Father's sister Jane, lives quite close to the Fulford family. They go to the same church, have dinner together, that kind of thing. Aunt's a widow and Pa asked me to visit her, since he's out of the country. Every time I called on her, Selina was there ... she's intelligent, we talked about books. I read a few myself, living alone. And then, Aunt kept telling me I must marry and produce an heir.' Tom paused.

'So duty calls.' Kate thought it sounded less than romantic.

'There was nobody else in view; I don't meet many young ladies out here. And Selina seemed quite keen, so...' He tailed off, then added brightly, 'She'll get used to living here in time, I hope, and I expect I'll have to get used to visiting York and Harrogate quite often.' He grinned. 'Maybe I should buy faster horses to cover the distance.'

Kate picked up the shopping list and added at the bottom: *2 fast horses.*

They both laughed.

'Now, Kate, can you make lunch for the

shooting party next Wednesday? Do you mind?' Tom looked at her anxiously. 'We haven't done it before, but they asked for it, easier for them than bringing a packed lunch. And they will pay for it, of course.'

'How many lunches, Thomas?' Kate mentally checked the stores.

'About ten guns, and there'll be a few beaters as well. Separate groups, of course. I can get a girl in to help if you like.' He paused. 'I will be in Harrogate of course, but Sam can look after things; he did very well on the last shoot.'

'You haven't quite got into the way of – er – directing your staff yet, Thomas.' Kate put on a gruff voice. '"Cooper, you will provide fifteen lunches at twelve thirty on the dot." That's the way to do it.'

'Nonsense, we know each other too well. You could give them something hot, maybe meat pie ... some shoots have elaborate meals with butlers in attendance, but our guns are sensible local people. They're prosperous men enjoying a day out, even though prosperity is relative these days. You make wonderful trifles ... is it too much to ask for trifles for dessert?'

Tom watched as Kate got out a notebook, selected a clean page and wrote out a menu.

'A girl to wait at table would be excellent if you can manage it, Tom.'

The boss nodded. 'I think we'd better look

out for a full-time housemaid to help you, but for now we can get Sally, the blacksmith's daughter. Sam will be guiding them round and perhaps loading for the shooters. If the guns invite him to sit at their table he may, otherwise he'll sit with the beaters. Some of the guns may know him, of course.'

'Very good. If you can spare Benson with the trap, I would like to go to Ripon for extra supplies. And I can buy material for sheets and so on if you like, but Miss Fulford should certainly choose the curtains.'

As Tom went out he put his hand lightly on Kate's shoulder. 'You'll make some lucky man a wonderful wife, Katherine dear.'

'I expect you say that to all the spinsters you meet.' Kate's voice was not quite steady.

The sun had risen above the mist and the crisp November day was exhilarating as Sam came back from the fields to see the boss.

'Sam! How lovely to see you! What are you doing here? We're looking for the game-keeper.' The cheerful young voice rang out and stopped Sam in his tracks.

'Evie!' Evangeline Somers herself, leaning out of a trap on the drive as Sam went up to the manor. A small, dark girl, very animated, Evie was a family friend. Although they hadn't met for some time, Sam still thought about her. 'How are things over at Masham?'

Charles Somers, Evie's father, managed to bring the trap to a halt. 'Good day, young Sam. Things are going well, I'm getting plenty of commissions and Evie here has been selling her watercolours to the summer visitors. Now, can you tell me where to find the keeper?'

'I am the keeper, sir. How can I help you?' Sam walked up to the trap, his gun broken and over his arm. 'I've been out after crows; we have too many at the moment.' He was aware that in his tweed coat and breeches he must look very rustic.

Father and daughter were surprised. 'You're a gamekeeper? But – I thought you'd be at the university. What happened?' Evie asked, looking rather embarrassed. 'And where's Kate? I've been meaning to write to her, but I don't know her new address.'

'I'm afraid that Kate and I both had to find work, after Father and Mother died,' Sam swallowed; it was still hard to talk about the weeks last year when both loved parents had died of influenza within a few days of each other. 'Can't afford university. Kate was working at Bellwood Hall, but she's house-keeper here at the manor now.'

'Kate's a housekeeper! How amazing! Could I see her, do you think?' Evie hopped down from the trap nimbly in spite of her long skirt. 'I will walk up to the house with you, Sam.' She linked her arm through his.

156

Mr Somers drove slowly up to the house ahead of them. 'Now I understand why we haven't seen you.' Evie sighed. 'We used to so enjoy the picnics on the common, your family and ours, in those faraway days ... Papa teaching us how to sketch.'

'It seems such a long time ago,' Sam agreed.

Evie looked at him anxiously. 'But we must keep in touch. Our family knows about poverty; we understand. In some years Papa hasn't sold enough paintings. I know how you must feel, but do you enjoy the work? You're not treated as a menial?'

'I do like the work,' Sam said truthfully. 'You'll remember Tom Ridley, he was always with us in the holidays. Tom is now running the estate and we work for him.'

Evie's father joined them, having tied the horse to a rail. 'I'd better explain why we're here, Sam: a commission for several oil paintings of game birds – pheasant, partridge, grouse, quail. I've been told that the estate might sell some birds to me. It's hardly possible to paint them in the wild, so I want to buy fresh dead birds.'

Sam said it was possible, but there were no grouse on the estate. 'You'll have to go over the moor for those.' He took a pheasant feather from his hat and gave it to the artist. 'This might help you with the colours ... the male birds are so beautiful, I always feel sorry they have to be shot.'

'But they taste so good!' Evie was a realist.

Tom came riding up and invited the visitors inside for a hot drink before their return journey. The day was growing chilly. Sam went off to find Kate and Evie said she'd like to go with him, to have a look at the house if Tom didn't mind. She skipped along beside him. 'Do you remember, Sam, when we were – oh, about eight years old – we were going to be married when we grew up?' Her little face was alight with mischief.

Sam had never forgotten Evie, but now she was out of reach. 'There's no danger of that as you can see,' he said quietly. 'I was going to be a famous doctor and now I'm a keeper. Here she is. Look who's here, Katherine.'

'Kate! You look so ... professional in that black dress!' He left the girls together, both exclaiming with delight. It would be good for Kate to see an old friend, especially one who wouldn't patronize her now that she was a servant.

The November days were short and Charles Somers was keen to get back to Masham before dark. Tom arranged to deliver a selection of game to him and, as Somers picked up the reins, Evie called, 'Will you deliver the birds, Sam? Let him come, Thomas, and we will give him lunch! Mama will be so pleased to see him!'

Tom laughed and nodded. 'Sam works at night quite often, he can have a day off.'

Will was well fed and better clothed than he had been for years, and he enjoyed working for young Ridley, but his life was not quite right yet. He had visited the Queen's Head every week and knew that the Taylor gang were quietly making raids on the Wiggins pheasants and others farther afield, but so far had no plans to invade the manor coverts. That was all very well and good information for Sam, but Will was now suffering for it.

Taking rabbits to Judith, Will had been invited inside, but she was very distant. 'What's up, lass? I thought you'd be pleased to see me.'

'You're nothing more than a poacher, Will,' the woman said fiercely. She looked wonderful when she was angry, the grey eyes sparking. 'What's more, you're taking money from Mr Ridley, pretending to be a keeper, which makes it worse. And spending it on drink.'

'What do you mean?' William asked irritably, although he knew. Somebody had been talking. 'Just because I take the odd pint to ease the loneliness? That ain't a crime.'

'Spending time drinking with that Taylor and his men, you should be ashamed of yourself. I've nothing more to say to you. I don't want to see you again.'

159

Will felt the injustice of it, that she would condemn him because of what she'd heard. She should have asked him first. When she found out that he was not poaching she might be sorry, but it was a question of trust. There was no future for them without trust.

On the next Wednesday Tom rode off to Harrogate, to see his lady, Sam said. That night, Will learned that Taylor had his eyes on the manor pheasants. 'There's been a few shoots, there might not be much left, but the Wiggins birds have mostly gone over the hedge. I was round there on the quiet last night. There's better cover in the Manor woods and more feed,' Ben had reported. 'That's where Wiggins's birds have gone.'

The domino players kept their eyes down. 'Thursday night it is then, lads,' Taylor said briefly. 'Full moon and it should be clear, enough light to shoot. In and out fast, before they hear us.'

'Poacher's moon,' Shorty whispered. 'We'll make the most of it this year. I'll let off a shot at t'other side of wood, to draw them that way, then work my way round to you.'

Damn! Will knew that he and Sam would have to handle the gang between them. It would have been much better to have Tom there, but he wouldn't be home until Saturday at the earliest.

'They will have guns,' Will warned, when the manor gamekeepers discussed the

160

coming raid. 'Taylor plans to shoot the birds this time, it's easy by moonlight.'

'You should know!' Sam grinned. 'We'll have to rely on our wits, make them think we've got a whole gang of men and chase 'em off before they manage to kill a bird.' He thought for a moment. 'But we won't take guns. We don't want a gun battle. Not many poachers around here would fire at a keeper I should think, although you hear of it happening near the big towns.'

'Hope not,' Will said grimly. 'But I've known plenty of keepers would pepper a poacher.'

On the Wednesday, William drove the cart to pick up game after the guns. He took it to their cold game larder where the birds were hung before dispatching to various hotels. It was nearly dark before Sam came in and counted the birds. 'I've got to deliver some of these to Masham tomorrow,' he told Will. 'We have to pick out the best looking ones as an artist wants to paint them.'

'Think on and get back well before dark,' Will warned him. 'We'd best be in our places nice and early and let the birds settle down.' He didn't want the Taylor gang to catch him with Sam, although in his good keeper's breeches and jacket – kept for shoot days – and with a big hat pulled well down, he wasn't likely to be spotted.

The next morning Sam set out with a light

heart, driving the young horse Jasper in the trap on his way to Masham. After a warm welcome at the artist's house, he was given lunch and shown around the gallery, where both Charles and Evie had work displayed. Sales of paintings had been quite good over the summer months. 'I'm going to try still life this winter,' Evie told him.

They helped Charles Somers to prop up a pheasant in a lifelike position in his studio, with some vegetation round it. Time went by and all too soon, Sam realized that he would have to drive back to Kirkby quickly if he were to be there in time to join William in the wood.

'Please come again,' Mrs Somers smiled, 'and bring Kate too, if she can get away.'

'Yes, do come. We've missed you, Sam.' Evie walked with him out to the stable and watched while he yoked up Jasper. 'Will you – will you write to me?'

Sam hesitated, acutely aware of his lack of prospects. If he and Evie became close, it would spoil her chances of a good marriage; but perhaps the future could take care of itself. 'I'd love to, if your parents are happy about it. You can send me sketches, Evie. Thank you all for a very pleasant day!' He turned the horse's head towards the winding road home. It wouldn't do to linger.

Over the common where they'd had such good afternoons as children, the sun was red in the west and the sky above was a pale green, graduating to deep blue. The air was sharp with the tang of woodsmoke as people in the little town below began to cook the evening meal. Sam drove quickly, thinking of Evie and whether he would one day be able to earn enough money to support a wife. Tom's plans for the estate were ambitious. If they were successful, Sam would be given a manager's place – would that be good enough for Evie Somers's husband?

Sam never saw the bird that caused the accident. It ran out suddenly from a bush and he heard it whirr away flying low, almost under the horse's hoofs. Poor Jasper was terrified. He reared, danced sideways and then fell with a sound of splintering wood.

It took some time to calm the horse. Sam realized that with broken shafts it would not be possible to drive home so he unyoked Jasper and felt his legs. 'Can you walk, lad? I think we'll both have to walk home, I'd better not ride.' Leaving the vehicle just off the road on the short moorland turf, he set out to lead the horse home, walking as fast as he could. The light was already beginning to fade; he should have been back with William Thorpe by now. William, alone in a wood full of poachers.

Before long the light had faded from the sky and the moon was rising, lighting his path with silver, so bright that the stars were hard to see. He could just make out the line of the Plough constellation above his head.

As he reached the outskirts of Kirkby, Sam saw a light coming towards him. People who passed in the night often spoke to each other out of curiosity, so see who it was and where they might be going, so Sam called 'Goodnight!' as they drew level.

Poor Jasper was limping along and the man with the light stopped to sympathize. 'You've had a spot of trouble? It's Sam Cooper, isn't it?'

It was PC Rodney Smithers, a young and energetic constable who'd recently come to the village. 'Yes, Constable, and I might be heading for some more. There's poachers about, expected down our way tonight. I don't know whether Mr Ridley has mentioned them.'

The policeman looked down at Sam from his considerable height. 'Aye, he did have a word with me a week ago. We know who they are o' course, but unless we catch 'em in the act there's nowt we can do. I'm right sorry for keepers like you, trying to do the right thing.' He thought for a moment. 'Tell me where you think they'll be and I'll come down there with me truncheon. How many do you think there is?'

This was heartening; many village bobbies turned a blind eye to poaching, not wanting to get into fights in the middle of the night.

'At least three,' Sam assured him. 'Can you bring your brother? Sim would be very handy tonight.' Sim Smithers was as tall as the policeman and had rather more weight.

By the time Jasper was back in his stable and handed over to a horrified Benson it was fully dark, so Sam went straight to the wood, only pausing to pick up his dog Chloe and a thick stick. Will had taught Chloe to unbalance people, by running between their legs – he said it was a trick his old dog used to do, no doubt to gamekeepers in Will's young days.

ELEVEN

'I am deeply in love with you, my dear,' General Ridley murmured to his partner, as they revolved slowly round the ballroom. Candles gleamed from crystal chandeliers, the orchestra fiddled energetically and the ball was in full swing. The Crown Hotel at Harrogate had excelled as usual. The charity ball would bring in money to ease the plight of orphans and the rich were enjoying the evening, especially Major-General James Ridley (retired), with his loved one in his arms.

The lady was speechless; she had not expected this. Was it just an old-fashioned compliment? The general sounded like an impetuous young man and she was getting into deep waters. Besides, she had other obligations.

'You look so lovely tonight ... and you dance so well, so gracefully. We dance well together, do we not?' They did. James Ridley was a good dancer and he evidently enjoyed the music. 'But of course you are musical, I admire your piano playing.'

What should a woman say in such a situation? She looked down modestly at her beautiful white ball gown, with pink trimming. The trimming had been inspired.

'I always enjoy a ball, with such a good partner,' she ventured. They were floating round the room to The Blue Danube waltz.

The general's son was watching them from across the room; he would be surprised if he could hear this conversation.

'I would not have spoken seriously to you yet, but there is so little time,' the general continued urgently. 'Next week I leave for Jamaica, my passage is booked, unless – unless an urgent matter needs my presence. I need to know how you feel.' He steered her deftly through a knot of dancers.

'These last two weeks at Harrogate, in your company, have been among the happiest in my life. I would like to spend the rest of my life with you. Now, I realize there are obstacles to be overcome ... my age of course, is one of them. What do you think?'

The lady leaned back on his arm and looked at him carefully. The general was quite slim and fit for his years. He could dance all night, as she had discovered the previous week. If her mother was surprised at the way the general was constantly at her side, she never showed it. General Ridley was well bred, respectable and rich. He was also just old enough to be her father; there could be no danger from his company in her mother's eyes, which was how he'd come to spend so much time alone with her.

She looked into his eyes and realized that he was in earnest, agonizing, waiting for her answer. It gave her a feeling of power. 'Do you know,' said Selina dreamily, 'Thomas has never said he loves me? He pays me attention, but there is no real ... intimacy.'

The general's arm tightened around her waist, just a fraction. 'Are you very fond of him?'

'Thomas is the obstacle, of course. I am promised to him, as you know. I would not want to hurt him, but...' Selina smiled. Things were happening very quickly. The general had flirted as a privileged older man, but she had not taken him seriously until now.

'I have worried about your burying yourself on a country estate, although of course my main – ah – preoccupation is my feeling for you, Selina.' He was watching her expression. 'Could you really enjoy the life? You would have to entertain shooting parties in the pheasant season and the fox hunting set all winter, of course. You could in time develop an interest in sheep farming, or even forestry, but it would be a great sacrifice for you. It is still not too late ... to change your mind.'

'But Thomas ... what will he say?' Selina blushed. He understood her feelings exactly, about the mud and the boredom at the manor.

'I was going to find an excuse to visit you in York, Selina. I had to see you again – it was wonderful to meet you here! It was meant to be,' the general said earnestly.

'Perhaps.' Such determination was rather overwhelming, but also flattering, in a way. 'But I can't see how it could be arranged, General. You will not wish to quarrel with your son.'

'I am beginning to form a strategy. If you will consent to marry me, Selina dear, provided you are free, of course, well then, I think matters can be arranged. Will you?' The general held her close. 'Will you, my darling? It's now or never!'

'James, this is rather sudden. Yes, I will.' Selina leaned back and allowed her suitor to whisk her faster, right round the room until the dance came to an end and the men led their partners off the floor. She felt slightly giddy with the speed of events, as well as the dance.

The general guided Selina to her mother and their circle of friends, squeezed her hand and went off to find ices for the ladies.

Selina was trembling slightly. She was strongly drawn to the general. He was appealing in a way that Thomas was not and although they had the same charm, there was a slightly dangerous edge to the general's presence, an urgency that excited her. And then there was the lure of Jamaica, a tropical paradise so different from the manor's damp acres – and the general's social position, too.

Where was Thomas, while his father was wooing her? She looked round and saw him across the room, deep in conversation. Handsome in evening dress, Thomas looked most distinguished, but he could hardly ever be persuaded to dance.

Thomas was too serious. At a ball like this, with dancing, music, sophisticated society and a wonderful supper, he was only interested in sheep! Or wool, to be exact. Apparently he wanted to talk with leaders in the woollen industry, with the idea of selling his wool to the mills instead of the factor in Ripon.

'It's an ideal chance to meet people from the West Riding,' he'd explained apologetically. 'There are several mill owners here doing their bit for charity. I must speak to them.'

Selina had raised her eyebrows. It seemed that the mill owners, too, would rather talk business than dance. But now, she felt guilty when she looked at Tom. It was going to be an awkward situation. What on earth could the general's 'strategy' be?

The ices arrived and there was general conversation for a while. 'Did you know that Lord Byron once stayed here, at the Crown Hotel? It was much smaller in those days, of course.' An older woman who looked like a duchess had proved to be an old school friend of her mother's and she knew Harrogate well.

'How romantic!' Selina sighed. It was proving to be a romantic evening.

As the mill owner moved away, the general closed in on Thomas before he could join Selina. 'I'll be gone next week,' he reminded his son. 'But before I go, I'd like a private word with you. Several, in fact. I suppose you'll be off home tomorrow, so there's no time like the present, hey?'

Tom saw Selina across the room with her mother's group. 'I really ought to dance again ... but, very well, Father. Come out on to the terrace, it's stuffy in here.' French windows opened out on to a paved area overlooking a garden.

They stood under the night sky and Tom took a deep breath of fresh air. He looked up at the full moon, low in the sky and shining through branches, silvering the foliage that surrounded the building. What was happening on the estate? He hoped Taylor wouldn't raid while he was away. This was the poacher's moon after all, Will had reminded him, a favourite time for taking someone else's game.

The general looked round, but they were alone. The sounds of the orchestra came to them faintly, muffled by the ivy on the old walls. *The old boy has found a new wife, that must be it. He's threatened to do it for years and now he's going to break the news.*

'Two things, my boy. But let us sit down.' Tom drew up two wicker chairs and the general lit a cigar. He sat back smoking for a few minutes, as if uncertain how to begin.

'First of all, the straightforward part. I have certain things in mind and if we can agree, then I will legally hand over the whole Manor to you, with enough capital to run it – even to buy more land. It will be yours when I shuffle off this mortal coil in any case, but you can have it now, if you agree. With no strings attached, run it how you will.'

What could the old boy want? Tom was puzzled. 'Of course I agree to take the estate, its where I want to spend the rest of my life. But – what's the catch, Father?' He didn't know his father all that well, but he expected an ulterior motive. While he was always cheerful, Pa tended to barge his way through life like a cavalry charge.

The general examined his cigar. 'Tell me, how fond are you of your fiancée? Could you live without her? She's not exactly keen on the rural life, you know.'

Lord, he didn't want Selina, did he? Tom suddenly remembered watching them dance together only a few minutes earlier. They'd been … gazing at each other.

'Selina? Well, we're engaged, you know that. She expects me to marry her.'

'That sounds rather lukewarm, if I may say so. I know you don't like to express emotion, Tom, but are you passionately in love with Selina? Be honest, now.' His father blew smoke rings.

What was a man to say? 'Well, perhaps not, to be honest, but, we get along well; I think we'll be happy. Selina has a pleasant nature…' Where was this going?

The general looked at him through half-closed eyes. 'Because – I am!'

Tom sat up with a start. *The poacher's moon … it's my fiancée that is being poached. By my father. The old villain!*

Tom looked at the moon again, serene in a cloudless sky. 'You are? Good lord.' He struggled to compose himself. *My girl, you're taking my girl … and I resent it.* 'But – Selina? What does she say? Does she know?'

'I told her I would prepare you for the news. She doesn't want to hurt you, Thomas, she is quite fond of you – perhaps as a stepson? She is older than you, of course.' He paused.

'Of course.' Tom was stunned, his plans for family life in ruins. Had he been too casual? In spite of their different interests, he'd thought that Selina and he would get on well and he was getting used to the idea of marriage in the spring. Of course he wasn't in love, but – how many couples were?

'The dear lady will marry me, providing she is free. If you will free her from her engagement to you.' The old boy could hardly hide his excitement.

'So she agrees. She's giving me up.' He felt unwanted.

'There is twenty years' difference in our ages, but we are perfectly suited, I feel,' the general finished smugly.

'It will take me some time to get used to this.' Thomas wondered where he could find a glass of wine. 'I'd planned to marry Selina and have a proper home for the first time, since I've never had one.'

'The second thing I want to talk to you about,' went on the general, gaining momentum, 'concerns your – ah – lack of home life, and has a bearing on the first. I have worried for years about this, and especially when you became engaged to be married.' There was a pause. 'The truth is, dear Thomas, that your mother and I were never married.'

Tom got up abruptly, went back into the ballroom and came back with two glasses and a bottle of claret. 'Two large shocks in one night... I don't know what to think.' He felt like screaming and shouting.

Poacher's moon ... he has taken away my girl and now my good name, in a few minutes.

The general went on as soon as Tom returned. 'Sit down, Tom. Of course, I owe you an explanation. Your mother was a servant at the manor ... when she became pregnant, I planned to marry her, but – she died when you were born, unwed. I had left it too late ... I never expected...' He looked up. 'She was a lovely young girl, Thomas.'

'So I'm a bastard,' said Thomas flatly, pouring the wine. His father had never talked about his mother, or about anything else, for that matter. Little Thomas had been reared by a nursemaid and sent off to boarding-school very early. He had spent the school holidays at the doctor's with Sam Cooper, where there was normal, warm family life. All Tom's life, the general had been away, in the army and then in Jamaica. Had he ever felt guilty about the woman he should have married?

'The only time it matters is when your birth certificate is required. And, of course, when you marry, your wife has to know the truth.' The general paused. 'Naturally, for your sake, I led people to believe that your mother and I had married.'

'You're telling me that Selina wouldn't like the truth. It's your second argument, in case I won't give her up.' *The wily old devil! He must have been a good general.*

'I admit it.' The 'old devil' sipped his wine complacently.

Not a word of remorse for any of it, the

whole sorry tale. Thomas was beginning to see the depth of his father's selfishness. He was pleased with the neat way in which he had tied Thomas up, presented him with the inevitable. Tom had the feeling that even if he'd been in love with Selina he would have lost her. Generals are used to having their own way.

His father had not quite finished. 'I'm giving you the estate because I can afford it and also because, if Selina and I have children, no one will disinherit you.'

Of course … a legitimate heir could claim the estate if it still belonged to the general. The old boy had thought of everything. 'So – what next?' Of course his father would have decided what should happen next. Thomas liked women, he'd always got on well with them and to be rejected was a blow to his confidence. 'I suppose I must speak to Selina … in the morning. I've had enough for one night.'

General Ridley had other ideas. 'I will leave you now – don't go away. Give me thirty minutes.'

Thoughtfully, Tom poured himself another glass of wine. The poacher's moon was higher now, floating among the trees. He could hear the night sounds of Harrogate, horses' hoofs and the jingle of harness as people went to and from their evening engagements.

The blank feeling persisted. Not only

would Selina have been horrified to learn that he was a bastard , but so would any well brought up young woman. It was going to affect the rest of his life.

To be really honest, he hadn't shown much enthusiasm for the marriage, had he? By contrast, James Ridley was energetic, forceful in everything he did. Women liked that, Tom supposed. It would have been easy, though if he'd had strong feelings for Selina.

Another thought occurred. The consolation prize was a good one: he had the estate in his own hands, for good. He would make the very best of it. Tom straightened his shoulders and thought about his acres, dreaming under the moon.

Exactly thirty minutes later General Ridley came back with Selina. She was flushed, almost beautiful, standing so straight by the door in the light from the ballroom, with her head held high. She looked a little nervous, fingering the pink trim on her skirt.

Tom stood up awkwardly, with no idea what to say, but, as before, the general took over. 'We need no embarrassment. Please sit down.' He held a chair for the lady. 'There has been no deception, it was only this evening that I spoke to Selina about my hopes for our future.'

Tom looked at her. 'You're feeling the shock too? I'm afraid my father affects people that way.'

Selina smiled faintly and looked a little more relaxed. 'It is rather sudden, I'm afraid, and I would have preferred to speak to you first, but...' She looked at him helplessly. 'The general took charge.'

'As he does.' Tom decided to make things easy for her; she almost seemed like a victim. 'I gather that you want to end our engagement? That's perfectly reasonable, Selina. Country life would probably not have suited you after all, especially in the winter. I think Jamaica will be a much more exciting place to live in!'

To spare her, Tom made it seem like a choice of locations, rather than of people. And maybe that's what it came down to, in the end. Kirkby couldn't compete with the lure of Jamaica.

The general had said he was passionately in love, but Selina was not a passionate type as far as Tom could see. His father was an elderly man who had decided to find a wife to comfort his declining years, but that was not what he'd told Selina.

'Thank you, Thomas, I was sure you would be generous. I hope you will not be too much hurt.' Selina arranged her skirt.

Tom gave her a slightly hurt, but not too hurt, look. 'No doubt I will get over it, in time. I wish you both well, of course. When is the wedding to be? Do your parents approve?'

178

Selina blushed. 'My father is very much shocked, I'm afraid. He feels for you, Thomas ... but' – she looked coy – 'by the time of the wedding, I hope he will get used to the idea.'

His father looked at Tom and added, 'I will instruct our solicitors to have the estate papers and so on, ready for signing.' Tom nodded. He wondered whether Selina knew of the general's arrangement.

It seemed that the general was to delay his trip home until after the wedding. 'We'll be married and I will take Selina on a honeymoon cruise, and then back to Jamaica. And now, let us go in to supper; the Fulfords will be waiting.' General Ridley stood up and gave his hand to Selina. The deal was done and the winner was ready to move on, taking his prize with him.

The thought of those stuffy rooms in the hotel and a rich supper made Tom feel sick. He wanted to get away, out of Harrogate. He shook his head. 'I must ask to be excused, I'm sure you will understand.' Might as well twist the knife a little. 'I intend to ride back to the manor tonight.'

'Oh no! It's far too late – and what about robbers? Please stay until daylight, Thomas.' Selina looked quite worried.

'There's a full moon, it's as bright as day. Did you notice the moon, Selina? I thought not.' He laughed. 'There hasn't been a high-wayman seen for over forty years! The distance is only about fifteen miles and I have a good horse, well rested.' He bowed over Selina's hand and then looked into her eyes. 'I do hope you'll be happy.' After shaking hands with his father, Tom walked away and he could feel them watching him go.

Tom changed into riding clothes, packed his bag, collected Samson, his big bay horse from the stable and set off up the hill. Father could pay what he owed the hotel. It was good to get out of Harrogate and on to the upland. The night air was cold but invigorating and away from the town lights, he could see the stars.

There were villages on the way, Killinghall and Ripley, where the folks had all gone to bed and there were no lights, even in the big castle. Then he swung across to the west a little, down into the river valley and steeply up to Grantley, where he reined in to give Samson a rest. He rode into Kirkby as the church clock struck twelve.

Smiling, Tom took the familiar road through the old stone gateposts leading to the manor. It was good to be home and even the horse quickened his pace.

To Tom's surprise, Benson was in the stables at this late hour, bathing the knees of the young horse Jasper. 'What happened, Jake?' Wearily he slipped off his saddle, looking forward to going to bed.

'Oh sir, I'm so glad you're back. It's been

a very strange night.' Benson's young face was white in the light of the hurricane lamp.

'It has indeed,' Tom agreed. 'And it sounds as though it's not over yet.'

'Mr Cooper's gone out after poachers, sir, and he said Will Thorpe would be there with him. Then a cart came by, right through our yard and on down to the fifty acre wood ... I daren't stop it, I was here on my own.' Benson saw Tom looking at Jasper's knees. 'And the trap's all smashed up, he left it on the common ... what shall we do?' It was a despairing cry.

'Don't worry, Jake,' Tom said soothingly, running his hands down the horse's legs. 'Jasper will recover, the grazes are not deep. Tell you what you can do – build up your fire and put the kettle on, we'll be in need of a drink of tea once we chase the poachers off. We will come back to your cottage.'

Benson's mother would never forgive Tom if he took the lad into danger, but poor Jake wanted to be part of the action.

The baleful influence of the poacher's moon was not done yet.

TWELVE

Kate was uneasy on the night of the full moon, waiting for her brother, pacing up and down the manor kitchen. Sam was late, very late. He should have been home from Masham before dark and although she could imagine how hard it would be for her sociable brother to get away from the Somers family, she was worried. Though quiet and calm, Sam was very conscientious and was always on time. Something must have happened to delay him. The fact that Tom was in Harrogate for a few days made it worse.

Kate had felt the weight of responsibility once Tom had gone. She was alone in the big house at night for the first time. Sam had offered his dog for company, but she thought Chloe would be restless, shut in a house. Once Sam was home, even though he would sleep in his cottage, she would feel less vulnerable.

The other cause for worry was the threat of poachers, always at the back of her mind. Every time she heard a pheasant alarm can outside her bedroom window, Kate remembered the dark shapes in the wood on the night she had gone out to try to help Sam.

Foxes sometimes disturbed the birds, but there was always the chance of a more sinister presence, stalking quietly through the dark trees.

Tom had made a point of not telling Kate anything about poachers. 'We don't want you running round the woods like Maid Marian again and getting in the firing line,' he told her, and although he was smiling, she knew he meant it. She decided not to be offended. It was men's way to keep women ignorant of any possible danger, because females were supposed to be fragile.

Sam had just looked mysterious when Kate questioned him as to whether the pheasants were likely to be raided. 'William Thorpe has it all in hand,' he'd said. He was putting a lot of trust in the former poacher and Kate hoped it was justified. She liked Will, but she'd heard him confess to Tom that he found going after game hard to give up.

Jake Benson, the groom, was worried too, Kate could tell, although he told her to go to bed. 'Mr Cooper'll be right, miss, never fear, it's a grand night for driving. I'll keep a look out and help him with Jasper, when he comes.' Jake had a small cottage in the stable block and would hear him when Sam came in.

Moonlight flooded through the thin curtains of her room and eventually, unable to sleep, Kate drew back the curtains and looked out onto a silvery landscape. The estate was a beautiful place, over 700 rolling acres of fields and woods sheltered by High Side, a ridge of moors to the west that divided them from the next valley, Nidderdale. But tonight she saw a menace in every shadow, a feeling that she could not quite shake off.

She thought about Tom at the ball in Harrogate, and hoped that he and Selina would come to some understanding. Perhaps tomorrow they would go shopping together. Although it was hard to imagine Thomas buying curtains, it was time he gave some thought to the running of the house, for his lady's sake.

From her room on the third floor Kate had a wonderful view of the grounds and woods. Over in the distance she could even see Bellwood Hall, although it was not visible from the ground because of an intervening ridge. Once more she wondered how George and Bella were faring with their new governess. They would be back from their visit – to Chester, was it? – by now and presumably at the Hall for the weekend.

All was calm and not a breath of wind stirred the trees. She was turning away with a sigh to go back to bed when Kate noticed something about the Wiggins mansion. Were they hosting a party? There seemed to be much more light there than usual. Dinner parties were often arranged for when there was a full moon to light the guests on their way home.

She could imagine the scene; Sir Titus fussing about, beaming with false goodwill, his cruel nature well hidden as it always was on social occasions. Sometimes Kate had taken George and Bella to the top of the stairs to watch dinner guests arrive. They had loved to see their mother looking regal and their father in evening dress, his hair and even his rough voice toned down for the occasion. In the pheasant season there could be a shooting party staying overnight and, if so, they would be well into the bottles of port by now. Maids would be washing dishes endlessly in the kitchen; it took them hours after a dinner party.

The light was increasing and it was now a reddish, flickering glow. Kate strained her eyes anxiously. Could it be a fire? The next moment a column of flames rose high in the air from the roof and she gasped in horror. Bellwood Hall was on fire!

With so many candles and lamps in a big house and so many servants, fire was a constant fear. Long, voluminous dresses and shawls could easily catch fire if women stood too close to the hearth, the material caught up in a sudden draught from the chimney. Kate shuddered as she remembered stories of fires, told by the doctor's patients.

What could she do? Tom was away, Sam was missing and presumably William Thorpe was at home in the village. Sadie went home to her mother at night, so she and Benson were the only staff at the manor.

It was unthinkable to stand and watch the disaster from a safe distance. Kate knew she had to go over to the Hall to see whether there was anything she could do to help. Those poor children they would be terrified. She scrambled to change her clothes, thinking of the children. George and Bella would have been tucked up in bed in the nursery long ago and the new governess would be in Kate's old room, which was next door. The woman would take the children to safety downstairs, of course, but Kate had to go there to see for herself.

Of course, the fire might soon be under control. There was supposed to be a plan at the Hall in case of fire, she had been told. Everyone in the building was to leave immediately and assemble on the lawn, to be counted. There was a flexible leather fire hose on a cart in the stables, to spray water by means of a manual pump from an ornamental goldfish pond. But in Kate's time at the Hall, no one had tried out the apparatus.

In the towns, if you carried out insurance you could call in the fire brigade to put out a blaze. But the Ripon fire engine, pulled by slow horses would take hours to call out and even longer to arrive. Country people had to rely on their own resources.

It was sensible to wear boots and an old black dress, tucked up and tied like a fish wife's skirt to give her room to move. Kate was soon letting herself out of the side door of the manor, her heart beating fast. That hose would probably be far too short, it would only reach as far as the ground floor, but Kate had seen flames erupting from the top, through the roof. It looked as though the fire had started on the top floor.

It was easy to see where she was going; along the carriage road and on to a small road to the village she hurried along in the moonlight. Kate remembered that Bellwood Hall was an old building and the roof timbers were ancient, dry, dating back to Tudor times. It would burn very easily, even though there was no wind.

Running, Kate hurried down the drive, the whole place lit by the flames. Pausing to catch her breath, she stared in horror at the scene. Fire raged across the top storey, out of reach, flames shooting up and dying through windows and through holes in the roof. A small crowd stood on the lawn, gazing up-wards. A woman was screaming. There was no sign of the children, as far as she could see. Perhaps they'd been taken away to safety.

Fletcher was doing his best, holding the hose in both hands, spraying water on the ground floor. He saw Kate and shouted to her above the din. 'Must keep it from spreading,' he panted. 'What about the maids – and the nursery, up all those flights of stairs? Are they out yet?' Two labourers worked the pump, sweating.

'I'll find out, John,' Kate promised and went to look for the housekeeper, who was presumably in charge.

A figure appeared at a top window: Polly, her clothes on fire, waving her arms and screaming. Those below looked up in horror. Fletcher saw her and heroically tried to reach her with the hose. 'Get down the stairs!' he shouted. 'Get down!'

Kate tried to call poor Polly, who was evidently panicking. 'Tie some sheets together!' she called. If she could climb down to the next floor, she might then use the stairs. 'Sheets! Make a rope!' Others tried to encourage her, but Polly made no move to save herself.

Instead, the maid stood on the window sill. 'I did it!' she screamed. 'Tell Wiggins I did it!' She jumped out of the window and, as the crowd watched helplessly, fell to the ground. Kate felt sick no one could survive such a fall.

It sounded as though Polly had started the fire, but what had driven her to such a horrific act? It was hard to believe. Kate had liked the little maid, who was quite good with the children. Polly must have been desperate, completely unhinged. Something must have happened to her. And she had mentioned Wiggins. A cold feeling came over Kate as she imagined what might have happened. After a shocked pause, people began to move towards the still figure on the grass.

The nursery was on the top floor; surely the children were out by now? 'George and Bella? Where are they?' Kate yelled above the screams and shouts that erupted again.

The housekeeper and the cook were going round the group, trying to account for all the people in the house. They shook their heads. 'Haven't seen them ... don't know where they are.'

Kate looked round quickly. All the other maids were sitting on the grass, weeping and the farm manager had just arrived. The children were not there: they must still be in the building.

Kate ran into the house and found that the main staircase was ablaze from the top, old oak ignited by ancient hangings. So were the twisting back stairs from the kitchens to the attics.

There was another iron spiral staircase, never used because it was said to be unsafe, although the real reason was probably because it went from the top floor where the servants slept, to a hidden side door. Kate had found it one day when she explored the house with the children for a history lesson. They'd discovered that at one time there was a priest hole in the passage wall. She ran for the old door and sobbed with relief to find it unlocked, though covered in ivy and cobwebs.

Up and up, round and round she ran, 'George! Bella!' she called. The lurid light from the fire lit the stairwell through slits in the stone walls. When she reached the landing, fire was licking the nursery door and the smoke made it difficult to breathe.

She must be too late.

Kate wrenched open the door with an effort and found the two children and their mother, cowering behind it. They were all coughing and choking, but they were alive. Lady Wiggins's elegant bed gown was streaked with grime and her hair was down over her back.

'Cooper ... what are you doing here?' It was a simple question, not a reprimand. 'We're trapped,' she whispered. 'Unless you can get us out.'

'Mama came to get us,' George choked. 'But then we couldn't go to the stairs. What shall we do, Nursie?' Bella was silent, with her thumb in her mouth. If the little ones panicked, precious time would be lost.

'We're brave explorers, remember? Get down on the floor!' Kate spoke firmly and obediently, Lady Wiggins got down and pulled the children with her. Shaking with fear herself, Nursie tried to smile at the children. 'We're going to explore, find a way out down the old iron stairs. It's quite easy, you've done it before. Keep your heads down, out of the smoke and follow me. We'll soon be outside. Tuck up your gown, Lady Wiggins.' The woman was a fire hazard in that bed gown.

'Thank you, Cooper,' Lady Wiggins whispered, humbly doing as she was told. The hard part was to dodge the flames on the landing, but Kate pushed them along, out of the fire's way. Slowly they crept down the smoke-filled passage, a strange procession on all fours, near the floor where the air was slightly clearer.

'What about the governess? Will she be up here?' Kate suddenly remembered, as they passed the door of her old room that there might be another person in danger, possibly overcome by smoke.

'No. I looked, she's not in her room.' The lady looked murderous.

Bella started to cry and Kate picked her up, marvelling at her own strength. 'Keep a firm hold of George,' Kate said to their mother, as she wrestled with the door to the iron staircase, which she'd closed behind her. When they got to the narrow stairs, Kate took George on her back and helped Lady Wiggins to do the same for Bella, who was lighter.

'Mama, you came for us, you came! You're here!' Bella wriggled and her mother nearly fell, clutching the metal banister for support.

A tear rolled down the sooty face. 'Yes, darling. I'm here, we're going to be safe.'

Kate turned her attention to getting them down the staircase, a tricky operation. Down they went, inch by inch. George held on to her so tightly she thought he would choke her. 'Oh, Nursie, where's Papa? Will he be cross? We didn't make the fire, truly.' The poor child was worried about future punishment.

Bella piped up, 'Polly burned the curtains with a candle! I saw her on the landing!'

Kate realized then that Polly must have been driven to the point of insanity. The little maid she knew would never have put George and Bella in danger; it was unthinkable.

Where, indeed was Sir Titus? Kate had not seen him on the lawn with the servants. He should have been putting all his baleful energy to good use, directing and helping the fire fighters. There had seemed to be no one taking charge, although Fletcher had evidently dragged out the hose. Where was the new governess? Surely she wouldn't have got out herself and left the children?

They heard a loud crash; part of the roof must have fallen in. 'Faster!' Kate cried.

'But be careful where you put your feet...' It would be easy to miss a step and put a foot through the gap between them.

Lady Wiggins was panting and looked ready to faint. 'I failed,' the older woman muttered. 'I should have thought of this way out.'

Kate looked round at her as they went down the stairs. 'You were the only person who went to help the children, ma'am. Don't forget that.' She was seeing the formal, distant Lady Wiggins in a new light, as a mother at last.

Kate felt her legs were turning to jelly, but she forced herself on and then suddenly the stairs ended, there was a breath of fresh air from the open door and they were out on the gravel in the moonlight.

They stumbled out and fell onto the grass. Their mother held the children tightly, one on either side of her. Kate went by herself round the side of the house, where poor Polly was being gently carried away. The children had seen enough horror for one night.

The fire was dying down as it reached the stonework. The roof was gone, but it looked as though the lower part of the house would survive. Kate went back to the children.

'I will not forget tonight, Cooper,' Lady Wiggins whispered hoarsely. The smoke seemed to have taken her voice away. 'When

I can find my husband, he will organize where we and the servants are to go. Would you be so good as to find out whether everyone is accounted for? I can scarcely stand.'

George looked up from the shelter of his mother's arm. 'Tell Papa we didn't do it,' he begged. 'He'll be so cross, he'll hit me again.'

Kate put her hand lightly on George's sooty curls. 'Of course you're not to blame. Don't worry about it, Georgie boy. Or you, Bella.' The little girl was half asleep.

At the front of the house, Mrs Mason, the housekeeper, took Kate aside. 'The children are safe? The governess should have been there ... I was hoping she'd look after them. You're a wonderful woman, Kate. I can't think how you did it.'

'The old staircase right at the side of the house. What about the others?'

'All the maids are here ... except poor Polly. It seems that she started the fire. Polly was very strange, these last few weeks. I've been worried that she was losing her mind.' She paused and then said wearily, 'You will understand – she was being harassed. It got too much for her.'

It made Kate sick to think of what had happened to Polly. 'The children and their mother are on the grass at the side of the house. But I'm not sure about their governess ... is she here? I don't know her, of course.'

Mrs Mason had turned to look over at the line of stone buildings across the drive, the stables and other outhouses. Kate followed her gaze and they saw two figures creeping along the side of the wall. The shadows split up and one came towards them, while the other stood watching from a distance.

'The new governess is over there. I expect she has been entertaining Sir Titus.' Her normally soft voice was hard. 'There's a room over the laundry and he visits her there sometimes. He'll have got a shock just now … must not have noticed that the place is on fire.'

'When the governess doesn't sleep near the children, then who looks after them in the night?' George used to have bad dreams sometimes and call for Nursie. It was appalling to think that they were being so badly neglected.

'Polly is … was to see to them at night. I'm not happy about any of it, of course. Every night I go up to tuck them in, poor little mites.'

'Well.' Kate sighed with weariness. 'Their mother went to them; she's with them now. I think she may take more care of them in future. At least they don't seem to be afraid of her.'

Wiggins came up to them, blustering. 'Mason, what's going on? What's all this? My house – it's ruined! Somebody will suffer for this!' He glared at Kate. 'What are you doing here? You have no right! Have you caused this – disaster?' This was just as George had feared; someone was to be blamed.

Kate glared back at him, furious. 'Sir Titus, presumably you want to hear that your wife and children are safe. Go to them. They are at the side of the house, outside the dining-room windows.' If she'd been a man she would have knocked him down.

Instead of going to his wife, Wiggins strode off, bellowing, 'Fletcher! You idle dog, how could you let the place burn down? You deserve a flogging!'

'Poor Fletcher did what he could. I think he helped to save the lower rooms,' Mrs Mason murmured. 'I'm leaving, Kate. I can't stay here, working for a man like that.' She paused and then dropped her voice even lower. 'Polly was raped, you know, several times. Wiggins is a monster. Last week she told me she was pregnant. She thought he would kill her if he found out. And she was probably right. I was trying to find a safe place for her. Now it's too late.'

'I was nearly raped myself, the day he found out about the stolen silver,' Kate admitted. To banish the memory, she changed the subject. 'I know of a very good position for you, Mrs Mason. Mr Ridley will be looking for a housekeeper; he's getting married in the spring.'

The other woman looked shocked. 'But that's your place, I can't take that. Where will you go?'

'I'd like to teach, if I can find a decent household with some good children. I have missed these two, I admit. And I've wondered how they were being treated.'

'Well, I hope you're right and that their mother will take more interest in George and Bella. I suppose they'll stay in Bradford, until all this damage is repaired. The roof will need replacing and it will take time.' Mrs Mason looked round. 'I'd better go with Cook to see whether we can make up beds in the stable block for tonight. And then – I don't know what we'll do. In the morning we'll be able to see the damage and try to find our things.'

THIRTEEN

Ill met by moonlight ... the words echoed through Tom's head as he crept through the wood. Shakespeare, wasn't it? The poacher's moon might have even more in store for him before the night was over.

Keeping to the shadows Tom tried not to disturb the birds, although one or two cackled as he passed. He kept moving to where he thought Sam might be. Sam and Will wouldn't expect him, but that might be a good thing.

He'd been longing to climb into bed, but although he was tired and aching a little from the long ride home, Tom was now fully alert. Jake had said that Sam was out after poachers, tipped off by William who was sure they would be there tonight. Trust them to choose a night when the boss was away from home. He wondered whether one of them had seen him ride off on the Harrogate road.

For the first time he wondered whether he should trust Will Thorpe, or whether he was really working for Taylor's gang. Will could have told them that the boss would be away. If so, what would his purpose be tonight –

did he want a share in the profits? It was hard to fathom for a straightforward man, but perhaps Will had a devious side to him. If he was in with the poachers, he surely wouldn't have told Sam to expect them – unless that was a bluff, to prove his own innocence. It was enough to make a man's head ache.

The main thing now was to find Sam, to make sure he was safe. Tom stood quiet, listening to the night sounds of the wood and watching the pattern of moonlight under the trees. Nothing stirred. Perhaps he should have brought a gun, but that would be taking things to extremes, although it might scare off the thieves – if they were here. So far, no sound had reached him. Perhaps it was all over.

The loud report of a shotgun suddenly shattered the silence echoing through the trees and making Tom start. It was followed by another, presumably the second barrel. There were more shots from a slightly different direction, echoes rumbling round him. What was going on?

Tom's precious pheasants took to the wing in dozens, clattering through the wood on heavy wings. The fight was on and Tom's heart beat faster. But what could he do against armed men? And where were his keepers?

The whole thing had gone wrong. He should never have gone to Harrogate in the first place. It would have been far better to be told of his fate in a sweet little note from Selina, in due course. This was what you got for neglecting your duty.

Tom shouted, there was no point in silence now. 'Alan! John! To me!' There was little hope of frightening the poachers, but at least he could locate Sam and find out what Will was up to.

He heard an answering shout, Sam's voice. 'Coming!' from far away. And then there was another, Will's deeper tones. 'Here, boss!' A pause, another report, then a harsh cry of anguish; more than pheasants were being targeted tonight.

Tom stepped out into a moonlit clearing so that he could be seen. Surely they wouldn't shoot him? He was playing a game without knowing the rules. All was quiet, except for faint rustling of dead leaves. After a few minutes he could hear movement in the undergrowth and a man stumbled out, clutching his arm. 'They got you, Will?'

William Thorpe's teeth were gritted. 'The bastards got me.' Blood trickled down his arm, black in the moonlight. He rolled up his sleeve.

Sam arrived with twigs and cobwebs sticking to his clothes, followed by the faithful Chloe, breathing heavily with excitement and grinning from ear to ear.

'Taylor's here, of course,' Sam said breathlessly. 'Good to see you, Tom, we didn't expect you back tonight. I was late I'm afraid, but Will and I managed to meet up. Then we saw them. They had guns, so we scared some of our birds away, out of their reach. But they've got quite a few ... they've grabbed them from the branches. The birds were drugged, I think.'

'Raisins with rum,' Will told him. 'I found some under a tree.'

'Let's get William bandaged up,' Tom said crisply. 'That's the priority at the moment.'

Will looked at his arm. 'Its full of pellets. He was not far off me when he fired, but some of 'em missed.' He looked round. 'Watch out, sir, they're not far away and they're very poor shots.'

'William, I'm sorry you're injured. It's the doctor for you and no arguments this time, as soon as we can get you to the village.' Tom realized that he sounded just like his father, taking charge. Had those men shot Will deliberately, as soon as they realized that there were keepers about? But now they were all vulnerable, because Tom had called out.

The next moment Taylor and Shorty came into the clearing, each with a gun under one arm and a bulging game bag over the other shoulder. Taylor was laughing. 'We knew you was running to Tommy boy here, telling him everything we said. Sorry you got shot,

Mr Thorpe. I thought you was a pheasant.'

'Get off my land.' Tom was ferocious. Poor Will was suffering once more and this time Tom knew it was his fault. It was too risky for Will as informer to be in the wood that night.

'Mr high and mighty Ridley, you can't do nothing about us. We've got guns and you have none. Then, of course, we have to tell you that these here are wild birds; they belong to anybody.' Shorty sounded smug. 'We've got plenty tonight, make us a quid or two and no—' He broke off as they were joined by two other young men, walking steadily up to them.

One was a policeman in uniform.

'Now, you two, put down your guns,' PC Smithers said firmly. 'And open those bags.' His large brother Sim edged nearer to them, fingering a thick stick.

The men slowly put down the weapons. It was a tense moment, but presumably they were not loaded, having just been fired. The policeman signalled to Tom and Sam and they emptied out the bags, which were full of dead pheasants.

'You can't prove anything—' Taylor began, but Smithers interrupted him.

'We've got the proof we've been waiting for, believe me. I can tell the court I saw your bloke with the cart taking pheasants with my own eyes. You are trespassing with firearms on private property and you have game in your possession.'

'And one of these rats has just shot at my gamekeeper, wounded him in the arm.' Tom glared at the poachers. 'I am glad you're here, PC Smithers.' He'd talked about game thieves at the police station often enough, but there was only one policeman in Kirkby. The man had been sympathetic, but had explained that he couldn't spend too much time lurking in the woods.

The constable nodded. 'Thanks, Mr Ridley.' He turned to the men. 'What's more, I know your names and addresses. Tonight you will spend in the cells. Give us a hand to cuff them, Sim.' He got out handcuffs looking very happy, but his big brother seemed to be rather disappointed there had not been more of a fight.

Taylor lunged sideways and turned to run, but quick as a flash Chloe was there. She ran between his legs and he fell heavily. 'Damned dog! Get it off me, it'll kill me!' Chloe was standing over him, teeth gleaming in the pale light, waiting for his next move. She looked menacing, but she only wanted to play.

'Good girl, Chloe! Stay! Hold him!' Sam told her and the tail wagged, but she still pinned the man down.

'Well, well, Mr Taylor's frightened of dogs. Useful animal, that,' the policeman said, as his brother put handcuffs on the man as he lay on the ground. In spite of his pain, Will smiled wryly.

Shorty dived away but Tom was after him, all his pent-up rage exploding as he tackled the man as though he were playing rugby at school, throwing them both to the ground. He too was handcuffed, but Shorty was large and powerful and it took two of them using, their whole strength. The cart came up, driven by Ben and he was quickly taken into custody, together with his load of birds.

'Where's Seth?' Will asked. He had the feeling that someone was missing.

Taylor muttered, 'You've got nowt on him. He's not here.'

'Where did you get this cart?' the policeman demanded. Tom pointed to the name on the side; it belonged to the coalman. 'Right, we'll take it back in due course.'

A strange cartload creaked its way down to the village: three handcuffed poachers, one injured man, the policeman and his brother and Tom as the driver, all with a slight coating of coal dust. Sam stayed behind to deal with the dead birds and reassure young Jake Benson that nobody had been killed. The full moon sailed on serenely through the night, lighting the pale road in front of them.

As they jogged along, Tom noticed a red glow in the sky. 'Looks like a fire somewhere,' he said to the constable.

'Bellwood Hall direction, Sir Titus must

be having a party. He has fireworks and all, they say, sir.'

Tom left the constable and his prisoners at the police station, where the poachers would spend the rest of the night in a very bare cell. He then used his persuasive powers to get the doctor out of bed to attend to Will. The injuries might not be serious, but the man was in pain. He shouldn't have been injured at all, Tom kept telling himself.

Tom had heard that the overworked doctor sometimes told people to go away and come back in the morning, when they threw pebbles at his bedroom window to wake him. Thank goodness, this time Dr Sherwood was quite civil, dressing and coming downstairs as soon as he heard the door bell. His wife was sympathetic, giving them hot sweet tea to revive them. 'Those pellets need to come out right away,' the doctor said.

To take his mind off the operation Tom talked to the patient. Will had been difficult to deal with after the mantrap episode, but this time he was relatively calm, just muttering, 'Another bloody setback. I don't blame you, Mr Ridley. It was my own fault, I should ha' kept out of sight.'

'How did the policeman and his brother come to be there at the right time?' Tom asked. 'Mind you, I don't know how we'd have managed if they hadn't turned up.'

'That was Sam's doing, he brought them

in,' Will said, and then gasped as the scalpel went deeper. 'He was coming home in the dark and he met Smithers on his way. Asked him to bring along his big brother.' He took a swig of the sweet tea. 'Now, boss, don't be carting me off to Judith Weaver again. She was glad to see the back of me. I can fare right well for myself, if you take me home.' He peered at Tom in the lamplight, which was centred on the operation, leaving the rest of the room in shadow. 'If you don't mind me saying so, Mr Ridley, you look a bit – worn, yourself. You must ha' galloped back from Harrogate.'

'It's been a long night,' Tom admitted.

'Please keep still, Mr Thorpe,' the doctor said firmly. 'I don't want to make bigger holes in your arm than is necessary.' He dropped a piece of shot into a basin.

'You look as though you'd had a bad night, sir, before you even got back home,' Will went on. 'None of my business of course ouch! But that's life, you get a rough patch sometimes. And we beat Taylor in the end.' He looked down at the arm under the knife and quickly away again. 'Although I do feel sorry for the bugger, there was no call to go shooting at folks.'

'Aye.' Sighing, Tom took refuge in the old Yorkshire, noncommittal expression. It said it all. He was not going to lie to William Thorpe and Will nodded.

This was a strange conversation to have with a poacher turned gamekeeper, but at the poacher's moon it seemed that anything could happen. Tom realized that by coming home early from Harrogate, he had made the staff wonder whether there was a problem with Selina. It was good to have such loyal servants, but they did like to know the details. 'Thank you for the tea, Mrs Sherwood.' It was time to change the subject.

At last the probing was over and the arm was swabbed with disinfectant. Dr Sherwood expertly wrapped it in a bandage. 'You will need to change the dressing every day for a while. Get someone to do it for you,' he advised.

'Thank you, Doctor, I'll manage,' Will muttered. Tom paid the doctor and drove the cart quietly up the village to Will's cottage, where a faint light showed through the window. A low fire still burned; the house would be warm. That was good because the man was suffering from shock. In the moonlight his face was haggard.

'You go home, Mr Ridley.' Will got stiffly out of the cart. He managed to drag the door key out of his pocket and then looked up. 'Thank you.'

Tom plodded round to the coal yard, where he unyoked the tired horse and put it in the stable. Walking home down his drive, he was startled to see a bulky shape on the road in front of him. Keeping to the grass, he silently overtook the shadow. 'Good night, enjoying your walk?' he said ironically. Was this a stray member of the poaching gang, the missing Seth? He felt his fists curl in his pockets; another fight would be almost welcome.

The dark figure gave a little scream and Tom realized with a shock that it was a female scream. He strode up and in the faint light he saw that it was Kate, but Kate as he'd never seen her. She was filthy, covered in soot and with her skirts bunched up to her knees.

'Lord, Kate, where have you been? What happened?' Tom put his arm round the drooping girl.

Kate passed a grimy hand over her eyes. 'Oh, Tom ... a fire at Bellwood Hall!' She staggered and almost fell. 'You gave me a fright; I didn't know you were behind me.'

The groom's cottage was only a few yards away and soon Tom and Kate were sitting in Benson's kitchen. The young groom heated some milk for the lady, while Tom rather awkwardly sponged her hands and found that her fingers were burned. Benson brought her some comfrey salve, which was used for the horses.

'I don't remember ... maybe I was burned when I opened the nursery door,' she explained. 'The – knob was hot.'

'You? Do you mean to tell me you went up

to the nursery – during the fire?' What a night it had been. 'Tell me what happened,' he commanded.

Kate shook her head. 'Tomorrow ... not now. The children are safe,' she added. 'But Polly, she's a maid, she – died.' Helpless tears poured down her face. Then she sat up straight. 'Sam? Where is he?'

Tom stood up, went over to Kate and took her in his arms. 'Sam is quite safe. He's probably in bed by now. We've had a night of it, but the poachers are safely locked up. Don't cry, Katherine. Drink your milk and I'll take you home.' He knelt beside her chair and looked at her sooty, beautiful face. It was like Kate to go rushing off to help the Wiggins family.

They walked down the drive like tired children, their arms round each other. 'Do you remember,' Tom said mischievously, 'the night you fell into the river and we had to fish you out, and we all three went back to your mother dripping wet and worn out?' That had been a moonlight escapade before Tom went to university. They'd been trying to find out whether eels were going up the river at night.

'You mean that it seems we're still getting ourselves into trouble, Tom.'

The Manor house stood grey and solid, dreaming under the moon and, tired as they were, Tom and Kate stood for a moment to look round before they went inside. An owl hooted from the wood, answered by another with a faint echo floating over the fields and woods. In the gardens the lawns were etched with white frost; a peacock called plaintively.

'It is so lovely,' Kate said softly. 'Just to be here makes me feel calmer.'

'Wiggins didn't annoy you, did he?' Tom asked fiercely. 'I can imagine that when you saw the fire you felt you had to go over there, but – oh lord, you should keep away from him.'

Kate shook her head. 'He only appeared at the end. George and Bella had a fright, but they are with their mother. Let's go in, it's cold. I think I can sleep now.'

Tom tried to force his tired brain to think. When would he tell Kate that Miss Fulford was not to be the future mistress of the manor? There had been too much happening, too many emotions tonight. It would be best to focus on the practical. He shrank from the idea of telling people at home that he had lost the lady to his father, of all people. Leave it for a while; they would have to be told in the end, but not just yet. He would never forget the night of the poacher's moon.

FOURTEEN

The next morning the tired household met for a late breakfast. They ate in the kitchen, the warmest place in the house, gathered round the big scrubbed kitchen table.

After a warm bath Kate felt more normal, but had found that her hands and arms were blistered. She treated them with lavender oil, which is what the herb woman recommended for burns.

The memory of Polly falling from the window was far worse. She kept hearing the girl's shriek and seeing her jump. Then her mind turned to the horror of the trapped children, cowering with their mother – and how they would have died, if she had been there only a few minutes later. Kate did not want to talk about it, but Tom and Sam had to hear the story, as brief as she could make it.

'You are a brave girl, Kate,' Tom said quietly. 'Where was Wiggins in all this?'

'In the stable block.' Kate could hardly believe herself that Wiggins had not noticed the uproar at the hall until it was almost over, but it was just as well. He would have made the crisis even worse, judging by his usual behaviour.

As soon as she could, Kate changed the subject. 'More porridge, Sam? Now, why were you so late back last night?' So Sam explained about Jasper's accident and the talk turned to consideration of how they could bring the damaged vehicle home.

'Could do some repairs, enough to be able to yoke up and bring it home, and then get it properly mended here,' Tom decided. He took another piece of toast. 'Better do it to-day, Sam – you and Jake, if Jasper's fit enough.'

'How was Evie?' Kate asked mischievously, but Sam was unwilling to talk about Evie and his visit to the Somers family. 'It was good to see their paintings,' he said briefly.

'And what about the poachers?' Kate looked at the two faces across the table. Tom was serious, whereas Sam was very happy about last night's arrests and cheerfully told his sister that he thought they would be rid of poachers for some time to come. 'Pity they don't still send felons to Australia, it would have been good to get rid of them.' Sam shook his head. 'They should do a spell in prison, though – shooting a keeper is a serious crime. They shot poor Will in the arm, Kate.'

'Goodness! Where is he now?' Kate was horrified.

Tom looked at Kate and his dark eyes were

sombre. 'He's at home, after we took him to the doctor. He wouldn't hear of going to Judith's again. I blame myself, Kate. I shouted, Will replied and they then worked out where he was. I think they went for him on purpose, because he works for me.' There was a silence and then he added, 'Will should never have been in the wood last night.'

Kate still couldn't quite understand what had happened. 'But – we thought you were not coming home until today or tomorrow, Tom.' What had happened to the shopping trip? She had thought he would have stayed longer with Selina.

It seemed that Thomas, too, had something he didn't want to discuss. 'It was a fine night ... so I came home and went straight to the wood. That's all.' His face was closed, grimmer than she remembered seeing it. There was another pause and Kate began to clear the breakfast plates.

It was Tom's turn to change the subject. 'Will you be able to visit William today, Kate? I'll get Jake to drive you to the village – but no, we have no trap at the moment and Jake has to fetch it back. Perhaps tomorrow? Will should be able to manage on his own for a day, he's used to it.'

Kate wondered how badly Will was injured, but she would have to wait to find out. It would take too long to walk through the village to his house. 'I'll go tomorrow, then, if you like.'

'Good, take him some food from the kitchen – you could get Sadie to make a stew or something. And you'd better take bandages as well.'

The trap was recovered and repaired by the village joiner, but it was not until the Saturday afternoon that Kate was able to go to the village. She was driven by Sam, since they had discovered that Jake Benson was to play in the Kirkby football team against Fearby, their old rivals. He usually had Saturday afternoons off and so Tom let him go. 'Make sure that Kirkby wins,' he told the lad.

It was a cold, misty day and Kate was wrapped in a thick shawl against the chill. It would soon be winter now; the last leaves were drifting down from the trees. They called at the village shop and Kate bought a newspaper. 'It's time I started to look for a place,' she told her brother. He started to protest, so she explained. 'Miss Fulford will want to choose her own staff, Sam, when she comes to live here.' She didn't mention the fact that she would rather not have Miss Fulford as her mistress.

Sam laughed. 'Miss Fulford might want to change the gamekeepers, come to that.'

'I doubt it ... she's not very interested in the estate,' Kate told him.

When they drew up at Will's cottage, one

of a row in the village street, Sam stayed with the horse in the road outside, since Jasper was restless. 'Tell Will I hope he's feeling better,' he said. Kate knocked at the cottage door, wondering what sort of a state Will might be living in. The place could be a pigsty; some men were incapable of making themselves comfortable at home.

'Come in and wipe yer feet on the mat.' That sounded like Will, though he hadn't yet seen his visitor. Kate dutifully wiped her feet on the door mat in the little entrance hall and went into the kitchen.

Rather to Kate's surprise, Will's kitchen was clean and neat; the slate floor was swept and a bright fire was burning. The grandfather clock in the corner had a deep, slow tick. Horse brasses adorned the mantelpiece and a shelf held a few books.

In front of the fire was a large rug made from rags cut into strips, the traditional hooky rug which he had probably made himself. Thrifty folks in Kirkby never threw away old clothes; they cut them up for rugs and worked on them in long winter evenings. Dr Cooper's house, where Kate was brought up had just such a rug in the kitchen, she remembered.

The keeper stood up politely and then sat again in a Windsor chair by the fire, his bandaged left arm on the table beside him. 'Now, lass,' he said, moving aside his newspaper. 'I was just wondering, what would your Pa have said to this arm? What would Dr Cooper say? You used to help him, you'd have a good idea.'

Kate put down her basket. 'But, Will, Dr Sherwood has seen it. What did he say?' Gently, she took his arm and began to unwrap the bandage.

Will's arm was a mass of bruising, peppered with holes made by the scalpel. Some of the wounds were turning septic; something more needed to be done.

'Doctor said to keep quiet. And to change bandage. As I did, but – it's not right, Miss Cooper, as you can see ... and it feels hot.' The blue eyes looked up at her, guileless. 'But it's nowt – doubtless it will heal up soon.' He wanted her to reassure him. 'I'm right sick of being a patient.'

'As I recall, you're more of an impatient.' Smiling, Kate took the kettle from the hearth. 'Has this boiled? I'll just bathe your arm with water, Will, and wrap it up again. I think you should see Dr Sherwood, though. To be on the safe side.' She didn't want to alarm him, but the wounds looked angry.

'Nay, I won't bother Doctor again. Jim next door, he's the postman and he brought me this paper ... he said same as Dr Cooper said to me, that most folks recover on their own, given time. That's worth knowing... By, something in that basket smells good.'

Kate knew that it was useless to argue with Will and she decided not to mention Judith Weaver. She bathed the arm and rebandaged it with clean cotton, then gave him Sadie's stew. It was a thick mixture, mutton with plenty of carrots and potatoes, in a pot kept warm in a box of hay. Kate took out a loaf and cut him a slice of fresh bread.

'Best dinner I've had for a long time,' Will admitted after the first mouthful. 'I was just thinking about boiling an egg.'

'I'll collect the pot another day,' Kate decided, realizing that he probably wouldn't eat it all at one meal. She put on her shawl. 'I hope that Taylor gets a long prison sentence for this. So will you, I expect.'

Will put down his knife and fork. 'Well, it's not that simple,' he said slowly. 'Taylor's a broken man: he's been turned off his farm and his lass interfered with. Stands to reason he's making a bob or two where he can, and he's not particular whose property he takes. I just stood in the wrong place. I feel sorry for him, in a way.'

'You're not a bit sorry for yourself, with all this pain?' Sometimes Will Thorpe surprised Kate.

'Nay, lass, I'll be back at work next week. I've got a right good boss, now – young Ridley's a grand lad. I'm doing well. I'm going to lamb all manor ewes, in spring.' Will went back to his stew cheerfully.

Kate found that Sam had walked up the street a little way to keep the horse moving. 'Have we time to see Judith Weaver?' she asked her brother. Sam nodded, helped her aboard and turned Jasper's head for the village outskirts. 'I want her opinion.'

Judith was pounding dried sage and rosemary leaves, making packets of mixed herbs for sale and their fragrance filled the kitchen. A small cat sat beside the fire with a bandaged paw. 'It was burned in the Bellwood Hall fire, the cook brought it here. Who's with you, Kate? Bring Samuel in, I'll make tea for you both. It's a raw day.' So Jasper was tied up under cover of Judith's large shed and Sam came to join them in the kitchen.

The fire at Bellwood Hall was apparently the main news in the village and Judith shook her head sadly over Polly's death. Kate was thankful that her own part in the rescue was apparently not being reported.

Judith looked serious when they told her what had happened to Will. 'He wouldn't hear of us bringing him here again,' Sam confessed. 'Said you were pleased to see the back of him.'

Judith said nothing for a while and then she looked at Sam. 'I was told he was drinking with the poachers... I'm sorry he was shot, but I don't want anything more to do with Will Thorpe and he knows it.' She turned back to the teapot and cups.

'Well,' Sam began, 'Will has actually been talking to the poachers to find out what they were planning. He went to the Queen's Head because that's where they get together.' He spoke slowly; it was important to put the record straight. 'He's not a drinking man, at all. He was trying to help me and Mr Ridley, but on Thursday night he was shot by one of them as we were trying to save the manor pheasants. So don't think too badly of Will, Miss Weaver.'

There was dead silence and Judith sat down suddenly in her chair by the fire.

'That's – it's a different story, then. I see.' She looked into the fire with a strange expression. 'Will was only doing his job.'

Kate took up the story. 'I would like your advice, Judith, that's why we're here. Doctor Sherwood dug out the shotgun pellets, but it's very swollen and he seems to be getting feverish. I think some of Will's wounds are going bad. I bathed them with boiled water, but they need something more.'

Judith considered. 'He's hot. That's not good.'

'His arm is very hot and he said it was throbbing. He's breathing quickly.'

Judith seemed to pull herself together as she poured the tea.' I can give you a few things... He probably needs willow bark, it helps to bring down a high temperature. And honey might help the arm itself. Maybe you should wash it first with something to clean out the badness, like lavender water.'

'I'm sorry, Judith, but I can't go back to look after Will, I'm on duty at the manor. It's Sadie's day off and I have to cook the dinner. Mr Ridley is very concerned about Will; he feels responsible. I am sure the manor will pay you if you can visit him... He's our game-keeper.' Kate looked at her with wide eyes.

'Me!' Judith gasped. 'I don't think he'd want to see me, Kate.'

'But,' Kate said persuasively, 'if you mis-judged him, you can – er – start again. It would be good to help him, wouldn't it? You must feel unhappy about Will – this would be the best way to make amends. And there's no one else in Kirkby who could do it.'

Sam agreed, and by the time the tea was drunk, Judith had said she would visit Will in the evening after the goats were milked on the next day, Sunday. 'I can't manage it before, I've promised to do other things, but if he won't see me, that's the end of it,' she said. Kate hoped he would not be so stub-born, but she realized that it was quite possible. There always seemed to be some sort of trouble between those two.

As they turned in at the gates on the way home, Sam and Kate saw two small figures trudging up the drive. One carried a bag. 'Sam, it's George and Bella,' Kate groaned. 'What now?'

Sam pulled up beside them and Kate got down into the road. George looked scared, his face dirty and his clothes torn. 'Nursie, we came to find you, it's not nice at home. Where's Uncle Tom?'

Bella nodded, just as dirty but not so upset. 'We've run away from home,' she announced. 'So we're exploring, like before.'

Kate's own eyes filled with tears. Sam jumped down from the vehicle and lifted them both into it. 'We'll take you for a ride,' he said cheerfully. 'See if we can find Uncle Tom.'

George looked round at Kate. 'There's men trying to mend the roof at home, but Mama says we'll be living in Fletcher's house for months. Mr Fletcher has to live in the village now, 'cos we've got his house. And Miss King is cross ... that's our governess, you know. And Papa is cross. He's very cross, all the time.'

Bella reminded him of the bright side. 'Cook is good to us, she gives us cake. And Mrs Mason.'

'Why are you so dirty?' Kate asked gently. smoothing Bella's tangled curls.

''Cos Polly washes us and she's gone to heaven.' This was quite matter of fact. 'Mama used to, sometimes, but she's sick since the fire. She's in bed. We're supposed do it but we hadn't any warm water.'

Uncle Tom was dismounting from his horse

outside the stable when the trap rolled into the yard. 'What's this? The young folk from Bellwood Hall come to visit?' He looked at Kate. 'They're in need of a wash and a good meal, if you ask me. Sam, would you be so good as to ride over to the Hall and let somebody know they are here? Take my horse, I'll look after Jasper.'

Kate led the children into the house and gave them a drink of milk. She stoked up the cooking range and then ladled hot water from the big side boiler into a tin bath. George's bundle held a few clean clothes, so by the time Tom came in, George and Bella were quite ready to be sociable.

'Can we see the peacocks?' Tom promised that they should on their next visit. The birds went to bed when it got dark.

'We haven't had a visit from the Hall before,' Thomas smiled. 'We'd better feed these two before they go home.'

It was good to have the children with her, but Kate knew that they had to go back. Sam thought that their escapade had probably done some good. 'The Hall was in uproar when I got there,' he said, while Kate was preparing the meal and the visitors were on a tour of the house with Tom. 'They were annoyed that I hadn't brought the children straight back. No sense of fun, those people. The house itself is in a mess, of course.'

'The children were missing and there was

222

blame all round?' Kate guessed.

'Sir Titus was just about foaming at the mouth. Lady Wiggins was truly anxious – and maybe she was feeling guilty. Mrs Mason told me that her ladyship had kept to her bed since the fire – her bed in the groom's house, that is. And it was getting dark.'

'They could stay in Bradford until the Hall's repaired, but Wiggins wants to be a country gent,' Kate said. 'I worry about George and Bella, they're too young to be left to themselves. We were lucky, Sam – we had so much love and care when we were that age.'

Sam nodded. 'I think Mama will take better care of them in future. She's realized that the governess is not a responsible person.' What she had said to Sam about the governess was not repeatable to Kate. Her vocabulary was astonishing, even more so since it was delivered in that upper-class drawl. She must have learned how to swear from the grooms and she obviously felt very strongly. 'I would hate to work at Bellwood Hall! Thank goodness you got away, Kate.'

After dinner two sleepy children were driven home by Uncle Tom himself, with a promise that they could visit again. George undertook not to run away. Both George and Bella clung tightly to Nursie before they were lifted into the trap.

Brother and sister sat by the kitchen fire,

looking back over the last few days. 'John Fletcher's had enough of the Hall, he asked me whether Mr Ridley needed a groom. He said Sir Titus has joined the West of Yore hunt, so he'll be chasing foxes this winter. Bought another horse, a heavy hunter – more work for Fletcher, of course.' Sam sat back in his chair. 'On top of all his other jobs.'

'I don't remember Tom ever hunting.' Kate took up her sewing.

'No, he doesn't, but, of course, they ride over his land sometimes,' Sam reminded her. 'I wonder what's worrying Tom? He's rather quiet lately.'

Uncle Tom was driving home in a sombre frame of mind. He had just been insulted by Sir Titus Wiggins. It was hard to take the man seriously. He was clearly mad. On the other hand, he could do much damage if he repeated his lies to everyone he spoke to.

The children had been met by the house-keeper as soon as they arrived home. 'Don't scold them,' Tom said persuasively. 'We kept them. It wasn't their fault they were late.'

'Oh yes it was!' That was Bella, the fearless one. 'We ran away from home and we weren't going to come back, but Uncle Tom and Nursie said we should!'

'And we've got a new uncle – Uncle Sam!' George chimed in.

Mrs Mason smiled at Tom and he saw that

they had one friend at the Hall at least. 'I wish I had more time to give them, Mr Ridley. Thank you for bringing them back. And now you're ready for bed. Come along, children.' They thanked Tom and went off quite happily, to his relief.

Tom was stepping into his vehicle when Sir Titus Wiggins came dashing up, the chestnut mare drenched with sweat. Tom watched him bounce awkwardly up the drive, elbows flapping and wondered why he didn't take a few riding lessons.

'You! Ridley!' Wiggins shouted. 'What do you mean by keeping my bairns? They should have been whipped for running away and instead, we have a man here saying that you're giving them supper! I never heard owt like it!' When he lost his temper, his speech seemed to slip back to that of his working-class days.

'We hoped you wouldn't mind if they paid us a short visit,' Tom said quietly.

'I do mind, and I'll tell you to yer face. Yon's no place for my children. It's well known that you are openly living in sin with a woman of loose morals.' He rolled the words round his mouth.

Tom stood stunned. 'What?'

'That woman I paid to nurse my children, until Lady Wiggins turned her off without a character.' The flat West Riding voice rose a little. 'I know for a fact that instead of doing her job she was meeting you on the sly. I saw it. And now she's living with you the whole parish shall know. The name of Ridley shall be dragged in the mud. She's a slut, she even tried her sluttish ways with me one day ... and then you take my bairns. Just you wait, everybody will hear about this.'

Abruptly, Tom turned his horse and drove off down the drive without answering. He had been tempted to smash his fist into Wiggins's coarse red face, but it would only make matters worse. Poor, innocent Kate! Surely, no one would believe what Wiggins said. That was some comfort.

Cold rain began to fall; Tom turned up his coat collar and quickened the horse's pace. It was better to forget Wiggins, think of something else, but that brought no comfort. Thoughts of Selina and his father came back, as they always did when he was alone. Since the ball at Harrogate, Tom had been angry and sad by turns as he went over the evening's events. Should he have handled things differently; should the general have been allowed to get away with it?

He realized that his pride had been wounded, not his heart. He'd never really loved the girl, but he'd thought they were good friends. To think that a woman would choose the general over himself – and that his father would cut him out – was hard to swallow. It had deeply upset him; the old devil had enjoyed it too, that made it worse. And almost casual, the sting in the tail– 'By the way Tom, you're a bastard. Sorry about that.' No wonder he was angry.

All the time Kate had been there, sweet Kate. He had loved her company when they were children, but he'd been away from the village for years, at university and then in Scotland. Meanwhile the little lass had grown into a beautiful woman, but by the time he met her again, Tom had been engaged to Selina.

Well, he had no fiancée now. The resentment was fading and for the first time Tom could see clearly. It was a blessing that he was free of any obligation, to either Selina or his father as far as he was concerned. It was a blessing that the estate was his.

Tom wondered about Kate. They were friends, but even when he flirted with her a little, she had hardly responded – except that time when he'd kissed her. She'd often reminded him that he was almost a married man. But in the last few months he'd grown very fond of her, beginning on the day when she brushed off her treatment by Wiggins. He had wanted to hit the man ever since and today ... he didn't know how he had restrained himself.

Tom's confidence was bruised; would Kate be likely to consider him as a suitor? He unyoked the horse in a lighter mood. It would take time, he would go carefully. He didn't want to be rejected again. And then there was the problem of legitimacy to be overcome.

By the time he stabled the horse, Tom had decided that Wiggins should not be allowed to insult Kate. He would have to do something about it.

FIFTEEN

Dusk was falling on Sunday evening as Judith Weaver set out with a large basket to visit William Thorpe, for the first time in her life and against her better judgement. A shawl covered her head and shoulders and more than one villager on the way to evensong wondered who she was, an old lass with a youthful stride, until they realized it was the herb woman. No doubt she was taking her medicine to some poor soul in need. Those who couldn't afford the doctor were grateful for Judith's help.

Only a mile separated their houses, Judith's at the moorland end where the houses gave way to small fields and Will's lower down the village, opposite Church Street. But Judith had resolutely kept away from William and Lily. She would have kept her distance from Will in any case, but his marriage had put him firmly out of reach. Will's wife had been civil enough if they happened to meet, but she'd never bought herbs or cheeses.

Will himself had not spoken to Judith after she came back to the village until he was forcibly taken to her house by those well-meaning lads, Thomas and Sam. What followed had ruined her peace of mind, brought back the past and the pain.

Kate had persuaded her to break with convention to visit Will, which was what it amounted to. Heads were shaken and tongues wagged if a woman visited a lone man in his house after dark. Her mother, even now, would be horrified if she knew. But the mature Judith Weaver was the herb woman, respectable and with nothing to fear from gossips.

Kate's pleading eyes had overcome Judith's resistance. It was hard to refuse Kate, who was so concerned about Will. That, and her own feeling of guilt. She had condemned Will too quickly, but harsh words could never be unsaid. Judith sighed as she knocked at Will's door. She had no idea what to expect, but meeting him on his own ground gave him an advantage ... if it came to another clash.

'Come in and wipe yer feet,' she heard him call. Hesitantly, with far from her usual confidence, Judith stepped into the room.

Will was sitting by the table, shoulders hunched. The soft lamplight fell on his face and she could see beads of moisture on his brow. He was clean and shaved, but the hostile blue eyes blazed out from a flushed face. He looked up at her, clearly surprised.

'Come to see me death throes, then?' Will laughed grimly. 'There's nowt you can do, I won't trouble you. Go home, or they'll talk

about you in the village. We can't have that.'
He turned his shoulder away from her.

Judith took a deep breath and set her basket on the clean table. The room was homely; she was glad to see that Will lived in some comfort. 'I'd like to dress your arm, Will. Kate is worried about it. But first...' She faltered. 'Before anything else, I want to say sorry. Sam Cooper told me how wrong I was – about you.'

'Young puppy should mind his own business,' Will growled. He shifted the bandaged arm restlessly. 'It doesn't matter.'

'It does. The worst thing about it was that I believed the tale. I should have known you better. You're a wild lad, but you're very loyal. You would never have let Mr Ridley down and joined the Taylor gang.'

'It makes no difference what you think of me, Judith. You turned me down before – before all this and I was beginning to get used to it.' Will stood up shakily. 'I suppose I'm pleased that you see fit to say sorry. Now go home.'

It was time to be firm. 'Will, sit down. I think your temperature is high... Let me see your arm. Please let me treat you and then I'll go.'

Will stood there leaning on the table for support, his mouth in a straight, stubborn line, glaring at Judith.

Firm, but she must also be honest. 'I still ...

have a great deal of feeling for you, William. You are ... very dear to me, you always have been. Let me do it ... please.'

'Could have fooled me,' he muttered, but he sat down and held out his arm. He was hot to the touch. Judith suppressed a gasp; the wounds were much worse than when Kate had seen them. Quickly she wiped away all the infected matter with diluted lavender oil, until she could see the bruised skin underneath. She plastered the whole area with honey and bound it with a pad and a clean bandage.

'Now my lad, you'll have willow bark tea and no complaints.'

Will drank obediently, although he shuddered. 'Must be good for you, it tastes so bad.' He'd said that before. There were dark rings under his eyes and Judith was reminded of that night at her cottage when she was afraid he would die. She glanced at the grandfather clock. The godly would be coming out of church very soon; she would wait until they had all gone home. She would wait a little, to see if Will showed any improvement. They sat in silence for a while.

'Could you eat supper, Will?' From her basket Judith took a curd tart, a traditional recipe she had perfected in the bakery days. She had made it with curds from her cheese making, currants and egg, baked in a pastry

232

case. The top was fragrant with powdered nutmeg. Curd tart was just the thing for Will, easily digested and full of goodness.

They sat down with a cup of tea, real tea this time. 'This is grand,' Will conceded, helping himself to a second slice of tart. 'My ma used to make it when the cow calved, first milk's got all the goodness. She called it beestings pie.'

Judith sat quiet, listening to Will talk about the old days and this time, she didn't try to stop him. There was a sort of peace between them. After a while, she laid a quiet hand on his head and found he was cooler. She made up the fire and he fell silent, but he was not sleeping. He was watching her across the hearth.

The clock struck eight and Will roused himself. 'What about your reputation, lass?' he asked with the ghost of a smile. 'You'd better go, but if you come back tomorrow, I want you to tell me the truth, Judith. To talk to me.'

'Yes.' Judith realized then that one reason she had sent him away over the drinking incident was to avoid answering his questions about the past.

After a restless night, Judith milked her goats the next morning, fed the poultry and returned the small cat to the cook at the Hall, who came to collect it.

'Thanks so much, Miss Weaver,' the woman

said. If you hear of anyone who needs a cook, let me know, will you? I can't stand much more where I am.'

After some thought Judith packed the basket with more medical supplies and added a sage cheese and a loaf of bread. A light drizzle started to fall as she set out.

All the way down the street, rain intensified until by the time she reached Will's it was a downpour. Judith had steeled herself for the visit, but when she got there Tom Ridley was with the patient. Although it was only delaying her time with Will, she felt a sense of relief. They were deep in talk about estate matters and Judith waved to them to continue while she took off her wet coat.

Will was clean and cool; her treatment seemed to be working. She looked at his upper arm for evidence of poison but there was no thin red line, much to her relief.

'We'll have to make some arrangement for when the hunt comes through,' Tom was telling his worker. 'We can't have them galloping through the ewes when they're lambing. The season's started and they'll be down our way soon, I've seen a few foxes about.'

'Sam and me have shot a couple of foxes that were after the birds, but of course hunting folks don't like it. We didn't tell you, sir, in case they asked.'

'Of course, it's always the same,' Tom, agreed. 'The hunt went anywhere they liked in my father's time, he was keen, kept two hunters. But I think they'll be reasonable about it if I talk to them, keep them out of the sheep pastures. They can always ride around, if the fox goes that way.'

'I've wondered why you don't hunt, Mr Ridley. I would, in your place – it must be grand to chase over the country on a good horse, whether you kill a fox or not.' Will smiled. 'Jumping hedges and gates and all, taking risks, riding fast. I'd love it.'

Judith unpacked her basket. Will was always one for taking risks.

'Afraid I've never taken to it. But – I want to run the farm properly, with your help.' Thomas walked up and down the kitchen. 'Improve the quality of crops and stock. I suppose we can't turn the hunt away, but we can ask them to let us know when they're likely to ride all over us.' He frowned. 'There's a big field this year, they tell me, Wiggins and a few more newcomers are keen to hunt.'

'He'll maybe do away with his mantraps then, there'd be terrible trouble if the master fell into one,' Will said grimly. 'Couldn't have that.'

Tom moved to the door. Judith went with him and as he stepped into the street he said, 'Thank you for looking after Will. We were very worried about him. How do you find him, Judith?'

'Much better than yesterday, the fever's gone down, I think, although of course I haven't seen his arm today. It's very wet – have you a good cape, Mr Ridley?' His horse stood in the rain with its head down.

'I do, thank you. Y'know, Judith, I would rather lose all the birds than have this happen.'

The swelling was going down, but the patient had to suffer another cup of willow bark tea. Eventually he said, 'Well? What have you to tell me?'

Judith sat down. 'You'll live, if that's what you want to know.'

The blue eyes were fixed on her. 'You know what I mean, Judith. You need to tell me about the past. I want to know what happened to you, lass, about the baby and your situation, all by yourself with such a burden to bear. I've felt sorry for myself, but for a mother to give up a child ... it was hard. I blame your family, you know – they were too respectable by half.'

Judith told him about her beautiful baby, her little girl with blue eyes like his, and fair hair. It was painful, but it was also a relief after all these years to talk to the only person who had the right to know.

'I was staying on a farm near Pateley, with kind people – they didn't judge. But the wife said I should give up the baby as soon as possible, before she – knew me, so she

236

wouldn't grieve. They'd find her a wet nurse. We had her christened, and then – she went.'

The memory of that day still seared her, the feeling of holding the little mite in her arms for the last time. They had only two days, but they should have been able to stay together. The fire crackled in the silence as Judith paused.

'After that, I stayed for a few years, learning all the time. Mrs Gill was very clever, knew a lot about herbs. And she taught me to make cheese.' Thinking of the practical, such as making cheese, kept Judith from crying. She felt that she must not cry; with Will in his weakened state, it might affect his health. The first rule of medicine was to keep the patient warm and cheerful.

Will wiped away a tear. 'So – how did it happen, lass?'

'Doctor Cooper had found me the place, he rode over and delivered the baby. He used to see patients over there sometimes. They sent a lad on a pony to fetch him.' Another pause, while Judith tried to slow her breathing. 'Doctor Cooper said ... he said all mothers think their babies are beautiful, but this one was special. He would help with the adoption.' Judith looked at him. 'He ... said he knew it would be hard for me to forget her. And, of course, I never did. It hurts to talk of it, even now.'

Will was speechless for a while. 'Does the

bairn know? I suppose not.' He smiled, a gentle smile. 'And you won't know where she is now. They never tell, in case the mother comes back to claim them.'

Judith shook her head and swallowed. 'Doctor Cooper said it was better not to know. As soon as she was old enough, she would be told she'd been adopted.'

'And when you came back to the village,' Will said slowly, 'nobody knew there was a bairn at all. So you kept your respectable character, but you broke your heart. Poor lass.' He came across, scooped her up with his good arm and pulled her into a fierce embrace. Judith didn't think of resisting – it might have reopened his wounds. No nurse could allow that.

After so many years without Will, Judith felt her heart melting. So many emotions had been shut away, for so long. This was where she belonged. She felt whole again. Both her arms went round his thin frame and she hugged him gently.

Judith was astonished that Will had appreciated her feelings, in spite of the fact that he'd felt shut out for so long. Most men she knew only really thought about their own side of things. It made all the difference; it wiped out all the resentment she had felt over the long years on her own.

'So,' Will murmured when she was finally sitting close, 'we could have had twenty years of happiness, with our little daughter.' They were silent for a while, thinking of the lost years.

Trying to be practical, Judith slipped away from him and put the kettle on the fire. She looked out into Will's back garden, where the rain still teemed down. It would be foolish to go home in this weather. And in any case, they needed more time together before she left.

For a while they were both quiet, content to be together. At length, William came over to Judith where she sat and put his arm round her again. 'Please, Judith, will you marry me? I'm a bit the worse for wear after these two mishaps, but I hope you won't turn me down.' Will was smiling at her now, a different man to the one who'd greeted her when she walked in.

'Well...' Judith wanted a little time to get used to the idea. Only that morning she had assured herself that it would never work, that she must keep away from Will Thorpe once he was well again. But now, things were different and some invisible barriers between them seem to have melted away.

Will held her more tightly. 'Of course we'll get married, lass. No arguments, I won't have them. So when we get married, we'll have Kate there and young Tom – sir I should say – and Sam.'

Judith realized that the question of marriage was not if, but when. 'We'll get married quietly, please. No fuss. We are old, of course – in the eyes of the young folk, at least.'

'Just you wait until I've got two arms, young Judith. I'll show you who's old! We're nothing of the sort.' Will grinned. 'We might even make a baby, in due course, although I'm not sure whether it would be fair to a bairn to land it with old folks for parents.'

Judith doubted whether it would be wise or even possible to have a child at her time of life. It was a tempting thought, but...

'Let's be sensible, Will. Where will we live? I don't want to give up my goats and my herbs...' She realized that the new Will she had discovered wouldn't want her to give up anything.

'I hardly dared to think it would happen, so I haven't really planned anything,' Will confessed. 'But if you could bear to live with me in your house, I could let this one, it belongs to me – was my ma's. It might bring in a bob or two a week in rent. Handy for our old age.'

Judith looked round the kitchen, where everything was neat and in place. Will had taken a pride in his little house. If it were hers, she wouldn't want to give it up, but he was right, it was the sensible thing to do.

It was past noon and time to eat; Judith was surprised to find she was hungry, in spite of all the emotion of the morning. She sliced the bread and with her cheese and an apple from Will's tree, it was a good meal.

'When do you think I'll be fit for work? I worry about the pheasants and Sam working on his own.'

Judith handed him a cup of tea. 'Don't worry about it, lad, leave things be.'

The next afternoon Judith was making cheese in her dairy and thinking about William when he appeared, in his long poacher's jacket and a cap. 'I've just realized that after all these years, I can come to see you any time I like. So here I am.' He was freshly shaved and looked better than he had for some time.

It was strange, but her heart lifted at the sight of him as it used to do. 'You're very welcome, lad, as long as I can keep working. I've an order to fill.'

Judith lifted down a bag of curd, one of a row that had been suspended over a bucket to drip. She scraped the curd off the cloth and turned it into a fresh cloth, then hung it as before.

William politely removed his cap and took off his coat carefully, easing it round the bandage on his arm. Judith frowned when he dived into the hidden pocket and then smiled when he brought out a rather battered bunch of flowers. 'The last chrysanthemums; better than a rabbit, maybe?'

'As long as they're not poached from somebody else's garden.' They could joke about it now, his poaching.

Judith knew why he'd squashed them into his pocket; of course he couldn't walk the length of Kirkby street with a bunch of flowers in his hand. Folks would think he'd gone soft in his old age. Ah, well, they'd know soon enough what Will Thorpe was up to now and it didn't really matter what they thought.

The flowers were put into water and then Judith turned to the next batch of curd. This she scraped and turned into a bowl, where it was mixed with a little salt and a handful of chives.

'Well, I spoke to Vicar, and he read me a little sermon about married life, and then shook my hand and wished us happy. Said it was very good news.' He laughed. 'The old lad's glad to have me back in the fold. I was with the Methodists for years, of course. But my folks were always Church of England. And quite respectable, you know. I was the black sheep, as your mother pointed out.'

'As soon as banns are read, everybody will know,' Judith reminded him. 'They'll be talking about it in Kirkby.' But she thought the talk wouldn't last long. It was quite common for older folk to get married, after all. So many women died in childbirth, and a lot of men were carried off by pneumonia in a wet winter, when they couldn't afford good boots. You just had to look at the inscriptions on the gravestones in the churchyard to see how many lives had been cut short by fate. Will himself, as he'd once said, could have been there by now, but for willow bark and a bit of luck.

'It's something to be proud of, on my side at least.' William watched her working for a while. 'I thought it might be as well for you to get used to seeing me, and to see if we can talk together without fratching like bairns,' he announced. 'It's too cold to walk out down the green lanes–'

'Or lie in the bracken,' Judith finished for him. 'I haven't much time for walking out these days. But we'll see what we can do, next summer. We'll be an old married couple by then and nobody will look twice at us. Pass me that blue dish, will you?'

While the cheese was being packed William pulled the kitchen fire together and agreed to put the kettle on to boil, so long as he didn't have to take willow bark tea.

When Judith had finished in the dairy she looked at Will's arm. 'I'm off back to work,' he told her. 'Light duties, that's what Sam said. We've got to keep an eye on pheasants right until February, end of the season. And,' he said seriously, like a seasoned game-keeper, 'we need enough breeding birds for next year.'

'You'll be lambing after that, I expect,' Judith reminded him. 'Are you sure you've got time to get married, Will?'

SIXTEEN

The lovely autumn was dissolving into the gloom of damp dark days and long nights. The poacher's moon had waned and the skies were cloudy. There had been a lightness in the atmosphere at the manor, which had carried Kate through the hard work, but it was gone. Tom gloomily shut himself in the farm office when in the house and Sam was mostly outdoors, busy with mending fences and planting trees on the estate.

A woman from the village had been employed to help Sadie, who was now 'living in' and this made the housework easier, especially as more fires were needed as the weather turned cold. It was time to move on, Kate decided sadly. She wouldn't wait until Miss Fulford made the decision for her.

A few days after the children's visit, Kate sat by a fire in the housekeeper's room after dinner, carefully analysing employment vacancies in the newspapers. There were one or two requests for refined ladies of good character and she had written several versions of a suitable reply, a letter that would quietly let them know she was the right person for the job.

A family in Ripon was looking for a governess for one small child. The father was Canon Wilkinson of the cathedral; it sounded quiet and respectable, just what was needed. She started to copy out her letter.

The fact of leaving, of going among strangers had to be faced. She had done it before, when the doctor and his wife died and she and Sam had no home. This time was different, because she had been weak. She had fallen in love with Tom Ridley, a foolish thing to do.

A few tears fell on the page and Kate had to start the letter again. She hardly ever felt miserable like this, but now there was no bright side.

There was a light knock on the door and Tom strode in, looking harassed. 'Kate, the hunt will probably be riding through here on Saturday, I thought you should know. We can't predict which way the fox will take, but we must make sure the gates into the gardens are shut and that the peacocks are inside.' He sank down into a chair with a sigh. 'The West of Yore has a big following; there will be people everywhere. My father knew them all in his day, of course,' he finished with a bitter note in his voice.

'Yes, I've seen it in the past, its one of the biggest hunts in Yorkshire, I believe,' Kate agreed. There was a silence. Should she speak? She decided to plunge in.

'Tom, what is the matter with you? You don't look happy.' Kate spoke gently but she felt impelled to say it, had been wanting to say it ever since the night of the poacher's moon. He'd been worried about Will, but Will was on the mend and the gloom hadn't lifted.

'Should have told you before. A few things have bothered me lately, to be honest, Kate ... including my father.' Again, the bitter tone. Kate began to wonder what had happened on the night of the ball ... a quarrel, perhaps. 'The thing is, I don't know what to do about Wiggins. He was furious when I took the children back the other night and I'm afraid he spoke about you in a most insulting way. It can't be allowed, Kate. Something must be done.'

Tom was most agitated and she had to do something to calm him down. 'There's no need to worry; he's mad – didn't I tell you? He called me a slut, I suppose,' Kate said casually. 'He's done it before, to my face. I don't think anyone will take him seriously.' Wiggins was not a threat: she didn't work at the Hall any more.

Tom jumped up. 'He's done it before? You never told me! Kate, that man must be stopped. I must either hit him hard, or take him to court. This could affect your repu-tation and that is very serious.'

Kate tried to calm him down. 'Yes, Wiggins

looks for sin everywhere.' A thought struck her; she knew Wiggins. 'Did he suggest that you and I – we are living in sin? I suppose people might think that, since I moved to the manor.' She smiled with mischief. 'Refined young ladies shouldn't mention such things, I know.'

Tom turned a bright red and choked. 'Heavens, Kate, you should not have to even think such a thing. Your good name must be protected! It's my fault, I should have thought of it. I blame myself.'

'Please don't worry about him, Tom. I won't be in Kirkby for much longer in any case – I'm in the process of applying for a job in Ripon.' Perhaps that was too abrupt. 'Of course, my position here has always been temporary and you were very good to give me a place when I left Bellwood Hall. But I don't think you need me now. There's a family looking for a refined lady, will you give me a character? You can say how very respectable I am.' Kate tried to speak lightly.

Tom looked stricken. 'Kate! You're not going to leave Sam and me, surely?' He sounded like a lost little boy, like George was sometimes when he needed a cuddle. 'Kate, you can't do that!'

He looked so miserable that Kate nearly changed her mind; her arms almost went out to him. But then she thought of Selina Fulford's bright, fashionable presence, the sharp eyes that looked her up and down, noting her dowdy clothes. She had to leave, for her own sake.

She still didn't know why he had been so gloomy of late, but Tom had always been reticent about his real feelings. When anything troubled him, he kept it to himself.

Kate tried to sound cheerful. 'Now, Tom, Sam's a grown man and so are you! And remember, Mrs Mason at Bellwood Hall would love to be your housekeeper. You don't need me at all and in any case, Ripon is not so far away. Do please forget about Wiggins. I mean it.'

Tom Ridley was very even tempered, but he had evidently reached his limit. 'It's because of Wiggins you're going to leave us, I know – and you want me to do nothing, just give in to an evil slanderer. You don't realize the damage that man could do. To others, as well as to us. He must be stopped, I tell you.' He faced her across the table, glaring. 'You won't tell me what to do, Kate! I will take him through the courts!'

'You will do nothing of the kind!' Kate felt her own face flushing with anger as she faced him. 'I will not be the subject of public ... ridicule! It would be my name in the papers if you did that and I will not have it. Just forget about it. Go away, Tom, I don't want to talk to you. I resign. Find another house-keeper you can order about.'

Tom went out, banging the door and Kate sank down on a chair. She wept as she had not wept for years, sobbing for their lost happiness. She and Tom had never quarrelled before. Nothing had been the same, since that night of the poachers and nothing would ever be the same again.

For the next few days, Kate busied herself with turning out cupboards and drawers, intending to leave the house as neat as possible for the next housekeeper. When Tom was in the house, she worked in the attics. She wrote a formal letter of resignation and left it on his desk, feeling that it might seem childish to him. But another confrontation must be avoided.

The penny post brought an answer to her application letter with amazing speed. Canon Wilkinson hoped she would pay him a visit as soon as possible. It sounded as though he were desperate, with a small child to cope with.

Ripon was only about seven miles away, but getting there was another obstacle for Kate. Luckily, one day Sam was sent to Ripon with the trap to collect various items for the estate and bags of flour and dried fruit for the kitchen. Sadie was about to make the Christmas puddings, a serious undertaking.

Kate showed her brother the letter and asked for a ride and Sam agreed, but grudgingly. 'Why do you have to leave, Kate?

What's gone wrong between you and Tom? He's as grumpy as an old bear, these days.'

'I thought you of all people would understand, Sam. I have to earn my living and when Miss Fulford becomes Mrs Ridley...' Kate felt weary. 'She's a strong minded woman and she will be very much in charge, I'm sure.'

With her fair hair scraped back into a bun and her heavy grey winter coat and hat Kate jogged down to Ripon through the frosty lanes, feeling as subdued as she looked. All cheerful thoughts were gone, as though the frost had entered her soul. Even so, she felt that every turn of the wheels was taking her further away from Tom, fatally so, as though she would never see him again.

Sam set her down outside a large grey stone house near the cathedral and promised to call back for her in about an hour. He looked down at her as she stood on the pavement and grinned, 'You look the very picture of a good governess! I'm sure you'll be hired, lass, but I really wish you'd stay at the manor. Tom does, too.' He drove off and left her staring after him. What had Tom said?

As soon as Kate rang the bell, the door was opened by an elderly maid in starched cap and apron. 'Miss Cooper? Please come in, Canon Wilkinson will see you now. I was asked to take you in whenever you arrived.'

The hall smelled of polish and soap, a

fresh smell. Brass doorknobs twinkled, windows sparkled and the tiled floor gleamed. Kate thought as she was led to meet the reverend that it was very obvious this wasn't a farmhouse. You could never keep the manor up to this standard, what with bits of harness, muddy boots, cats on cushions, the occasional dog tramping over the floors and wet coats left to dry in front of the fire. It was a different world, but the manor was somehow warmer, more human. Or it had been, until recently.

Mr Wilkinson stood up to shake hands, a very small man, pale and anxious. He launched immediately into an account of the problems that beset the household and Kate listened patiently. He spoke very fast and used scholarly language, but the simple truth was that he had a child he couldn't understand. And neither, it seemed, could anyone else.

'Please say you will start at once. I will pay you very well, of course.' He named a sum that was twice her wages at the manor, and Tom had been generous. The child must be very badly behaved indeed, Kate thought wryly.

The man hadn't asked her a single question. Didn't he know how to conduct an interview? 'But you know nothing about me.'

Mr Wilkinson waved the letter she'd written. 'It's all here, my dear. Now, I will ask

Fawcett to show you the nursery and the governess's room.' So Kate was taken on a tour of the immaculate house. There was no sign anywhere that a child was living here; it was rather chilling.

Questioned, Fawcett said that there were four Wilkinson children. That sounded alarming, but three were at boarding-school and also boarded out for the holidays; their father visited them from time to time. 'Have they no mother?' Kate asked nervously. No family life...

'Well, aye, but after the last bairn was born Mrs Wilkinson was taken queer, you might say. She's in a hospital, like but ... well, to tell the truth she's lost her wits. It's dreadful.'

'Very dreadful, with young children. So, the youngest, what of him?'

Fawcett blinked and smoothed her apron. 'I think the canon is afraid for Sebastian.' She closed her mouth firmly as if she had said too much.

'Afraid of what?' The woman shook her head and Kate thought for a moment. 'Afraid he might take after his mother?' Insanity ran in families, she knew. This sounded like a difficult case.

'Aye, well, he's heading that way. He's a strange little mite. He's been staying with the canon's sister ... she can't make owt of him, either.' The woman dropped her voice

253

to a whisper. 'Truth is, Sebastian has been left to himself too much. He's coming home today.'

Fawcett, the undermaid called Mary and Mr Wilkinson all put great pressure on Kate to stay and in one way it suited her; it was awkward to go back to the manor. Sam could bring her trunk down. It was a leap into the unknown and although Mr Wilkinson was as unlike Wiggins as a man could be, there were many questions. For one thing, she had not yet seen the child.

Sam was most upset to hear that Kate was not to go home with him. 'I think Tom was going to talk to you tonight,' he told her. 'Said he had something to tell you.' He looked at Kate. 'He doesn't say much these days, but I think there's a problem somewhere. He'll be most upset that you're not coming back.'

'I've promised to help these people, Sam. I will have to find another home, you know and it might as well be now.' Kate gave him as good a smile as she could manage. 'In one way it's easier for me to make a clean break, with no goodbyes. This will be a good place, I think, and I'll earn some money.' It hurt her to see Sam so sad.

'If it doesn't suit you, send a message and I'll be straight down here to collect you,' Sam said as he shook the reins. 'Take care, Katherine.' Through tears, she watched him out of sight.

The first evening, Kate decided to watch and wait, to see how things worked in this house. The child was delivered by a servant at about five o'clock, in time for nursery tea.

Sebastian was thin and pale like his father, but much quieter. He hardly spoke at all. Seven years old, a little older than George, but more like a shy three year old. He'd been neglected, Kate could tell. The servants fed him, but they didn't talk to him – there was no real contact with him.

Looking at Kate, Sebastian had no re-action. When she spoke to him he whispered, 'May I go to bed?'

What shocked Kate the most was his diet. Fawcett gave the child a bowl of thin gruel, made with water. 'No milk – he's not allowed to have milk,' Kate was told.

The next morning it was difficult to get Sebastian out of bed, and no wonder. Break-fast was the same thin gruel and he pushed it away after a few spoonfuls. He was not allowed eggs or meat, Fawcett said, because the doctor advising the canon had said that he needed a 'low diet' for his health.

In the kitchen the servants ate good, plain food and Kate was relieved that she was not expected to keep to a low diet. She could take meals in her room, but it seemed best at first to eat with the others in the kitchen, to get to know them a little.

After a few days, Kate was sure that one of Sebastian's problems was his food. The child needed better food and also, he needed someone to play with, or at least someone to talk to. Nobody read to him. 'Papa teaches me,' Sebastian said, 'but it's all Latin and Greek and I don't know what he's saying. I don't like lessons. And now you're going to give me lessons, miss. I won't like them.'

The new governess felt like saying, *'You will enjoy them!'* but he was scared enough already. She read to him, but he fell asleep. Thinking to interest him she tried a game using arithmetic, but he seemed to have no concept of numbers. He looked at the page blankly.

'Papa gets worried, but I can't do sums,' the child mumbled. He seemed at times to be only half conscious. Was it possible that he had a serious problem?

Kate tried something else the next day. She took him for a walk, wrapped up against the cold wind, but Sebastian didn't really like walking and asked several times whether they could go home. For most of that night she worried about him. Then she had an idea.

The next day they took another walk, this time in the direction of the river. An old friend of Dr Cooper, himself a doctor, lived in a tall grey house by the bridge over the River Ure. Kate looked down into the dark water and shivered. She had been pushing thoughts of Kirkby and Tom to the back of her mind, but the river reminded her of Tom's estate and his ambition to buy land next to the Ure.

Doctor Jameson and his wife were pleased to see Kate, who had sometimes called on them when she was in Ripon. 'This is Sebastian,' she told them, and they looked the poor child over. 'I'm his governess, for a while.' By this time, she was not sure how long the job would last.

Mrs Jameson looked at her carefully. 'You miss the country, Kate? I'm sure you do. And the canon's house will be very ... quiet, I expect.'

The canon's house was suffocating, but Kate didn't say so.

'Do you like dogs?' The doctor asked and Sebastian nodded. 'But I'm not allowed to have a dog.' His face lit up when he saw a puppy on a cushion by the window. Mrs Jameson led him over to it and Sebastian was 'allowed' to pat the soft little head. For the first time, Kate saw him smile. He sat on the floor beside the puppy while the doctor's wife smiled at them both.

Looking up, he said, 'I'm not allowed to touch a dog because they bite.' The dog licked his hand. 'Look! He likes me!'

'Of course he does, Sebastian.'

Left alone with the doctor, Kate wasted no

time. 'I would really like your advice about this child,' she said very quietly. 'He's not normal. He sleeps a lot and can't seem to do his lessons. They give him what they call a low diet ... a lot of gruel and not much else. I would like you to take a look at him, if you don't mind, Dr Jameson.'

The doctor smiled at her. 'Kate, you're a good soul. I know his father. The canon is an intellectual, you know and he has some odd notions. My advice to parents is no doubt the same as your father's. Growing children need good food and plenty of fresh air and exercise. This young man looks as if he doesn't get outside very much. And a low diet – that's nonsense. It leads to pale cheeks and low spirits.'

'That's what I thought, but can I change his whole regime? I might not be allowed.' The doctor grinned at her. 'I took the job because they seemed to be desperate, but I haven't made any progress yet, even with lessons.'

A maid brought in tea and milk for Sebastian, who was put on a chair by the table. Kate watched as he drank it down. He looked at her guiltily over the rim of the glass. 'It's good for you, Sebastian,' she reassured him, as she offered him a plate of biscuits. He hesitated, then took one.

The doctor took the chair next to the child. Gently, he put his hand under Sebastian's chin. 'Let me have a look under your eyelids, my lad. Yes, it's as I thought – anaemic. He needs a stronger diet, Kate. Now ... for another thought.' He went out and came back with a child's picture book.

Sebastian ate his biscuit and then looked longingly at the puppy. 'Yes, you can talk to Fido again, but before that, I would like you to look at this book. What can you see, Sebastian?'

The book was evidently designed to test eyesight; Kate thought it was clever. Each page carried pictures of animals, including puppies, the pictures increasing in size as the pages were turned.

Sebastian sat silent for the first half of the book, just as he had when Kate had tried to interest him in reading. Then Dr Jameson turned to a large, clear drawing of a dog. 'I think that's a puppy!' Sebastian brought his face closer to the page. 'Yes it is!' He could see the larger pictures, but when the doctor turned back to the smaller ones, the child turned away. 'I can't do it. Am I allowed to go back to Fido?'

'The lad has poor eyesight, Kate. He needs spectacles.' He sighed. 'I will talk to the canon. He means well, of course, but he can't be very observant.' He thought for a while. 'Sebastian might be better off at school with his brothers; they are quite lively boys. I will suggest it.'

'He's not allowed to go to school,' said Kate with a straight face. 'His father thinks he's too delicate. He worries because Sebastian can't read ... no wonder he can't read.'

Kate took the child home, feeling more optimistic than before as Sebastian trotted beside her, talking about Fido. 'How big will he grow, Miss Cooper? Can we go to see him again? I like that puppy.'

SEVENTEEN

Thomas Ridley felt that things were sliding from bad to worse as time went by. He'd been planning next season's crops quite happily until the night of the poacher's moon, but since then there was much more on his mind.

He felt Kate's absence so much: it was ridiculous and also unexpected. They'd always enjoyed each other's company, but in the last few weeks he had come to depend on Kate's quiet organization and her presence at the end of the day. She was interested in his plans for the estate and she loved the old house. The manor was gloomy since they had quarrelled; he hadn't realized until then how much she meant to him.

They should never have quarrelled – and it was over Wiggins, of all people. He should have looked at Kate's point of view. Perhaps he should try to see her and have a quiet talk. Sam knew where she was working in Ripon.

The loss of Selina, he admitted to himself, was just a matter of a blow to his pride. She had been Tom's girl and easily, how easily she had changed allegiance and dropped him. It was probably a lucky escape. Selina was quite determined and she would have expected him to spend more time in town, to go to charity balls, perhaps even to travel abroad – too much time away from the estate. He couldn't imagine her riding round the estate with him, enjoying the changing seasons.

Then the next thing happened.

The day after Kate left, Tom had a letter from his father, the final straw. At some length it explained that Selina's father was still objecting to her marriage to the general and so was her mother. It was probably because of his age, Tom thought, but perhaps they had some sympathy for his son as the disappointed suitor. Mr Fulford had always been very friendly to Tom.

This disapproval meant that they would not be married from her home in York, so an alternative was needed. '*We will be married at Kirkby church. I have told Selina what a beautiful old place it is,*' he wrote. '*The Ridleys have been married there for two hundred years.*'

Except for one wedding that didn't happen. What about my mother? Tom felt his anger rising as he read. Pa could only see one point of view, one person's convenience. How was Tom supposed to feel about the old man marrying *his* fiancée in *his* village? Like his father, Tom had been away from Kirkby for years, but now he was back and ready to settle down. He went to church occasionally and knew a fair number of his neighbours. None of them had met Selina, but if they had it would have added to the humiliation.

'Then we will provide a wedding breakfast at the manor,' the general went on in his flowing handwriting. 'Naturally I will pay all the expenses, and I am sure your admirable Miss Cooper will be able to organize the affair. A small group, of course, just a few close friends.'

Tom wondered how many; he had met some of Selina's friends in York. There would be few close friends in Kirkby since the general had been an absentee landlord for so long. Presumably there would be no time for his close friends in Jamaica to make the journey.

The wedding was to be in early December, just a few weeks away and there was no admirable Miss Cooper to help. Blast and damn! Tom threw the letter down and then felt ashamed of himself.

It was Saturday, the day of the foxhunt. Tom realized he was still in a low mood when Sam asked him quietly whether he could share the problem, but he felt unable to talk except to say briefly, 'Saddle the horses. We'll go up to Bell's Hill in good time and watch the hunt from up there.' From the highest point on Tom's land they would have a fair view of the route that the hunt would probably take. The fox, if one was found, wasn't predictable, but they usually put hounds in at a covert over the hill at the start, because that was where foxes lived.

Sam rode Jasper and Tom was on his big bay; he was still finding it hard to talk to Sam, but knew it had to be done. The day was cold but fine, with high cloud. They reached the hill, from where they could see some of his fields and woods and in the distance, the spire of Kirkby church. That reminded Tom of the impending marriage and he drew his father's letter out of his pocket.

'I should have told you before, Sam, and Kate, too. But I felt – oh, it was pride, I suppose. The fact is, Selina has ended our engagement.' He saw that Sam was looking concerned. 'Don't worry, I'm not too devastated. In fact, it's a good thing in the long run. It was a shock, that was all and so I kept quiet for a few days to let it sink in.'

'She would probably not have enjoyed country life,' Sam said cautiously.

'You're right. It did upset me at first though, mainly because the thing is, she's going to marry my father.'

He saw the shock on Sam's face. 'The general? Goodness, you will feel let down. How could he...? And he's much older than she is. Well, no wonder you were shocked.'

From far away on the other side of the hill they heard the huntsman's horn; the hunt was under way. 'To make matters even worse, this letter informs me that the marriage will take place at Kirkby.' Tom felt a certain relief Sam now knew the worst.

'Here? Oh lord, the manor will have to host the wedding party ... and no Kate. This sounds like a recipe for disaster.'

'No Kate. I feel much worse since Kate left and it's only a few days. I took her for granted, Sam. That's the trouble.' Tom sighed. 'She's made such a difference to the manor.'

'Never mind, lad, we'll get through, we always did, remember? We were in a few scrapes when we were young and we always found a way out.' Sam was obviously trying to be cheerful. 'I think you've got to see it as a lucky escape, wish them well and be happy! Do you know, Kate was anxious to leave before Miss Fulford took over as the lady of the manor. She told me so.'

'I thought it was because of Wiggins... Sam, we had a disagreement.' Tom cursed himself for keeping silent. If Kate had known that Selina was not going to be his wife, she might still be there.

The hunt was drawing nearer; hounds voicing, obviously on the scent of a fox but they were out of sight round the shoulder of the hill. Down a slope in front of them rode a horseman apart from the group, a groom by the look of him. 'Somebody getting there early, to watch the circus from that hedge. I do hope they don't cut up the ground too much ...' Tom got out his field-glasses. 'I suppose it's a very old tradition and it does give some of the country people employment.'

'There wouldn't be so many grooms, or blacksmiths without hunting,' Sam agreed. 'There he goes!' He pointed and Jasper danced a little, as though he wanted to join in the chase. The fox was loping quite steadily down the slope. He paused and looked round, unperturbed and then he vanished. Below them, a little while later the procession passed by, hounds and horsemen hunting the fox according to ritual and riding according to their varied abilities.

Well up with the hounds were the good horsemen, fearless riders who flung themselves over every obstacle. More sedate were two ladies, riding side saddle. 'I don't know how those women manage,' Tom murmured. 'It must be hard for the horses as well.'

In among the red coats were black ones and at the rear, trailing a little, a bunch of men who looked as though they were new to hunting. One man seemed to be impatient with this group and cantered forward, but he rode badly and his horse was skittish, dancing sideways as it approached another horse.

'That's Wiggins! He's got a new mount. And he's making a fool of himself.' Tom could not help smiling; this is what you'd expect from the man. They should never have let him in.

The big, unruly horse backed into that of one of the ladies and she nearly lost her seat. Wiggins's whip came down across his horse's flank, which made matters worse. It reared and the flow of riders was held up. Wiggins held on by clinging to its neck, an undignified figure with his rump in the air as the animal lowered its head and tried to throw him off. Tom looked round at Sam. 'Would you believe it? He'll be most unpopular, to say the least.'

Sam laughed. 'It's time people got to know him as he really is. Even his horse hates him.'

Riders spread out over the field, as far away as they could from Wiggins. As they got to the far side they had to slow down and wait to jump a five-barred gate. Over they went in fine style, red coats and black. Before the last group came up it was Wiggins's turn and in spite of himself, Tom held his breath.

Wiggins's horse was still capering and when it came to the gate, it took off badly. The man was reining it in fiercely, which hampered its movement.

Up they went, Wiggins half out of the saddle. The horse just cleared the top rail with its front legs and then crashed down into the gate. Wiggins was thrown clear as the horse rolled sideways. Hounds and the main body of the hunt had disappeared across a ploughed field in pursuit of the elusive fox. The stragglers came up to the gate slowly and dismounted when they saw there had been an accident. 'He asked for that,' Tom said. 'Did you see the way he pulled? A horse can't jump with its head pulled in.'

'We'd better go down, see if he's injured,' Sam suggested. The horse was up again, but not the rider. When they arrived, there was a still figure on the grass and the faces around him were grave. Fletcher, the groom, was kneeling by his master and Tom realized that it was he who had ridden in earlier. He looked up at the ring of faces, his own deathly white. The men took off their caps.

'He's gone,' Fletcher said. 'Broke his neck.' He choked with emotion. Wiggins lay with his head at an unnatural angle, the coarse face buried in the grass.

'Are you sure?' Another rider went forward. 'I'm a doctor.' But he shook his head as soon as he had examined the body.

Sam went to the horse, which was being held with difficulty by a hunt servant. There was no visible injury.

Tom took the lead, as the property owner. He sent Sam off for a vehicle and talked to the hunt officials about what should be done next and who would go to see Lady Wiggins. No one wanted to speak ill of the dead, but there was little sympathy for the man. 'Sorry about your gate, sir,' a hunt servant said quietly. 'We will repair it, of course.'

Gradually, the other riders drifted away. The body was eventually removed, a very subdued Jake Benson driving. Tom's main feeling was one of relief Wiggins would never cause harm again. He felt sadness too that there was nothing good to say of the man.

Fletcher appeared to be very shocked as Sam and Tom rode up the slope with him, slowly because he was leading the dead man's horse. He started to talk and at first Tom could make little of what he said. He made out the words 'it was meant to be.' Gradually Tom realized that the man was excited, almost overcome, but not with grief.

'This is for poor Polly,' Fletcher whispered. 'Knew it would happen, sir.'

Tom was puzzled. 'How can you say that? It was an accident, surely?'

Fletcher smiled and it was not a pleasant smile. 'Aye, an accident. I corned horse up for a week or more, so it was over fit and he couldn't handle it.'

Tom looked across at Sam, who shook his head. They had both heard of grooms that starved horses, to make a profit on the oats not used. Fletcher had deliberately overfed the horse to make it more difficult to manage. With a rider like Wiggins, it was dangerous. Wiggins was not safe on any horse,

269

especially one that had been given too many oats.

'Even so...' Tom looked at the groom. 'Why did you come down early, to this spot?'

Fletcher took a piece of white material out of his pocket. 'I was ready to wave a flag to frighten horse,' he whispered. 'When he went over. I reckoned he was bound to be on his own, the others would avoid him. But I needn't have bothered, Wiggins did it himself. He couldn't get horse over gate. Cruel and bad-tempered, he was and the poor horse suffered.'

Tom patted his own Samson, plodding along at walking pace as they talked. 'And – you mentioned Polly? The servant who died in the fire, wasn't she?' Kate had told him about Polly's last moments. 'What did you say about her?'

'Polly was walking out with me, sir. Until' – the man choked – 'until Wiggins raped her, and then it was all over with us. He took her over, like, and she said she felt ... bad. But I never knew what was wrong until the last.'

There were no words to say; Tom was silent.

'You don't mind me talking, sir? Polly, she fell pregnant, after Wiggins had forced her time and again. That must be why she set fire to the Hall. She couldn't see a way out. She wanted to get even, like. She'd told Mrs

Mason her life was over. I would have stood by her, but I never knew.' A sob escaped him. 'At the end she was out of her wits, though she'd been bright enough before. Like, as normal she'd never have put those bairns at risk. But Wiggins had driven her out of her mind. Mrs Mason knows that, she told me after. There was nowt anybody could do, sir. Except – I should have taken her away. I can see that now.'

'It's a terrible story, Fletcher. I hope it's over now.'

'Aye, he did enough harm. Thrashed the childer and he attacked Miss Cooper, one day. Polly told me.' Fletcher paused. 'If it weren't for Miss Cooper, the bairns would be dead.'

Both Sam and Tom shouted together, '*He attacked Miss Cooper?*'

Fletcher looked nervous. 'I shouldn't ha spoken ... it was when he beat poor George for stealing and Miss Cooper waited outside for the little lad – and Wiggins dragged her into the library. Polly saw it and Mrs Mason knocked on the door, just in time. Polly said, Miss Cooper's dress was all torn. He was a monster, that one.'

'If I'd known that, I've have killed him myself,' Tom growled. 'Now, John, don't you tell anyone else what you've just told us. It was a hunting accident, pure and simple. Several people saw what happened.'

'Thank you, sir.'

'And ... I'm sorry you lost your girl.'

Soon after this Fletcher rode home slowly, leading the other horse while Tom and Sam went back to the manor, still shocked that a life could be snuffed out so quickly.

'Poor Kate.' No wonder she wanted to get away from Kirkby. 'Do you think she'll come back, now, Sam?'

Sam sighed. 'You know Kate ... I think she'll have taken on this job and she'll already feel responsible. She's like that: she stayed at the Hall until she was dismissed, just for the children. Even in spite of Wiggins.'

On the Monday there was a meeting of staff at the manor, in the kitchen with tea and scones. Tom treated his servants like human beings, a very new idea for Kirkby. Living at the doctor's with Sam and Kate as a boy, he had learned to appreciate all classes and to talk to them easily.

The new owner of the estate looked round the table. Jake Benson sat next to Sam, then Will Thorpe, looking healthier and almost happy. The gardener, Wilson, was there and a boy called Zeb who worked with him, then 'Arry, who worked on the farm and a couple of other workers. Sadie and Mary in the kitchen completed the little group.

After mentioning briefly the sad accident of the previous day, Tom told his people that there was to be a wedding before Christmas.

'So we will all have to work very hard, to make the manor look as good as possible. I have to tell you that my father the general is to marry ... his bride will be Miss Fulford, who was formerly my fiancée. And whom you have met.' He looked round the shocked faces and smiled. 'Don't worry, we are all happy with the arrangement.' It made him feel lighter to say so and he saw Sam's smile.

'The other piece of news is, that my father has given over the estate to me. With your help I intend to make many improvements. With time, we will need more staff.' The servants looked at each other. 'The general and Mrs Ridley will live in Jamaica.' Was that a sigh of relief that went round the room?

Sadie spoke up. 'If I might say so, sir, we'll be needing more supplies for pantry, I'll have a sight of baking to do if there's to be a wedding. What about a big cake, for a start? Eh, it's grand to bake for a wedding!' Everybody smiled.

Tom thought for a moment. 'That's true, you need to start right away with food that will keep a few weeks. Now ... 'Arry, have we a pig fit to be killed?'

'Arry thought there was a grand pig, fit to make hams for a wedding, but they'd need time to cure. 'So we better get pig sticker in right away,' he advised.

'One last thing,' Tom said as the meeting broke up. 'The general will expect to shoot pheasants while he's here; he's coming a week before the wedding. Will and Sam, you'll have to rustle up a few birds for him.'

The gamekeepers looked at each other. 'We've already sold a lot of ours,' Sam said. 'We need to keep some for breeding.'

'But there's plenty in Wiggins's place, sir,' Will added. He was still a poacher at heart.

Tom looked at him severely. 'William Thorpe, do not even think about the Bellwood Hall birds.' Will gave him a grin and he realized that the man had been teasing him. What were servants coming to, these days?

On Thursday Sadie went to Ripon, driven by Benson, in her best bonnet. She was entrusted with buying the ingredients for the wedding feast, cakes and puddings. 'And fancy stuff as well, pastries and such,' she said happily to Benson. 'And you'll need to clean up all brasses on trap and varnish woodwork,' she added, looking critically at the blistered varnish and the traces of Sam's mishap with Jasper on the common. 'They'll likely drive to church in this here trap.'

'Well, aye, and I'll come and tell you how to bake pies,' Benson grinned. He was getting to be a cheeky lad.

Jake dropped Sadie on the market-place and said he would meet her an hour later and go with her to pick up the goods. 'I have

274

a job to do for Mr Ridley,' he said importantly.

It took rather more than an hour to buy everything on Sadie's list and she hurried back to the market-place from the grocer's shop, worried about keeping Jake waiting. She almost bumped into a woman with a little boy. 'Good day, Sadie! You're in a hurry!' It was Miss Cooper.

'How are you, miss? I can't stop, Jake won't want the horse to get cold. I've been shopping for the wedding!'

'I'm well, Sadie. The wedding – is it to be soon?' Miss Cooper looked alarmed.

'Aye, before Christmas!' With a wave, Sadie hurried off.

It was not until they were halfway home that Sadie realized Miss Cooper might have thought it was Mr Tom's wedding she was talking about. That was a pity, because Miss Cooper was sweet on Mr Tom. Anybody could see that.

EIGHTEEN

'I give you full charge of the child,' the canon said with a sigh. 'He is not afraid of you.' It was startling to hear a man of the church admit he was beaten, but it was good and also a little daunting that he had confidence in his new governess.

Kate was sitting opposite him in his big, intimidating study, surrounded by leather-bound volumes of sermons. Gold lettering on the book spines glittered in a ray of sunshine from the window, but it was a gloomy room, with heavy velvet curtains that kept out draughts, but also most of the light. No wonder Sebastian was afraid when he had lessons there. It would be difficult for a normally sighted child to learn his letters in that room, or to see anything there that he understood.

'Make whatever changes you see fit. I will ask Fawcett and Mary to follow your instructions.' That was a relief. The servants were always ready to tell her the canon's ruling on every aspect of life.

He was giving Kate the responsibility, but he evidently didn't hope for much. 'Unfortunately Sebastian is a stupid child. I say it with sorrow, but we must face the fact that he has, and will always have, very limited abilities.'

Kate clenched her teeth. We shall see, Canon, she thought furiously. 'Thank you, sir.' It was time to get out of that stuffy room.

She stood up to go and the canon added, 'Please let me know of any progress you might make.' He didn't ask what she proposed to do and that too was a good thing.

Kate walked upstairs to the nursery and looked round the room. If she took down the curtains and moved the table nearer to the window, the light would be much better. But the first item on the agenda was to get Sebastian fitted with glasses. The Jamesons would know where to get them.

To his delight, Sebastian visited the puppy dog again that day. He was keen to put on his outdoor coat and little boots; he wanted to go out. That part was easy, but some of the other changes might be harder.

Sebastian played with the puppy as Kate talked to the doctor about getting spectacles for him. He offered advice on diet and exercise and what was good for growing boys. Until now she had taken it for granted that parents gave their children good wholesome food when they could afford it.

'That business about a low diet ... it's nonsense,' Dr Jameson fumed. 'The doctor who suggested it has a practice full of obese aldermen – he makes money by starving them, and in their case it's good advice. So he thinks it's a cure-all. Narrow thinking, in my opinion.'

Kate laughed. 'I hope we will take more walks. I would love to buy him a dog, but...' She hesitated.

'Why not?' Mrs Jameson asked.

'That house – it is spotless! So clean and tidy, it feels unnatural. A dog would never fit in.' Kate added, 'In any case, my aim is to get Sebastian ready to go to school with his brothers. I think that would help him more than anything else, but there's a long way to go.'

The doctor looked thoughtful. 'I agree. But that would mean you'd have to look for another place, Kate. I wish we could help.'

Kate took Sebastian to be fitted for spectacles and on the way home, she suggested that he could count the horses he saw and tell her the total later. He was absorbed by this and she realized that he could actually count quite well. 'I'll count white ones and dark ones separately,' he said. He was a little more confident than before.

As so often, thoughts of Tom came back to Kate with a now familiar ache. She wondered why his marriage was to be so soon; something must have changed. Sam had promised to come to see her, but so far she'd heard nothing of Kirkby except for the fleeting scrap of news from Sadie.

It took some perseverance to change Sebastian's diet, since Fawcett and Mary, although passionate about cleaning and polishing were not very interested in cooking. Of course, they wouldn't allow the new governess to cook anything in their kitchen. The other problem was that the child recognized very few foods and was wary of those he didn't know.

Kate started on easy meals. At the end of a week, Sebastian was eating eggs and cheese and found to his surprise that he liked apples. It could have been imagination, but Kate thought there was a little more colour in his cheeks; he was certainly not so anxious.

Mrs Jameson sent a note one day, inviting Kate to supper. 'I hope you can be spared, after Sebastian is in bed.' The canon gave his consent and Kate changed into a prettier dress for the occasion.

The supper was informal and enjoyable and Kate found herself relaxing; for once, she was not on duty. The other guest was a young man introduced as 'my nephew' by Mrs Jameson, a likeable young man who was working as a doctor in the hospital. Dr Mark Forester was interested in everything Kate had to say, and agreed with her that living in the country was preferable to the town, in spite of the drawbacks. 'I am hoping to buy a country practice,' he said.

It was only a short walk back to where she lived, but Dr Forester insisted on walking with her, talking all the way. When they reached the canon's house by the river he raised his hat and said he hoped to see her again.

The Jamesons, Kate decided, were matchmaking. They had obviously decided that Kate needed a husband and they knew that the young doctor was looking for a wife. Tom's aunt had introduced him to Selina and there must be many couples who married because their well-meaning friends had decided that they should. Tom had been trapped in this way, she was now sure. Well, it wasn't going to work with Kate Cooper, she told herself.

Every day brought a new experience for Sebastian. With the aid of a magnifying lens, they looked at leaves and insects in the winter garden. Kate wrote large letters on sheets of paper and encouraged him to form words with them. She read to him a book she found in a cupboard in the nursery, *Children of the New Forest*, which Sebastian took very seriously.

'We don't have to do Latin?' he asked anxiously and Kate reassured him. 'No Latin with me, although once you go to school, you may have to learn it there.' She spent time talking about school as a great treat for the future, and all the adventures he would have with his brothers.

The spectacles made a great difference to Sebastian and he seemed brighter, more eager to learn once he had them, although Kate hoped that other children wouldn't tease him about wearing them. One day he brought a letter upstairs. 'I can see COO – P-E-R. It's for you!'

Kate was as pleased as he was that Sebastian was making use of his letters. She drew the single sheet out of the envelope and unfolded it slowly. It was a wedding invitation. Her heart gave a lurch – This must be it, then, Tom had invited her to his wedding – and then seemed to right itself. She was invited to the marriage of Mr William Thorpe and Miss Judith Weaver. Things had evidently moved on in Kirkby since she left the manor.

Kate smiled, thinking of the day they'd taken Will to Judith's house and he'd said it was the last place on earth he wanted to be.

She started to plan; she wanted to be there and share in their happiness. To get to Kirkby church for the wedding, Kate would have to travel in the carrier's cart from Ripon on its Saturday run. She could stay at Sam's house that night and try to find a ride back to town the next day.

The canon said he was happy to give Kate two days free of duties and suggested she come back to work on Monday morning. 'I do feel easier in my mind about Sebastian,' he admitted. 'Possibly because I am not trying to teach him.' He said he would take the boy to visit his brothers on the Sunday, which was a rare occurrence.

Saturday dawned with rain, but then the clouds rolled away and, as the carrier lumbered slowly up the long slow rise out of Thieves' Gill, Kate was dazzled by the light on wet leaves dancing in the sun. She felt happy for Will and Judith, but very apprehensive too. No doubt Tom would be there, but it would be far better not to meet him. She snuggled deeper into her warm shawl.

By the time Kate reached the village, guests were already assembling outside the ancient grey stone church, standing in groups among the tombstones. She walked through the gate a little shyly, but soon hands grabbed her from behind and she turned to find Sam laughing at her. 'I knew you'd come! You can stay with me tonight, of course.'

'Where have you been?' his sister demanded severely. 'I'd hoped you would visit me before now.'

'Oh lass, we've been busy! I'll talk to you later.' He rushed off, to be replaced by Tom, who took both her hands and looked down into her eyes anxiously.

'Kate? Are we still friends? How I've missed you!'

A rush of emotion took Kate by surprise. She was speechless, looking at Tom with eyes that filled with tears. It was cruel of him to show her such affection, when Selina would soon be his wife.

'I have so much to tell you, Kate. It will have to wait until after the wedding ... perhaps you and Sam would have supper with me tonight?' Kate nodded and as someone called Tom away, she struggled to stay calm.

Judith and Will made a handsome couple, Kate thought, as she watched them standing at the altar. The church was decked with greenery and flowers, an achievement in the month of November, but Tom's gardener always had flowers in his greenhouses.

Judith wore a blue dress and hat, perfect for the occasion. She looked quite calm and very happy, although Kate knew that the goat lady was usually not at ease on public occasions. The service was a simple one and the sermon for a change was not about hell fire but about love.

As Mr and Mrs Thorpe came out of church, blinking in the sunlight, Tom stopped them at the porch with a box perched on a tripod. 'He's just bought a camera,' said Sam happily. 'He'll be able to record everything that happens.' Kate was amazed; she thought that a camera had to be operated by a proper photographer. The couple had to stand very still to be photographed and then it was the turn of the wedding party. Even Judith's mother managed a smile for the occasion.

When they could move again, Judith threw her bouquet over her shoulder in the traditional way and it was caught by Sadie, Tom's kitchen help. Sadie blushed bright red as everybody cheered.

The wedding feast catered for about thirty people, with Judith's sister Bessie in charge. It was a traditional village feast with ham, chicken, tongue and a wide variety of cakes held at the Mechanics Institute. A monumental wedding cake, three tiers high stood as the centrepiece of the table. It had been made by the village bakery, where once Judith had worked. A number of Judith's grateful customers had got together to buy it.

'Miss Weaver saved my boy's life,' one woman told Kate. 'We wanted to make a really big cake for her.'

'Please go and tell her mother your story. Mrs Weaver is sitting over there,' Kate directed. Judith had told her that her mother had never approved of Will, or of Judith either, and it was time that she heard the other side of the story.

The happy couple were toasted in sherry and the ex-poacher even made a short speech, telling everybody how lucky he was. Will looked distinguished in his best suit, with a white shirt and a new tie. You shouldn't judge people by their clothes, Kate thought, looking at him, but they certainly make a difference.

By early evening it was time to go home and Kate found herself in Tom's trap, travelling with him back to the manor. Sam was driving another vehicle, taking the elderly guests back to their homes.

Wrapping her shawl closely round her, Kate could find nothing to say. To her surprise Tom passed the entrance gates. 'We'll go the long way round, in at the far gate,' he said. From the far gate you had to travel across the whole estate to reach the house.

Tom drove slowly, pointing out various improvements and work in progress as the sun went down over the moor. Homing pheasants crossed their path. He reined in the horse on Bell's Hill, from where Kate could see the land falling away to the Vale of York, with the river winding down the valley.

'I won't keep you long, Kate, you're tired, but it's not often we can have a quiet talk.'

Kate looked straight ahead, willing herself not to be emotional.

'I apologize, Katherine dear, I should have told you straight away, I realize that now. My pride was hurt, to be honest. Truth is, Selina has ended our engagement.' Tom was looking almost sheepish. 'If you'd known, you might not have run away. I blame myself for that.'

'But – I thought – Sadie said there's a wedding soon?' Kate's heart started to thump alarmingly. She looked at him carefully for signs of grief.

Tom took her hand. 'Not mine, sweetheart. I'm free, I'm thankful to say.' His dark eyes never left her face. 'The night of the ball – and the poacher's moon, of course, a dreadful night – my father told me that he wanted to marry Selina. Since then, they've decided to marry here. In Kirkby Church.' He imitated his father's military style of speech. 'The admirable Miss Cooper will be able to arrange it all.'

'Tom ... were you very upset?'

'Only because she gave me up so easily! You see, the woman I love is you, Kate. It crept up on me gradually while we were working together, and now its incurable.'

'Tom...' Kate was thoroughly shocked, but underneath the shock, joy was rising, followed by despair. She was in turmoil.

Tom kissed her in a most determined way. 'And you? Could you put up with me?' He looked round at the darkening fields. 'There is a consolation prize, I'm pleased to say. Pa has given me the estate and a chunk of capital, so we'd be able to run it properly, with enough people to do the work. We could have a wonderful life together, Kate.'

Despair had now surfaced, fleeting joy had subsided. She couldn't marry Tom because of her birth. 'Tom,' she began, 'let us be practical. You will need a wife from the right level of society, with a proper pedigree –

you're a county gentleman, after all. You have an obligation to marry well.' That was what people believed.

He stopped her with another kiss. 'Katherine, do you love me?'

'Yes, Tom. But I can't marry you. I've loved you in one way or another since I was five, but – it's no good, we can't marry.' Kate was trying not to cry; the shadow that had always been there in the background was now overwhelming her.

'We'll see about that,' he said, and moved the horse on with a set face.

After a few minutes of silence, Kate tried again to set the record straight. 'The reason I say this is painful to me, but you have a right to know. In fact you've always known that I was adopted by the Coopers. So was Sam. The problem is that we're – we are probably illegitimate. That is a barrier to marriage into a respectable family; your children will be heirs to the estate. There's another barrier, too, you know. For good or ill, people like to know who your parents and grandparents were ... whether there's insanity in the family, or an inherited fault–'

'Such as a tendency to make mountains out of molehills.' Tom was smiling now, he wasn't taking her seriously. He turned skilfully into the stable yard where Benson was waiting.

At the stable, Jasper was handed over to

Jake Benson and they went into the house. Sadie had left a cold supper for them and Sam was hovering anxiously, but he didn't ask where they had been. There was no chance for more private conversation that night, but Tom was cheerful and talkative. Kate made him a list of things that would need to be done before the general's visit.

It was good to know that Selina would never be the mistress of the manor. Some other young lady would come there in the future; dark-eyed children, like Tom when he was small, would run through the corridors. It would be a real family home at last, if he could find the right wife. Kate, trying to be unselfish, hoped he would find a lady soon. He'd said he loved her, but if she went away he would soon forget.

'You're quiet tonight, Sis,' Sam said, helping himself to another piece of apple pie.

'And you'll get indigestion,' Kate said automatically. 'I was wondering where Will and Judith will live. It was a shock when I got the wedding invitation.'

'They'll be at Judith's, with the goats. Will says he'll help with the milking. I gave them a goat as a wedding present, as a matter of fact.' Tom laughed. 'You should have seen Sam bringing it back from the market. It was climbing all over him as he drove home.'

Kate smiled, thinking of her own modest

present, a flower vase. 'And the other thing you haven't told me ... what happened to Sir Titus? I saw a death notice in the paper.' Kate looked over at Sam. 'Did somebody finally strangle him? I wouldn't be surprised.' Kate still shuddered when she thought about the man.

'Er – no, not quite. Sir Titus Wiggins unfortunately died in a hunting accident and his funeral was held in Bradford,' Sam told her in an official voice.

'We saw the accident,' Tom added. 'He was riding in his usual fashion, half off the horse, and he came to a gate. The horse had already done its best to get rid of him, and then it finished the job. The sad thing is that no-one is sad about the affair. We've heard that Lady Wiggins is thinking about selling the Hall and the whole estate, so the servants are looking for new places, but I gather they always were.'

Kate looked at him. 'I'm afraid I was glad to hear Wiggins was dead. It's a relief to know that he'll never beat the children again, or assault women. Tom, I think you already have your eye on that property.'

'At the right price, it would make a good addition to the manor, but it's early days yet. You can't go calling on a new widow and ask if she's selling up.' Tom smiled. 'A few months ago I couldn't have afforded it, but now things are different.'

After supper Tom said quietly, 'I will talk to you tomorrow, Kate.'

Sam and Kate walked back to his keeper's cottage, where some of her belongings were still stored. She took a candle up to the little bedroom under the eaves and found a plain dress in the wardrobe that she would wear the next day. Then from the bottom of her trunk, she took out Dr Cooper's letter.

After he died, they had found letters in his desk for Sam and Kate. 'To be opened after my death,' the envelopes said. Sam had opened his some years ago, and found a loving message and hopes for his future. The Coopers had never known who his real parents were.

Kate had rarely thought of her letter, but now she had to open it. Perhaps it would be similar to Sam's. Her hands shook as she slit open the yellowing envelope.

My dear Kate, the doctor had written in his shaky handwriting, *We have both debated for years as to whether you should know who your parents were. You see, the chances are that you will know them both.* The candle flickered in a breeze from the window and Kate shivered.

In a perfect world, they would have married, but things went badly for them. I want you to know that they are both admirable people, Kate. Your father is William Thorpe and your mother, Judith Weaver. Neither of them know who you

290

are because I never told Judith that I had adop-
ted you. When she came back to the village, you
were a little girl of five or six. And, of course, by
then William had married someone else. It
seemed the best course to let people get on with
their lives. Judith had no scandal attached to her
and that was important. Unmarried mothers are
hounded and sometimes even take their own
lives. And for our part, we loved you and wanted
to keep you with us.

Now that you know, it is your choice whether
you tell them or not. It will depend on circum-
stances at the time. The letter ended with his
love and his gratitude that Kate and Sam
had been such a wonderful family.

Kate stared into space as the candle burned
lower. Will and Judith! This was something
she had never imagined. They were good
people and she had that day seen them
married. Her parents were together at last.
She wondered why, if they loved each other,
they had not been able to marry before she
was born.

What pain Judith must have suffered, giving up her baby and not knowing its fate!
Now, Kate was faced with a choice: to tell
them, or not to tell. She herself was relieved
and pleased to know who they were, but
what she had said to Tom had not changed:
she was illegitimate.

Holding the candle close to her face, Kate
looked in the mirror for traces of her

ancestry. Her blue eyes were like Will's; she was taller than Judith, but their bone structure was similar. Did she have her father's stubborn nature?

The question was what to do with her life. Tom loved her. He was not just flirting, he had been quite serious – and determined. But Tom really needed a 'county' wife. Kate would have to stay away from the manor.

Kate climbed into the high feather bed, but sleep only came with the dawn.

NINETEEN

On Sunday morning Kate woke with a head-ache. 'No, I won't go over to the manor,' she said to Sam. 'I've given Tom a list and that's all I can do for his father's wedding. He should get Mrs Mason in from the Hall, he needs more servants.'

Sam grinned. 'With more servants comes more responsibility. Now we have two maids living here, I have to drive them to church. Will you come? No?' He put on his coat and went off to the stables.

Kate had decided not to tell Sam that she had opened the doctor's letter, although the message was pounding through her head. Perhaps she should tell no one, ever, what she had learned last night. Will and Judith would want to get on with their new life to-gether, not to be burdened with a ghost from the unhappy past.

Tom was out of reach, just as he always had been. Even now, Kate wondered how deep his feelings for her were. He had always been affectionate, that was his way with his friends. He would realize as she had, that he would be expected to marry a well-bred young woman. He was the owner of Kirkby Manor and half a dozen other houses, an employer of servants and a member of an old family. He would be expected to set a good example in the parish. Queen Victoria's subjects put great emphasis on good breeding.

Sam was happy now that he was in touch with Evie again. Sam would have to face the same situation one day, the drawback of his birth, but perhaps a rather unconventional artist's family might not feel it was important. He would still need to earn enough money to support a wife and Kate hoped that he would find a way.

Kate felt alone, isolated. That was the burden of a secret – it cut you off from other people. She had always been open and honest; isolation was a new feeling for her. All her life until they died, the Coopers had made sure she was secure, part of a happy family.

The day was cold and clear and a good walk was probably the best tonic, Kate decided. In her old dress and shawl and her stout country boots, she went through the little gate in Sam's garden, into the small wood. There was a circular walk through clearings that would keep her well away from the manor house.

In spite of a headache that refused to go away, it was good to get back to the country, to breathe in the scents of the December woodland. The trees were bare but already she could see the swelling buds of next spring's leaves. A rabbit rustled through the undergrowth, intent on its own business.

Kate sighed and stood quiet, watching a robin on a fallen tree, but soon other thoughts intruded. Bright holly berries studded the bushes like jewels and they reminded her that by Christmas she would have no work. Sebastian was going away and next term, she hoped he would be going to school.

Some women might have seen the young doctor, Forester, as a solution and now Kate understood how reasonable people could make a marriage out of convenience and goodwill. Love hurt; how many men and women married the one they really loved, and even more unlikely, continued to love? Will and Judith had waited a long time and there had been a lot of pain on the way. Quiet affection was probably easier to live with.

Kate couldn't tell herself that her feeling for Tom was a passing phase; she had loved him, underneath it all, for too long. It wasn't honest to encourage anyone else, such as young Forester, when she felt as she did. Her only option at present was to come back to live with Sam, but that was too close to Tom. She would look through the newspapers again, she thought wearily.

Her eyes on the ground, Kate didn't notice that she had been followed until a twig snapped and she looked round. Tom stood on the track behind her, almost invisible in his riding breeches and brown tweed jacket. She felt like running away, but that was childish. Kate waited for him, watching a spider descending from a branch.

'Kate – please may I talk to you?'

Taking a deep breath, Kate faced him. 'For the last time, I can't marry you and the less we see of each other, the better.' Better to be abrupt, rude even than to prolong the pain. Surely he would go away, but Tom still stood there, tall and straight with his dark eyes fixed on her face. If only she didn't feel so weak ... most unlike herself.

Tom came towards her. 'But–'

'No, Tom, don't put your arms round me. Just listen for a minute. You see, it's for my sake as well as yours. If we married, I would be sneered at by the county people, the way Wiggins was. I'm not in that class.'

Tom was shaking his head, but Kate was determined to have her say. 'You perhaps didn't realize it, but you have been an exception because you spent so much time with us and even with village children ... and we were all treated alike. Sometimes I wonder whether Father – Dr Cooper – should have emphasized the difference between you and us, instead of ignoring it. But Father was like that, he saw the person rather than the class.' Kate stopped for breath, but Tom was still smiling at her.

'So rather than live as a social outcast, I'll go away and hope that you will find a nice girl. Better for me, better for you – and your children, of course.'

Tom swooped, gathered her in his arms and sat her down on the nearest log, displacing the robin. 'Watch out for spiders. Now, Katherine, if you'll allow me to get a word in, I've something to tell you. But first, I want to know – do you really love me? I'm honestly not sure.'

Tom Ridley, not sure? This was making the pain worse. Kate tried to stand up, but he pulled her back to him. Anger welled up as she said, very precisely for emphasis, 'I wouldn't be so unhappy if I didn't! You have no idea of the pain I feel and it seems you don't care! Here I am, trying to be sensible and look to the future for both of us and you are behaving like a spoiled child!'

The brute only laughed and hugged her. 'Did that make you feel better? Listen, Kate, listen to me. I have recently found out – informed by my dear father, that he and my mother were not married. So I'm a bastard, a love child. That upset me a great deal, especially thinking of my poor mother. She didn't live to marry him, of course. He said he intended to, might be true, but she was a servant, Kate. A poor little serving girl, my mother.'

Kate gazed at Tom, speechless.

'So I think I've demolished your argument, my girl. We're both in the same situation, and to hell with the rest of the world! Our friends of all classes will continue to notice us, as the saying goes. That – is – all – that – matters! Now, Katherine Cooper, will you marry me?'

The world swung round alarmingly, then steadied gradually. The headache was threatening to develop into a swoon. Breathless, Kate gave Tom to understand that yes, she would. She leaned against him, feeling faint.

Tom had swept away all her doubts and for the first time, she could allow herself to imagine a future with him. People might still talk, not knowing of his birth, but now, it didn't matter.

'Yours must be one more secret that Dr Cooper knew,' she said slowly.

'It was; he delivered me I believe.' Tom paused and then went on, 'Perhaps I should tell you that my prospects are bright. The old man has transferred the estate to me legally. Just as well, because I could have been kicked out, being illegitimate – if Pa has more children, or if my cousins got wind of the true situation. Bastards can't usually inherit. There would be a few beady eyes fixed on my land if that story got out.'

'Thomas, if I marry you it will not be in order to acquire an estate!' The very idea

298

was shocking. 'You must think I'm a calculating fortune hunter!' The world started swinging round again as Kate turned her head quickly. Was it emotion, or something else? She had no time for illness, especially now, when the world had just changed.

'You were calculating enough when you turned me down. Remember I'm fragile!' Tom looked the very reverse of fragile.

Eventually, Tom supporting Kate, they walked back to Sam's house. 'I feel so hot and my head aches,' she confessed.

'Goodness!' Tom was alarmed. 'Not the influenza, is it? I hear there are cases in Ripon. You'd better take a hot drink and have a rest. I'll call to see you later, darling.'

Sam came home, Tom called again but Kate was only dimly aware of her surroundings. Lying on Sam's couch, she was floating in a world of her own, frequently struggling to get up when she remembered poor little Sebastian and her duty to him. She had to get back to Ripon...

Will and Judith were making adjustments to their lives in the days after their wedding. Tom had given Will a week's holiday, with pay. 'I can hardly believe it,' the new husband said. 'Never had a boss treat me like this one does.'

'Troubled conscience, lad, that's what it is. He told me he feels guilty that you were shot in the wood.' Judith looked at him and added, 'Don't worry, I'll find a job or two to keep you out of trouble.' That was going to be her new mission in life: keeping Will out of trouble.

'Nay, young Tom needn't feel bad about it. They would have got me somewhere in the end once they'd worked out what I was up to.' Will flexed his arm and winced slightly. 'Risks of the job, they call it.'

With a cart and the help of Prince, an ancient Clydesdale horse borrowed from the manor, Will moved certain items of furniture from his house to Judith's, wrapped in blankets to keep them from scratching. He took the grandfather clock, his Windsor chair and a mahogany table on the first load.

'Making yourself right at home, then?' One inquisitive old man tried to see what was in the cart, but Will kept on moving at Prince's slow pace.

'Aye, why not?'

Judith had rearranged some of her possessions and moved some of the herbal material into an outbuilding. Will put up new shelves for her jars of salve and various potions, and gave the walls a coat of whitewash. 'I've been meaning to do this for years,' she said, wondering at her newfound energy. Everything seemed to have more meaning, even her daily work, now that she shared it with Will.

The more valuable items from Will's cottage were moved because he intended to find a tenant. He hoped to find someone quiet and respectable, but if they had bairns, furniture might get damaged. He'd never lived with little children, but Will had a healthy respect for them.

Will quietly put the word about in the butcher's shop and also in the forge for good measure, that the cottage was available to rent. Payable weekly, in advance of course. All breakages made good.

While he was on holiday, Will and Judith took the cart up to the moor to dig some peat for winter fires. Peat didn't burn very hot, but it lasted a long time and eked out the coal and wood. 'A peat fire's grand on a mild day,' Judith agreed when he suggested it. She loved the smell of burning peat, like that of the ancient farmhouses on the moor that had walls steeped in peat smoke. It was traditional on the moor.

The horse paced slowly up the hill, the cart creaking. At the end of the village, a man with a stick hobbled up to them and waved at Will. 'This here cottage – what do you want for it?' Prince looked at him and stopped.

Will glanced at Judith and saw she was trying not to laugh. The man was Joe Price, the gamekeeper who'd warned her long ago to keep away from poachers.

Will got down from the cart and stood in the road. 'What will you give me?' They haggled for a few minutes, then shook hands on the deal.

'I'm on the Azerley estate, these days. But I'm retiring next month, too old to chase poachers in middle of night. The young lads are too fast for me. And, of course, our house goes with the job,' he said. 'Missis is right worried; she'll be glad to get your house, right in village and all. We've always had to live on the job.' He peered up at Judith, chuckling. 'I see you didn't take my advice in the end.' He winked at Will. 'You don't deserve a good lass like yon.'

'I know it,' Will said humbly. 'Everybody tells me about it.'

'Do you mean my mother?' Judith asked him, as he shook the reins and they moved slowly forward. 'Don't worry about her. When she saw you at the wedding, she said she could tell you'd turned respectable at last. It must have been that new shirt that did it.'

Will let old Prince set his own pace as they jogged up the moor road. 'Good job it's downhill, coming home with the load,' he said. 'Peat's heavy stuff.'

Judith knew it was heavy and she was wondering how she could find the strength to cut the turf and then lift it into the cart. She wanted to help Will, whose arm was still troubling him a little.

They passed through the moor gate and

Judith felt the silence of wide open spaces surround her as the stone walls disappeared and the heather moor opened out on either side. Farm sounds were left behind and the sheep were quiet; the bubbling cry of the curlew wouldn't be heard again until the spring.

The day was fine and the thin winter sunshine warmed them a little, but the breeze was cold. Moorland ewes looked up for a moment to watch them pass, then went back to grazing the short turf. From russet beds of bracken grouse lifted, flying low. As she always did on the moor, Judith gazed across the wide views over Nidderdale, the far hills blue with distance and felt her spirits lift. Kirkby and village life seemed a world away. 'It's like a holiday!' she said and Will laughed.

'A very active holiday, I'd say, like walking across moors as some town folks do. We've peat to get yet, Judith!'

Soon William turned the cart down a narrow track to where there was a neatly stacked pile of peat sods. The heavy work was done.

'Who cut these? You wouldn't take another man's...' He shot her a warning look and Judith finished hurriedly, 'Of course you wouldn't. But when did you cut them? They're almost dry.' Peat was usually cut and stacked to dry out before it was used. In spite of her new resolutions, Judith doubted him.

Will wouldn't be able to cut these, he's been injured twice in the last few months.

Will jumped down from the cart and helped Judith down. 'You still don't trust me, lass, do you? You don't really think I'm honest.' His blue eyes were sad.

'I am so sorry, Will.' She wanted to take back the words and the thought. Judith realized that she would have to be careful what she said in the future – or perhaps, change her thinking.

'I suppose you realize that once Joe and Mrs Price take my house, you won't be able to send me away, Judith, if you change your mind about living with me. I'll have nowhere to go. But it is important to me that there's trust on both sides. Are you willing – will you promise to trust me?' Will waited for her answer.

That was what she had promised when they were married, to honour him, but already she'd fallen into her old, suspicious ways.

Will took both her hands in his. 'I want you to promise me right now that you do believe I am honest. That you will trust me always, for ever.'

Judith nodded. She wanted to believe in him.

Her husband smiled faintly. 'I cut these months ago, before I fell into the mantrap. It was something to do, after I was turned off.' Catching her eye, he added, 'And no, in case you're wondering, I wasn't poaching grouse at the time.'

Judith had no words. How would she feel if William decided not to trust her?

'There's a big difference, you see. Taking a rabbit or two, wild animals that run free on anybody's land, isn't wrong to me and neither is cutting turf on the moor as it's always been allowed. The ancient right of turbary, they call it. But taking turf another man has cut would be stealing – all his labour would be for nothing. You do see the difference?' Judith smiled, relieved. 'Now, will you promise?'

'I promise,' Judith said, and they kissed. There was much love in that kiss and the beginning of understanding. Under the pale, wide moorland sky, she felt this was a more solemn moment than that in the church. 'I won't forget today.'

Neither of them ever forgot that day. Tired after carting home the peat, Judith and William went home in the dusk to find a note on their door from Sam Cooper. 'Can you come to my house? Kate is very ill.'

TWENTY

'Dr Sherwood comes every day, but he can't lower her temperature,' a worried Tom told Judith as he met her at the door. William had driven straight to the keeper's cottage in the cart, Judith with a basket of remedies in case of need. 'She's been ill since Sunday, that's four days now. Sadie's been caring for her; she's been very good.'

Sam was hovering, restless. 'Thank goodness you're here, Judith. We thought you might have gone away for a few days after the wedding.'

'Nay, there's too much to do before the winter. Now, where is the poor lass?'

Kate looked very small in the big feather bed and seemed to be drifting in and out of consciousness. Judith was shocked to see how thin she was. 'Have you any ice, Thomas?' Some of the big houses stored ice in an insulated building after a hard frost, but perhaps it was too early in the winter.

Sam said immediately, 'We did save some, for making ice cream for the wedding. I'll go now.' He put on his cap and went out.

Judith bathed Kate's hot brow with cold water while Tom told her the details of Dr

Sherwood's treatment. 'We'll try willow bark tea. William, will you put the kettle on the fire?' she called down the stairs, where Will was waiting. 'Then you'd better stable the horse. We'll be here all night, I think.'

'Poor lass, she must be bad,' Will muttered. 'Ah well, the white willow did wonders for me.'

It was a long night. Kate was conscious some of the time and in one of these intervals, Judith gave her a cup of the tea. Ice fragments were wrapped in cloth and applied to her burning skin. Judith sat by the bed and Tom came in frequently, looking at Judith, willing her to give him good news.

'Why don't you go home?' Judith asked gently. 'Will's here, he can keep me company. It will soon be morning.'

'Judith, I can't leave Kate,' Tom whispered. 'Only on Sunday morning – it seems ages ago! she agreed to marry me. We were so happy...We have to save her, Judith – she has so much to live for!' He looked as though he hadn't slept since Sunday.

'The lass needs quiet, and sleep if we can manage it. Rest yourself in the kitchen then, even if it's just for half an hour.'

When Judith went down to the kitchen later, Sam was making toast at the fire and she realized that she and Will had not eaten since noon. She accepted a piece of buttered toast and the others did the same; she didn't feel hungry, but it was comforting.

Sam was sombre. 'When I went to Ripon to tell the canon that Kate couldn't come to work, he said that two people had died of influenza at the hospital. He didn't want Kate back in the house, in case Sebastian caught it.' Tom shuddered.

'I heard they were old folks that died, but Kate – she's young and strong,' Will told him. 'Isn't that so, Judith? Kate will come through?'

Looking round the three faces, Judith was hesitant. 'To be honest, I don't know. She could go either way. She's been hot for too long. And – her lungs might be affected.' It was better not to raise false hopes. She felt Tom's pain; life was cruel. Just as he grasped at happiness, it was fading fast, with Kate's fading heartbeat.

Going back upstairs, Judith heard Kate coughing and realized that she was awake. It was time for another dose of the herbal tea, willow bark, but this time with added cough mixture, horehound and coltsfoot. She'd never combined these plants before, but she couldn't ask the sick girl to take two draughts.

As she supported the drooping girl with one arm and held the cup with the other, Kate's blue eyes opened wide. 'Judith, it's you,' she whispered. 'What was it ... I must tell you?'

Was this the lucid moment before death, that Judith had seen before when nursing the dying? Should she call the others? Her supporting arm could feel the dangerous heat of the girl's body. The herbs might be too late.

Kate took a small sip of the bitter tea. 'I'm going to die, isn't that true?' Judith's eyes filled with tears and one splashed on to Kate's thin hand. 'It's time to speak ... I wasn't going to, but now...' She coughed again. 'There might not be another chance. Is Will here, Judith?' Shuddering, she drank some more of the draught.

Why did she ask for Will and not Tom? Judith called him up and Will tiptoed into the room at the foot of the bed. 'You'll do it, lass,' he whispered. 'Judith will have you right in no time at all.'

Kate tried to smile at him, but shook her head weakly and closed her eyes. She seemed to be sleeping, but then she woke again. 'There's something you should know. A letter from Father ... tells me who my real parents are. Judith, Dr Cooper adopted your little baby girl himself.'

There was total silence in the room; the candle guttered. Judith looked into the blue eyes that were so like Will's, and smoothed the fair hair back from Kate's brow. Will reached across and took her hand. 'Our little lass, growing up here in Kirkby and we never knew.'

'Did you know, Judith?' Kate's voice was weak, but insistent. 'Did you guess?'

Judith kissed the flushed cheek. 'I did guess eventually, lass, but I kept quiet. Doctor Cooper was so taken with you ... then he adopted Sam. When I came back to Kirkby you were five years old, just the age my bairn would have been. And your eyes are so like Will's. I did think – I hoped you were my little lass. I'm so proud of you, Kate.'

Kate closed her eyes again and a smile flitted over her face. 'I'm glad you know ... no one else does, it's our secret. I think I'll sleep now. I'm so tired.' Judith realized Kate was too tired even to see the men she loved and that she had quietly accepted death. 'Tell Tom...' She never finished the sentence.

Gently, Judith turned the girl onto her side. It was the rule for the dying.

After a few hours Kate was still breathing, more quietly than before. She was not conscious, but she seemed to be slightly cooler.

Sam looked in and Judith asked him to relight the fire in the tiny bedroom grate. 'We don't want her to catch pneumonia,' Judith warned.

The night seemed endless, but Judith could do nothing but watch and hope. Will kissed her cheek and went downstairs again. Would her old-fashioned remedies help in a case where the doctor could do nothing? It seemed too much to expect. She was not trained in medicine like the doctor, but she'd studied herbs for twenty years. This was one of the times when she had to trust the healing plants. Would they save Kate? It was the only hope they had.

Another hour, and Kate was much cooler and seemed to be sleeping naturally. Judith allowed herself to think of recovery.

Tom came in just before dawn as Kate woke and Judith whispered, 'I think she may be on the mend.' His eyes lit up.

By noon, Judith began to feel that they had won. She sponged down the tired girl with warm water and gently brushed her hair before giving her hot milk. The next day, Kate was in a clean nightdress, sitting up in bed and ready to tackle food. Sadie had made some chicken soup, singing as she worked because Miss Cooper was going to recover.

Tom took up her tray himself, smiling at Judith across the bed. 'I'll always be grateful,' he said quietly. Judith saw the way Kate looked at him with love.

'So will I,' said the patient. 'You've all been so good to me. But I have a few things on my mind. Thomas dear, what will happen to Sebastian? I'm supposed to be looking after him!'

Tom said firmly, 'I wrote to Dr Jameson and his wife – you told me they'd been kind to the boy – to ask them to keep an eye on him. Don't worry about him, sweetheart, the Jamesons will have told his father what he needs.' Judith nodded; Tom was saying the right things. Kate needed rest, with no anxiety at all.

'And the general's wedding...'

'You've been lying here thinking of things to worry about. Pa's getting married tomorrow; the manor is bracing itself for the fray and your friend Mrs Mason is here and loving it all. Only fifteen or so guests, it's not to be a big affair, thank goodness. Roast venison for the wedding feast, seven courses and champagne all round.' Tom took her hand, very gently. 'Do you approve? It will be good when it's over!' He dropped a kiss on her head.

Kate took a deep breath. 'Oh, Tom, you've a lot to think about.'

'Only you, that's all, Katherine. And just in case you think of anything else, your little friends George and Bella are thriving. Their mama has decided to sell Bellwood Hall and to buy a much smaller country house, with land where they can keep pets. Bella wants a tortoise, you see and George thinks a big dog would be fun.'

Judith relaxed and then she realized how tired she was. She would leave Kate with Tom for a while.

A few days after the general's wedding, when all the guests had gone, Kate was well enough to be driven over to the manor, where a huge log fire was burning in the drawing-room. 'Welcome home, my love,' Tom said with a catch in his voice. The room was welcoming and bright with flowers. Kate had believed she would die and was still amazed to find herself sitting in that beautiful room, feeling tired but happy, with a new life about to unfold.

'The next thing is Christmas, a family Christmas at the manor for the first time in my life,' Tom told her. 'After that, our wedding. We'll get married before Lent, of course. If you agree, I'll speak to the vicar and we'll make it January.'

Mrs Mason looked far happier than Kate had ever seen her when she came in to discuss the Christmas plans. Kate realized that to run the house properly, they would need Lizzie Mason as well as herself.

'Mr Ridley's planning a tea party, but he hasn't said who the guests are to be,' the housekeeper said. 'Neighbours, I believe.'

Kate and Tom sat by the fire, talking. Telling him the truth about her birth, Kate had wondered how he would feel about employing his father-in-law as a game keeper. But Tom just laughed. 'I like Will. In any case, nobody else will know the story. I'm glad you told me.'

Perhaps it was the effect of her illness, but Kate felt calm and happy. Instead of always being watchful and responsible, she was leaving everything to Tom. It was a strange feeling. 'Don't worry, you'll have plenty to do when you're well again,' Tom reminded her. 'It's your job to choose the new curtains.'

Tom persuaded Kate to visit the village dressmaker and she had several new dresses made. Instead of grey and the severe black that had been her housekeeper's uniform, she chose simple designs without too many flounces, in fresh colours, greens and blues. A wedding dress would also be needed, she told the woman, and saw her eyes open wide. Pattern books were consulted and lace examined. The next day, the whole village knew that young Mr Ridley was going to marry Miss Cooper, another Kirkby wedding.

Tom disappeared on the afternoon of his party and Kate went into the kitchen to find Sadie icing small buns and putting cherries on the top. Judith and Will were there, dressed in their best. 'It's grand to see you well again, lass,' Will said and kissed her shyly.

Snow was beginning to fall, drifting across the windows and lining the branches of trees. In about half an hour, Tom came in with a sprinkling of snow on his cape, leading a child in each hand. George and Bella had come to the party. 'Nursie!' they shrieked and threw themselves at Kate with such energy that she sank backwards into a chair. 'May we see the peacocks?'

She hugged them both. 'I think you've grown,' she told them. Soon the peacocks strutted by outside the long windows, the male bird spreading his tail in a cascade of iridescent blue and green, bright against the snow. George and Bella pressed their faces to the glass, entranced. 'I want one,' Bella decided.

A rattle of wheels in the drive made them look the other way and soon Dr Jameson and his wife came in with Sebastian, wrapped up warmly and with his glasses perched on a little pink nose. George and Bella took the boy off on a tour of the house. 'Are we allowed, Miss Cooper?' he asked, as he was dragged out of the door.

It was just as Kate had imagined; Sebastian came to life with the company of the two Wiggins children. School would do him good. She sighed with relief.

Judith and Will undertook to supervise and the afternoon went smoothly. The whole group, adults and children sat in a circle to play games, to Kate's amazement. Little George echoed her thoughts. 'We never do this at home!' Judith caught her eye and they both laughed.

Watching, Kate saw that when the meal was served, Sebastian ate everything available – another good sign. 'Thank you, Tom,' Kate said quietly. 'It is so good to see the children again.'

'I'm enjoying it too, the manor needs bringing to life.' Tom helped himself to another bun. 'Wait till we have three children of our own! That will brighten up the old place!' he whispered and Kate blushed.

The visit was cut rather short because the snow continued to fall, but also because Kate was tiring. Judith and Will had to go home to feed the goats. The Jamesons left next, promising to visit again. Dr Jameson had talked to Judith about her remedies and had made several notes, to her surprise.

Sam took George and Bella home and the manor was strangely quiet after they had all gone, the snow reflecting light into the rooms.

Tom was thoughtful for a while and then he said, 'We'll have to make one of the rooms into a nursery, you know. There are so many things to plan, Katherine, when you're well again. I'll buy Bellwood Hall if the price is right ... knock down the house, I suppose, and make another in the stable block.'

'That will give you more acres and more work, Tom. Is it a good idea?' Kate was not in favour of an over-large estate. Tom seemed to be out on his horse all day as it was.

'Of course,' Tom said thoughtfully, 'I do have an ulterior motive in wanting to marry you.'

Kate stared at him. 'What might that be?'

'If Sam's my brother-in-law, I could have some influence. I might be able to persuade him to let me send him to university, for the sake of the estate, of course.'

'He always wanted to ... but I'm not sure whether he'd accept, Tom. It would be expensive.' Sam was just as proud and independent as she was, Kate knew.

'We need a qualified man, you see. Things are changing, farming's a science now. He could study management as I did, or crops, or forestry – something useful that would help him to take over as manager – perhaps of Bellwood Hall. Do you think he likes that little artist girl?'

'I think he does. Tom, you're devious.' Kate shook her head at him.

'I do like planning, must get it from the old man.' Tom leaned back in his chair. 'If we do have Sam as a manager, we could leave him in charge and you and I could travel a little. Should you like to visit France? At the very least I'd like to take you to Scotland and show you where I used to work.'

Kate considered. 'I should like to travel, but on one condition, Tom: that we will never visit Jamaica.'

Tom gave a great roar of a laugh. 'I solemnly promise that will never happen. Now ... when Sam comes back, we'll get to work on him.'

The publishers hope that this book has given you enjoyable reading. Large Print Books are especially designed to be as easy to see and hold as possible. If you wish a complete list of our books please ask at your local library or write directly to:

Magna Large Print Books
Magna House, Long Preston,
Skipton, North Yorkshire.
BD23 4ND

This Large Print Book, for people
who cannot read normal print,
is published under the auspices of

THE ULVERSCROFT FOUNDATION